Take Two

Sawyer's Cove: The Reboot

Libby Waterford

Also by Libby Waterford

Sawyer's Cove: The Reboot

Take Two

Take a Bow

Take It All

Take a Chance

Take Me Over

Hot Take in Steamy Shorts: A Kissed by Romance Anthology

Take Another Look in A Kiss at Midnight: A Kissed by Romance Collaboration

Never a Bride

Can't Help Falling in Love

Can't Make You Love Me

Can't Fight This Feeling

Can't Hurry Love

Weston Reunion

Flirting with Her Professor

Her Reunion Fling

Falling for Her Ex

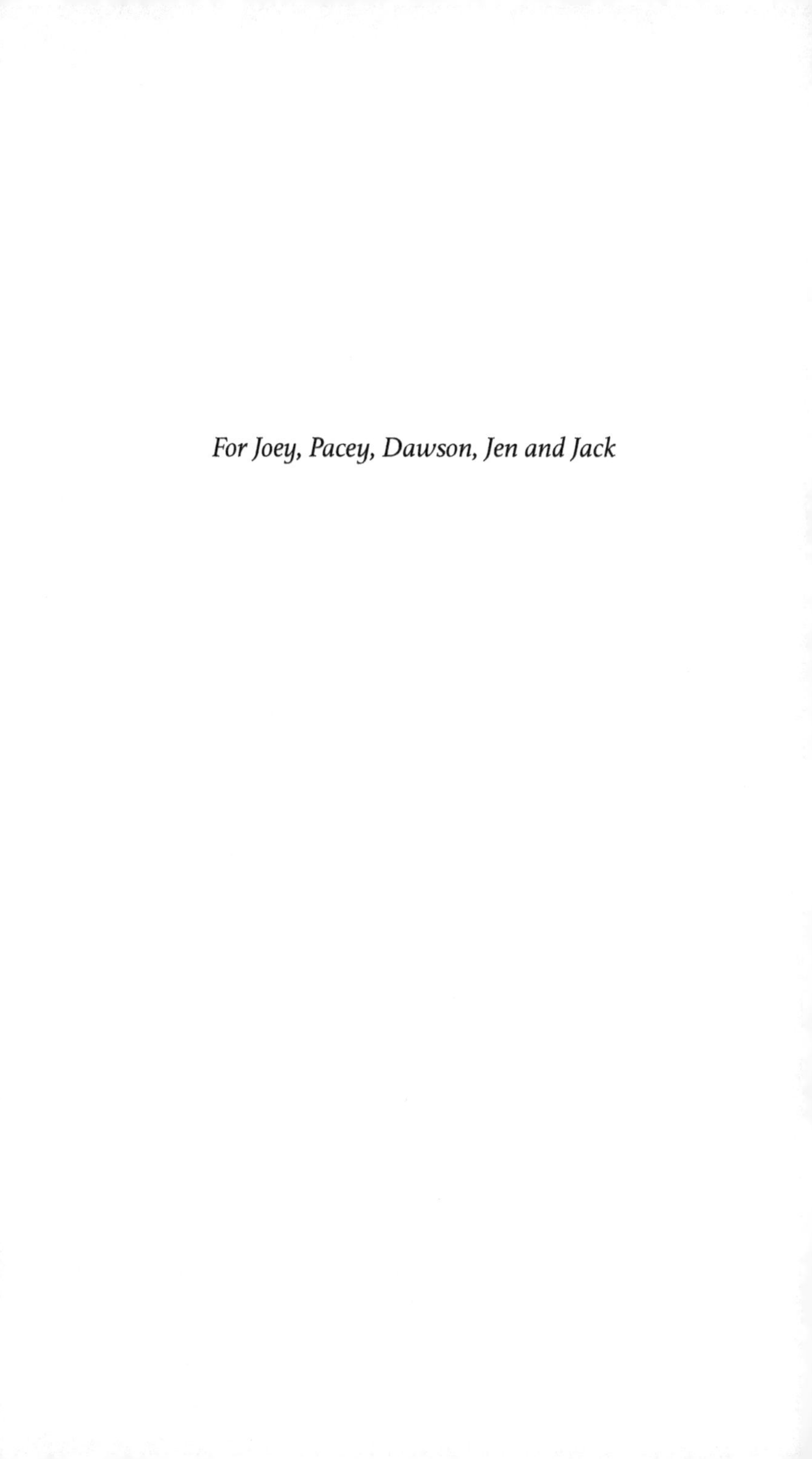

For Joey, Pacey, Dawson, Jen and Jack

"Love has nothing to do with what you are expecting to get — only with what you are expecting to give, which is everything."

— Katharine Hepburn

Chapter One

JULES: Okay, we're doing this. Are we doing this?

ERIKA: Hey, I bought this fancy microphone with my birthday money. We're doing this.

JULES: All right, then, let's go. Welcome to the first episode of *The Sawyer's Cove Rewatch Project* podcast. Jesus, that's a mouthful.

ERIKA: That's what Lily Fine said. Bah-dum-ch!

JULES: Wow, are we getting into the Lily-Fine-is-a-slut jokes already? Do we need to start some kind of counter?

ERIKA: Sorry, sorry. I'll be good. For those of you who don't know, *Sawyer's Cove* was a television show that ran for three beautiful, shamefully short seasons before it was canceled by evil television executives.

JULES: A lot of people became fans after it went to streaming, but Erika and I actually watched it live, being in the target audience of teenage girls at the time. But its cancellation broke my heart, so I left it behind and moved on to different pursuits. Erika, meanwhile—

ERIKA: I never stopped. I had all the DVDs, the sound-track, the Parker Wild posters, the whole shebang.

JULES: I haven't seen the show in over a decade, so we're both rewatching from the beginning.

ERIKA: Yeah, and then we talk about it and all you other *Cove* freaks can get your nostalgia fix. So, buckle up for drama, sex, tears, laughs, bad hair, and good chemistry. Let's do this.

FROM *THE SAWYER'S COVE REWATCH PROJECT PODCAST: PILOT*

Cami had expected Misty Harbor to be exactly the same. It lived in her memory as a static image, the quaint downtown with its brick two-story buildings frozen behind snow globe glass.

She remembered the narrow two-lane Main Street, anchored at one end by the Victorian-era mansion-turned-inn and at the other by the rocky beach and Atlantic Ocean, as it had been the last time she saw it, the final day of shooting *Sawyer's Cove*. Her father had rushed her to the airport right after wrapping so she could audition for a Spielberg movie she didn't get.

There had been a wrap party, eventually, out in L.A. She'd seen all her castmates again, when they were doing press for the series finale. Jay had even come, the first and only time he made the trek to L.A with her. But at the time, she'd wished she'd been able to say goodbye to the town itself.

She hadn't fully realized how much Misty Harbor felt like home until she left.

Twelve years had changed her. She was no longer a teenager, for one thing. As she left the inn on foot and wandered down Main Street, she shouldn't have been surprised Misty Harbor had changed, too.

Sure, the differences were small, but they were altering the image she'd held for over a decade. On this fine late spring morning, a handful of kids climbed over the new play structure in the park next to the library, their minders watching from gleaming benches. A colorful banner advertising something called Harbor Fest was fastened between two light poles behind the playground.

An attractive new sign invited people into the old-fashioned library. Cami was tempted, but her agenda involved a belated breakfast. She could have taken advantage of the inn's self-proclaimed impeccable room service, but she wanted to stretch her legs. Plus, Selena had instructed her to keep her eye out for possible filming locations. She didn't exactly have any expertise in location scouting, but she'd been on enough location shoots to know what to look for.

Wasn't there a diner on the block past the library? They used to hit up the fifties-style joint after shooting wrapped for the day, since it was one of the only places in town that stayed open past nine. She and Jay and Nash and Ariel would grab a booth and order malted milkshakes and gossip as if they were real teenagers out with their friends after a football game, instead of what they really were—actors who played them on TV.

She found the diner, a block farther down than she remembered, but hesitated when a cute bakery across the street caught her eye. She should have something more to eat than a pastry, but the bakery looked as if it might have a better chance of a latte than the diner. And yes, she was Hollywood enough to admit she wanted a latte.

Cami fell in insta-love with Misty Harbor Bakeshop the moment she walked in and discovered it smelled like cardamom and coffee. She smiled brightly at the young person behind the counter. The man was wearing a full face of makeup and he looked like he'd be more at home in Echo Park than Misty Harbor—yet another sign the town had changed even more than she'd imagined.

She kept the bright smile on her face as the employee said, "Welcome to the Bakeshop, what can I get you?" Then his eyes widened. "Oh, shit. Camille Corsair. Oh, shit. Shit. I need to stop saying shit." He clamped a hand over his mouth, as if that would prevent him from saying anything more.

Cami found herself giggling. Usually being recognized when she was trying to go about her business made her feel slightly vulnerable and off-kilter, but she had to admit that dynamic was different here. The residents of Misty Harbor had put up with *Sawyer's Cove* for three years, with the occasional street closures and calls for extras, and that one time they'd set up an entire fake carnival on the beach boardwalk. But the locals never made the cast and crew feel unwelcome. She hoped the hospitality would return if what she had planned came to fruition.

"Hi," she said, scanning the retro white-on-black letter sign hanging behind the counter. "Can I get the biggest latte you have? Skim, if you have it. And, um…" She inspected the glossy pastries in the case, and her mouth instantly watered. "I don't know. What else is good?"

The employee narrowed his magenta-shadowed eyes. "What else is good? Is this a joke? Are you actually Camille Corsair, or are you just a really good cosplayer?"

Cosplayer? "No, I'm Camille. What's your name?"

"I'm Trevor."

"Okay. You can call me Cami."

Trevor grinned with carmine-painted lips. "Cami, oh my God. Okay. Well, *Cami*, everything in this bakeshop is going to be the best thing you ever ate, so you can't go wrong. And we're still serving breakfast for—" he consulted the big analog clock on the wall behind him "—six minutes."

Cami ordered quickly. Eggs, toast, and a side of three berry jam.

"Zelda, she's the owner, makes the jam herself. And the bread, obviously. Prepare for a taste bud explosion." Trevor keyed in the order and started making her latte.

Cami laughed again. "Where was this place when I was young enough to actually eat croissants with no consequences?"

"I know, right?" Trevor nodded as if he was intimately acquainted with actress problems. "Zelda opened it about five years ago."

She paid in cash and dropped a large denomination bill in the tip jar. It never hurt to have a friend who worked at a bakery. She was already planning the standing order they'd have to treat the crew once a week. If everything worked out. She had to remember not to get ahead of herself.

Trevor handed over her latte, and she asked, "Why did you think I was a cosplayer?"

"It's Thursday," Trevor said, as if that explained everything.

She arched an eyebrow.

Trevor waved his arms theatrically as he elaborated, "Thursdays, Fridays, and Saturdays are *Sawyer's Cove* walking tours. Sometimes the guides dress up—usually they pick iconic outfits from the show, like the home-coming dance episode, or that horrible bridesmaid dress they made you wear in the one where your long-lost half-sister got married. But sometimes the people on the tour dress up, too."

"Wait. Walking tours? I don't get it."

"It's all part of, what is it called—fan tourism. *Sawyer's Cove* has a lot of fans, and we've got an entire cottage industry here in Misty Harbor to cater to them."

"That's what I'm counting on," Cami said under her breath. Louder, she asked, "Where does the tour start? Do I need a ticket?"

"*You* want to take the *Sawyer's Cove* tour?" Trevor asked. "This day is just too weird. Jay's in here all the time, but having you come in—it's like I'm actually living in Cloudy Cove."

"Life imitating art, again, I guess." Cami shrugged, even as her heart raced at getting confirmation that Jay was indeed in Misty Harbor. She sipped her excellent latte. "Trevor, this is exactly what I needed. Thank you."

"Anytime. Wait. Seriously, what *are* you doing here?"

A slim, dark-haired woman who looked about her age came out of the back holding a paper box. Her apron was embroidered with the name "Zelda."

"Stop interrogating the customers, Trevor. Here's your breakfast, sweetie."

Cami took the box, with a grateful smile. It wasn't that she didn't want to tell Trevor what she was doing in Misty Harbor, but it was for sure against the NDA she'd signed. "Thanks. Right now I'm going to eat, but I'll be back."

"We close at six." Zelda winked. "Tell your friends."

Cami took her breakfast and headed for the beach, considering the appealing storefronts she passed with fresh eyes. As the stand-in for the fictional Cloudy Cove, Misty Harbor had performed the role perfectly. She could all too easily see the town turned into a temporary backlot once again.

She was almost at the beach when she passed a bar. The simple sign on the weathered brick exterior read "The Cove" in a typeface reminiscent of the show's. Wow. The town had really gone all in on this fan tourism thing. This place probably served theme cocktails, like Sawyer's Angst or Amy Green Apple Martinis.

She made a mental note to check out the bar later, then spotted an empty bench where she could look out over the water and eat. Her brain whirred as she processed meeting Trevor and seeing how embedded *Sawyer's Cove* already was in Misty Harbor's DNA.

She was aware that in the years since it had been unceremoniously canceled, the show's audience had actually grown. They had always seemed to generate a lot of buzz, but the audience hadn't seemed to find it until it was off the air. Cami enjoyed hearing from fans who'd come to the show late, but she'd always assumed all that was ancient history. Then other cult favorites that spoke to some nostalgic part of the culture started getting revived as limited series and garnering nice deals. And about six months ago, Selena had called to pitch her on a reboot of *Sawyer's Cove*. She wanted them to do it together; Selena would be the showrunner, and Cami would produce in addition to reprising her role as Amy Green.

Speak of the devil, Cami thought as her phone buzzed. She set aside her breakfast box and pulled her phone from the pocket of her skirt.

"What's up, Selena?"

"You said you'd call me when you got there," Selena said in her usual no-nonsense tone. For years, Cami had assumed Selena had no use for her, but over the past few months, she'd learned that was just how Selena was— dry as dust, with no time for preambles or bullshit of any kind. Since Cami spent her life being professionally nice, Selena's lack of pretense was refreshing, now that she was used to it anyway. Selena didn't care if Cami was sweet or friendly. She didn't believe you caught more flies with honey, not in Hollywood. She'd parlayed her *Sawyer's Cove* assistant writer gig—her very first paying job in TV—into a full-fledged staff writer job by the time the show was canceled. She'd been a staff writer ever since, but she'd never been a showrunner. That was going to change as soon as the studio put its money where its mouth was and officially green-lit the *Sawyer's Cove* reboot.

And they wouldn't do that until Cami had Jay Orlando's signature on the contract.

"I'm sorry. I was so tired last night, I passed right out, then I slept in. I'm about to eat," she added pointedly.

"Well, I'm glad you got some rest." Selena didn't sound glad, but Cami knew that didn't mean anything. "So, what's the town like? Is this going to work?"

"The town looks better than ever, and I'm getting tons of ideas based on some new stuff downtown. The people are nice. They seem to have a whole little tourism thing built up around the show."

"I told you there was an audience for this. What's the deal with Jay? You close to tracking him down?"

"Give me more than five minutes, okay? I'll find him."

Selena had been more irritated than worried when they hadn't been able to locate Jay Orlando. He didn't have an agent anymore, and he'd never had a manager. None of his old numbers worked, and Cami had felt weird about randomly calling places in Misty Harbor, looking for a lead on him. When the project she was filming in Toronto was unceremoniously cut short, she'd had the idea of simply poking around Misty Harbor until he crawled out from whatever rock he'd been hiding under.

"Okay, text me the minute he signs the contract. I have a call with Brad and Krista tomorrow, and I'd love to be able to tell them we're set. Gotta go."

Selena clicked off before Cami could say goodbye, but she didn't take it personally. She put her phone away and settled back on her bench.

Her eggs were a little cold, but still tasty. The jam was sinfully good—tart and sweet. As she ate, she glanced around the waterfront. The June sun glinted off the Atlantic. To her left was the marina, with dozens of gleaming boats lined up like oversized toys in the bath. To her right was the boardwalk, with a parking lot on one side, the rocky beach on the other. A few joggers, a group of women chatting as they pushed strollers, and a galloping golden retriever playing fetch with its owner completed the idyllic picture of coastal New England.

Cami closed her eyes against the sun, too lazy to get her sunglasses out of her bag. She imagined the rays were powering her up to face the hardest part of her mission in Misty Harbor—convincing Jay Orlando, her first boyfriend, the boy who broke her heart, to co-star with her on a reboot of the show where they'd fallen in love, both on and off screen.

She smiled wryly to herself. It sounded like the premise of a bad episode of soapy television.

Chapter Two

ERIKA: What's amazing about Parker Wild in the pilot is that he's everything you expect—cocky, full of himself, knows how good-looking he is, the whole hot-guy thing—but he's got this vulnerability he can't hide, and that's why we fall in love with him almost from his first moment on screen.

JULES: I know—when he's trying to charm an extra coffee out of the lady at the donut shop because he doesn't have enough money for two cups, but he knows Amy won't take his if she thinks it's charity—swoon. And I know we're supposed to want Amy to get with Sawyer in the pilot, and, to be honest, when I first saw the show, I wanted that, too, but there's just something unforgettable about Parker there—and my God, his eyelashes. Are. A. Mile. Long.

ERIKA: Truly. Jay Orlando's eyelashes deserve an entire podcast episode.

Jules: Well, it's our podcast, so maybe we'll do one.
Erika: We make the rules.
Jules: Damn right we do.

From *The Sawyer's Cove Rewatch Project Podcast: Pilot*

Jay pushed open the door to the Bakeshop, pleased to see a couple of people in line ahead of him. Trevor was working the counter, and he waved in acknowledgment. A busy bakery was always a good sign. And speaking of signs, he abandoned his spot in line for the cork board on the back wall. There were fliers for lawn care companies, handymen, a couple of doulas, mommy and me yoga—Misty Harbor had so much going on, he had to move over a couple of fliers to make room for his poster advertising the first annual Harbor Fest.

The Pop-art poster design had been done by a friend of his sister Mimi; it added a contemporary look to what was basically a very old-fashioned idea: a town fair, with carnival rides and games, plus booths for local businesses, food trucks, and live music. Misty Harbor was going all out to celebrate the Fourth of July weekend, and hopefully draw some visitors from out of town in the process.

For a town whose economy depended on tourism, the declining numbers at local hotels had been cause for concern at the last town council meeting. Blame had been placed on the recent opening of a resort ten miles down the interstate. They boasted a waterpark and actual beach, instead of the rocky spits that made up Misty Harbor's shoreline.

Trevor was helping the customer in front of Jay when Zelda emerged from the back, wiping her hands on her apron. "Hey Jay, what can I get you?"

"I'll take a coffee and a dozen of whatever you want to get rid of for the library."

"I know what Mimi and company like," Zelda said. "Apple turnovers and chocolate chip muffins."

"Sold."

Zelda was new to Misty Harbor. Well, she'd been there for five years, but that was new in a town where most folks had been born in the local hospital and gone to one of three elementary schools before feeding into the single middle school and high school. Some went as far as UConn for college, a few escaped to New York or Boston and never came back. But not many arrived as adults and stayed, as Zelda had. Misty Harbor was too far for regular commutes to the big cities. Tourism was seasonal—most businesses needed to do well enough in the warm summer months and fall foliage season to make it through the cold winter. You had to make a point to come to Misty Harbor. It was one of the reasons Jay loved it.

"Be careful with that coffee, it's scalding," she instructed him as he balanced the cup on top of the box of pastries, a roll of posters stuck under his arm. "And you have a good day."

"Will do," he said, letting the incoming customer

hold the door open for him as he left the warm cardamom hug of the Bakeshop for the cool early June air of Main Street. He thought he heard Trevor say, "Do you think he knows?", but he was too busy keeping up his balancing act to wonder what that meant.

He avoided spilling anything for two blocks, where his next destination, Misty Harbor's only library, sat in all its gray stone glory. Jay used his hip to activate the automatic opener of the heavy main door, then walked through the lobby that always seemed to smell like Elmer's glue and construction paper. He nodded to the guy at the circulation desk.

"Morning, Colin."

"Morning, Jay. Mimi's in the back."

Jay knew where he was going. He let himself through a door marked "Employees Only" and found himself in the librarians' break room. A tall, handsome woman with curly dyed purple hair held back by a yellow scrunchie leaned against the counter, looking at her rose gold phone. She wore a bright red cardigan over the blue "Keep Calm and Ask a Librarian" shirt he'd given her for her birthday last year.

His sister was nothing if not colorful.

"Hey, sis." He set the box on the ancient Formica table. Hands free, he took a grateful gulp of coffee, wincing when he discovered it was, indeed, as hot as he'd been warned.

Mimi stuffed her phone in her sweater pocket, eyes lighting on the box. "Are those treats for me?"

"For you and everyone else."

She made a beeline for the box, making a *squeeing* noise as she pulled out an apple turnover.

"I'm going to put up some Harbor Fest posters."

"Just leave them, and I'll have one of my staff put them up."

"Thanks."

Through a mouthful of turnover, Mimi said, "Mom was looking for you. She just texted me to ask if I'd seen you."

Jay pulled out his phone, but he didn't have a similar notification. "Why didn't she just text me? Anyway, I'm headed there next." As a founding member of the Harbor Fest planning committee, he had plenty more posters to paper the town with.

Mimi shrugged, then took another bite and moaned. "Zelda must be some kind of witch. Why are these so damn good?"

"Must be her secret ingredient, eye of newt." Jay grinned when his sister stuck her tongue out at him. "I gotta run. You coming to see the band Friday?"

"I booked them, so I'll be there."

"Sweet. Be good, sis."

"Stay out of trouble, little brother."

Unburdened now by the pastry box, half a dozen posters still rolled up under his arm, and life-giving coffee putting a spring in his step, it took Jay only a few minutes to reach the Misty Harbor Inn. Maybe Zelda *was* some kind of witch. Her coffee put anything he could make at home to deep shame.

Jay had practically grown up at the grand hotel,

known locally as simply "the inn." His mom had worked there since before he was born, first as a housekeeper, eventually working her way up to the desk and guest services, until she became assistant manager. Transformed in the sixties to a hotel, the original mansion had been built in the 1800s by a man who'd made a fortune in transatlantic shipping and retired to Misty Harbor. The inn backed up on forty acres of preserved woodlands edged on the west by I-95 and on the east by the Atlantic Ocean.

Jay had been intimidated by the architecture when he was a kid—the place resembled a red stone castle, complete with bats in the belfry and ghosts in the dungeon. When he was old enough for his mom to start taking him along with her to work, he realized how mundane the inn actually was—dumpsters out back, laundry churning night and day in the basement—no dungeon. Maybe a ghost or two, though, in the form of memories of things he used to get up to after hours.

He checked his watch. If he hustled, he could visit Deb, then stop by the inn's co-op daycare and make sure they had everything they needed before his first meeting of the day. The Harbor Fest committee was getting together to make some last-minute decisions, and later the downtown development group was having a mixer at the bar. He'd offered up the space, since Thursdays were one of the few nights they didn't have live music.

He was about to try his mom's office when his phone buzzed. A belated text from Deb?

It was a message from Nash. He'd been shooting in

Bulgaria, or maybe it was Belgium, but his hours had been totally out of sync with Jay's, and they hadn't talked in a while.

> Dude you need to call me
>
> I need to talk to you
>
> Call me
>
> Seriously. Dude. Don't ignore me on this.

Nash had never mastered the art of putting all the info into one message, preferring a machine gun approach to texting.

Having no idea if Nash was even in the States, he figured he'd wait until after he'd checked in with his mom to give his friend a try.

His phone buzzed again. Impatiently, he looked at the text from his mom.

> Hey sweetie. Call me before you come by the inn, okay?

What the hell was wrong with everyone today? Did someone die? He couldn't imagine who in the world could have kicked the bucket that would have both Nash and his mother crawling up his ass. The only thing Deb Orlando, a fifty-two-year-old assistant hotel manager, had in common with Nash Speedwell, B-list television actor and C-list alt-country musician, was Jay himself.

He was literally a hundred feet from his mother's office; he wasn't going to call her when he could just get the bad news of whatever celebrity died and then get on with his day. He'd try Nash later if he had time.

He was about to pass the front desk when he heard the sweep of the inn's automatic door and glanced over his shoulder reflexively, noting the attractive blonde woman who entered the lobby. His head swiveled forward, then back again as he did an involuntary double take.

The woman was a head shorter than him and slightly built. Her shoulder-length hair leaned more toward butter than honey, and her flawless skin was several shades lighter again. She was dressed casually in a knee-length denim skirt and thin, girly flannel, rolled up to her elbows, in shades of purple and blue that he knew matched her eyes. She had sunglasses on, inside, which weren't doing their job because Jay would recognize her anywhere, with the glasses or without. He'd seen her dozens of times on screens large and small in the past decade-plus. But it had been that long since he'd seen her in the flesh.

"Cami."

Camille Corsair, child actor-turned-teenage-"it girl"-turned-big-screen-queen, stopped in her tracks and tipped her head back to meet his gaze. He imagined he could see her round blue eyes widen further under the tinted lenses of her Ray-Bans.

"Jay Orlando. Just the man I want to see." She didn't sound surprised to see him, her naturally cheerful inflection carefully neutral.

His phone buzzed impotently in his hand one last time, and he suddenly realized why everyone had been desperate to get in touch with him. No one had died. They had just wanted to warn him the ghost of girlfriends past was heading his way.

Chapter Three

Erika: Now we get Amy's introduction. Amy Green, shy overachiever, played by Camille Corsair, the quintessential girl next door, if the girl next door looked like a younger, shorter, curvier Nicole Kidman.

Jules: Nicole Kidman? Huh. I always thought she looked a little bit like Claudette Colbert if she was blonde.

Erika: No one is going to get that reference, you know that, right?

Jules: She's petite, heart-shaped face, cute and sassy and pretty. The kind of girl you want to make laugh.

Erika: Wow, that was an awesome description.

Jules: I may have had a tiny crush on Camille Corsair around the time she was doing those dumb rom-coms... okay, I might still have a tiny crush on her. Sue me.

Erika: Hey, I hear you. She's adorable. And how do we know Amy, the character she's about to play for three seasons, is a bookworm and good girl, everyone?

Jules: Because she wears glasses.

Erika: Because she wears glasses. Hoo boy, I wonder if we're going to see a scene with a cute guy sliding them off her face before telling her she actually has really pretty eyes?

Jules: No spoilers, E!

Erika: Oh right, no spoilers. Damn. First episode, and I already forgot.

Jules: It's okay. I forgive you.

Erika: But will the listener? Hi, Mom!

Jules: I think we're gonna find there are a lot of people thirsty to talk about Amy Green's glasses and which cute boy might end up sliding them off her face.

Erika: Fingers crossed!

From *The Sawyer's Cove Rewatch Project Podcast: Pilot*

Cami slipped off her sunglasses and thrust them into her bag. No point trying to stay under the radar, not if Jay was just walking around the inn as if he owned the place. Maybe he did. She'd had no luck finding out what he was up to these days. Hence deciding to track him down in person. It was good practice, anyway. If they were going to be working together again, she'd have to be able to have a conversation with him face-to-face.

Now, seeing him in person for the first time in twelve years, she had to admit—to herself, if no one else—she'd missed that face.

He looked older, obviously. He was almost thirty-three—their birthdays were within a few days of each other at the end of summer. She was going to be thirty-one, and she felt it in every newly developing line on her face, in the way she had to spend an extra fifteen minutes in the makeup chair to erase the rings that formed around her eyes if she didn't get her seven hours a night. Every day she spent in front of the camera was a reminder she was on borrowed time as far as Hollywood was concerned. She'd aged out of teenage roles about five years earlier, and the transition to adult roles had been precarious.

But Jay's adulthood looked good on him. At twenty, he'd been an appealing mixture of boyish and masculine. With his bee-stung lips, liquid brown eyes, and eyelashes for days, he could have been called pretty, but with his lean, muscled torso, strong shoulders, signature close-cropped brown hair, and sharp white canines, he had a masculine edge. At thirty-two, his hair was still shorn close to his head, like a baby lamb after shearing, but he didn't look particularly boyish anymore. Lines were around his eyes, still with an absolute plethora of eyelashes many a makeup artist had swooned over. Not to mention legions of other people.

It had never mattered how long the Connecticut winters were, Jay's skin was always a rich brown, and today, even though his famous arms were covered up by a long-sleeved T-shirt, the V-neck showed his complexion hadn't changed.

"What are you doing here, Cami?" He sounded the

same, too. For a second, she had a moment of vertigo, feeling sixteen again and hearing that warm baritone for the first time. The line could have been accusatory. It certainly wasn't original. But he sounded too surprised to be angry.

"I'm here to see you, like I said."

She'd developed a careful list of talking points, of numbers and dates and reasons he wouldn't be able to say no to her proposal. But in the face of him, the one and only Jay Orlando, she felt curiously ill-prepared. She straightened her spine in defiance. She wasn't a nostalgic fangirl. She was Camille Corsair, goddamn it.

He smiled, slowly, as if he was catching on to a joke. "You came all the way to Misty Harbor to see me? What is that, three thousand miles?"

It would have been if she'd been coming from her place in L.A. She couldn't even remember the last time she'd been there for more than a couple of nights in a row.

"Five hundred, actually. I was in Toronto for a shoot."

His smile dimmed at that. "And you never heard of a phone?"

"Look, I really do need to talk to you, and it might take some time. Are you free now, or can we set something up for later?"

The smile completely vanished. "Seriously, Cami, what's all this about?"

She glanced around the lobby. They'd been blessedly alone for the exchange thus far, but you never knew when a curious hotel guest with an itchy video recording finger would happen across them. "Is there somewhere we can talk? My room? I just ate, but I could order us some lunch."

He shook his head. "I can't. I have a busy day."

She grimaced. She should have known better than to think he would make this easy on her. She thought about Selena and how she had to be willing to get out of her nice girl comfort zone if she was going to be a producer.

"This is important, Jay. I'd really like to talk to you as soon as possible." She could at least get his phone number. She rummaged in her bag to find her phone. Somehow it always seemed to be the last thing she put her hands on.

"Camille?"

Dammit.

She turned to flash a professional smile at whomever had interrupted their moment of privacy, then felt her smile freeze on her face. The woman who'd joined them wasn't a random fan. She was possibly the person in Misty Harbor who might be the least excited to see her. After Jay, of course.

"Hi, Deb," she said, trying to infuse her voice with warmth instead of trepidation.

Jay's mom was an attractive woman, though she didn't look much like her son. The only trait they visibly shared was a proud nose. Deb's was centered on an oval face. With her freckled light skin, green eyes and thick curly brown hair pulled away from her face in a sensible bun, she looked much more like Jay's sister, Mimi. In fact, Deb and Mimi could have passed for sisters themselves. Jay had once told her Deb had only been eighteen when Mimi came along, nine months after prom night, to be exact, but her father had died before she was even born. Jay arrived two years later, the product of a brief encounter with a hotel guest who had never known about Deb's pregnancy. But Deb had never been one of those young moms who tried to be friends with her kids; Cami knew Deb was a protective mama to her core.

And Jay was nothing if not the dutiful son.

That was practically the only thing they'd had in common. Maybe it still was. Jay was a mama's boy, and Camille had always been her father's number one priority. She pushed away thoughts of her dad and the phone call she owed him.

Not for the first time, she considered maybe this detour to Misty Harbor was a way of putting off one uncomfortable conversation in favor of another.

"I heard you got in last night, and I hoped I'd run into you. You look wonderful, Cami," Deb said.

She sounded genuine enough, but in her role as hotel emissary, she couldn't very well spurn a paying guest, could she? Cami took a deep breath. Maybe she wasn't being fair. It wasn't as if Deb had disapproved, exactly, of Cami and Jay's teenage romance. More like lightly skeptical. But that was a long time ago. Cami hadn't had it in her to hope for a warm welcome from people she'd thought she'd never see again.

"Thanks. This place is so lovely."

"I'm happy to hear you say so. Staying long?" She

raised her eyebrows and glanced between Cami and her son.

"A few days. Maybe more."

"Well, I hope we'll see something of you while you're here."

Cami smiled weakly. "I'd love that."

"I'll catch up with you later, okay, Jay?"

"Sure, Mom."

They both turned to watch Deb stride away. Cami let out an audible breath.

"Still scared of my mom, huh?" The smile was back, and even if it was at her expense, Cami liked seeing it on him.

"Can I get your number?" Cami said, instead of reacting to the bait.

Jay recited a string of numbers, slowly enough that she didn't have trouble adding them to her contacts. She immediately texted him and saw his phone light up in his hand. Not that she thought he might give her fake digits. She wasn't that paranoid.

"I have a feeling I'm going to regret asking, but what's all this about?"

She looked around the lobby again. This wasn't the place, but maybe she needed to get it over with.

"Okay, here's the pitch. I'm developing a limited series reboot of *Sawyer's Cove,* and I want you to be in it. I've got a contract drawn up, and I need you to sign so we can finalize things with the studio and the production company. So if you want to put me in touch with your lawyer, we can move to the next step."

Jay had been looking at her steadily as she gave him the spiel she'd rehearsed. It came out drier than she'd practiced.

His mouth quirked. "This is a joke, right?"

"No. We're going to bring back *Sawyer's Cove*. And we need you, Jay. Everyone else has already signed."

He shook his head again. "No. That's impossible. Nash would have—"

She tipped her head to the side. *Nash and Jay were in touch? Huh. Nash hadn't mentioned that.*

"Well, he's been busy on that gladiator show. They're shooting in Bulgaria, right?"

"That explains it," Jay said absently. "Look, Cami, I get that you've come a long way—or, like, a medium-length way, to see me, and you probably have a whole batch of arguments lined up, but the short answer is no."

"No?" Cami refused to process the word. She heard "no" a lot as an actress, but she'd hoped Jay would see the possibility in the show. Would remember the fun they used to have.

Maybe she was the only one who still had fond memories of their time together. It had taken her months—okay, years—to get far enough past the hurt and remember the good times without feeling sick to her stomach at what she'd lost.

"No...thank you?" Jay said, as if this was all a joke.

"Let me take you to lunch, seriously, and we can talk about it. You haven't seen the contract, the numbers we're talking about. It will be worth your while."

"I'm busy for lunch," he said, clipped. "Harbor Fest committee meeting."

"Harbor Fest—oh, right, I saw the banner downtown. Nice artwork."

"Thanks."

"How about dinner?"

"I'll be working."

The man was infuriating. "And what work is that, exactly?"

He ignored her question. "The point is, you'd best head back to Hollywoodland, because I'm not interested."

"Maybe I haven't done the best job of selling the idea to you, but give me a chance. Do you know how popular the show has become in the last few years? It can't have escaped your notice that this town is already obsessed with *Sawyer's Cove*. They have walking tours for the people who come to visit Misty Harbor just because we shot here! There's even a bar called The Cove—I mean, how on-the-nose is that?"

He smiled tightly. "Yeah, uh. I own that bar."

"You do?" She absorbed that, trying to imagine Jay as a bar owner, as any kind of business owner, for that matter.

He looked as if he was about to take off in a run, and she put her hand on his arm to stop him. As soon as she felt the warmth bleeding through his shirt, she knew touching him was a mistake. She dropped her hand as if he was covered in toxic sludge.

"Then you must get how big this could be. The fans would go crazy."

"The fans already are crazy," he said dryly, but without malice.

"My point exactly. We have an active fanbase. We have the studio willing to put up the money. The production company is all ready to put things in motion. Nash and Ariel and Crosby are in. And me, of course." Her voice softened. "You're the last piece of the puzzle, Jay. Cloudy Cove needs Parker Wild."

As she name-dropped his fictional alter-ego, a scowl came over his face. "Look, Cami, Misty Harbor isn't Cloudy Cove. And I'm not Parker Wild. The answer is no. I gotta go."

He left her standing in the lobby, staring after him as if she'd forgotten her line and was waiting for a prompt from the stage manager.

Chapter Four

Jules: You know what I love about how they introduce us to Will O'Connell, played by Nash Speedwell?

Erika: Probably, but tell me anyway.

Jules: Television was far enough along with the gay friend trope that he's already out and we can skip some of the clichés. I mean, I love a well-done coming out story, but that's not what this show is about, and we can just appreciate Will as one of the Cove crowd who just happens to be gay.

Erika: True. And appreciate him, I do. Whew, Nash Speedwell was, what, sixteen, seventeen, and he's unfairly adorable. I don't remember any of the boys in my high school, gay, straight, or other, coming anywhere close to this cute.

Jules: And it's wild to see him here so young and little when on that historical epic show he's all huge muscle guy.

Erika: Totally bulked up. I like him better like this. Dreamy.

Jules: If anyone can pull off skinny arms, it's seventeen-year-old Nash Speedwell. Is it creepy that I'm this into him now that I'm an adult? Don't answer that.

From *The Sawyer's Cove Rewatch Project Podcast: Pilot*

Jay forgot about visiting the daycare and instead turned around and headed right out of the inn again. He couldn't be anywhere near Cami right now. He was still processing the fact that he *had* been near her—they'd been in the same room, practically shared the same air, for several minutes.

And the apocalypse hadn't begun.

Sure, it had felt like it might, for a second, when she started going on about the show and he'd internally freaked out. But he'd kept it together on the outside. Hadn't he? He'd forgotten when he was around her the rest of the world had a tendency to fall away. He'd struggled to understand what she was telling him about the show reboot while he processed the reality of her. She was as beautiful as he remembered, if not more so, but she had a confidence about her that was new to him.

He shook off the residual feeling of her hand on his arm and stalked across the green, gripping his phone aggressively. He had to get back to The Cove to pick up his Land Rover and drive to Melba's house for the

Harbor Fest meeting, but he had someone to berate on the way.

Of all the people Jay spent three years of his life making *Sawyer's Cove* with, Nash Speedwell was the only one who turned out to be more stubborn than him. Nash wouldn't let him give up on their friendship, and no matter how hard Jay tried to ghost him after the show was canceled and he had wanted to go back to being a quietly anonymous homebody, Nash was still there. Kind of annoying, actually.

He stabbed Nash's name on his phone screen as if he was poking his friend in the forehead and was mildly surprised when he picked up on the second ring.

"I have to tell you something," Nash said without preamble.

"You signed on to a *Sawyer's Cove* reboot and didn't warn me?"

There was a pause. "Pretty much, yeah."

Nash didn't sound nearly as apologetic as he should. "What the hell? First of all, when did all this happen? You just forgot to tell me?"

"Look, Selena and Cami called me a month ago, pitched me the idea. I was about to start all these night shoots, and I got totally wrapped up in work, and I actually forgot about it until Mary-Anne told me she had the contract all sorted out. Do you know how much they're offering? Even if I didn't think it was going to be a blast, I'd do it just for the money."

"Mercenary," Jay said, because that was the kind of relationship they had. But it got him wondering just how much they were talking about. He was fine, financially, but the provider part of him that never shut off knew there was no amount of money this town couldn't absorb. The senior center could use an update, and the town pool had seen better days. Not to mention The Cove did all right, but it wasn't as if there weren't some slow months. Maybe if he didn't contribute to his employees' retirements and pay for their childcare, there would be bigger margins, but that wasn't negotiable in his book, no matter how much hand-wringing his accountant did. He shifted gears. "Selena? The writer?" He remembered a curvy girl with masses of black curly hair.

"Yep, Selena Echeveria. She's gonna be the showrunner. You should look at the contract before you say no."

"I already did."

"What? You saw the contract, and you still said no?"

"I said no because I don't want to do it."

"Come on, the studio won't give the go-ahead until all five original cast members sign on."

"That's bullshit. They could just kill me off or write me out or something."

"Are you kidding? They aren't going to pass up the marketing opportunity of getting you back on screen. What a coup—Jay Orlando in his first role since his first role."

Jay imagined the headlines and shuddered. "No, thanks."

"And you'd hold up the entire thing, dash the hopes

of everyone who's working on this project because you want to stick it to your ex-girlfriend?"

"Jesus, it's not about Cami," Jay complained, stung. He didn't *think* it was about Cami, anyway.

"How's she doing? I heard she had a hard shoot in Toronto."

"What? She looked fine," he said automatically, then immediately wondered what she'd been shooting and why it was hard on her. "Except for the fact that she showed up at the inn out of the blue, and I had no advance warning from anyone," he said pointedly.

"Dude, I'm sorry. She messaged me a few days ago, saying she was going to Misty Harbor, but it's been bananas here, and I missed it until today. I tried to give you a heads-up."

Nash sounded genuinely contrite. And it wasn't his fault anyway. But Jay was still mad. He hadn't expected any of this.

"You really think this is a good idea?"

"Yeah, man. It's good money. Selena's a boss, so you know the scripts will be decent. Cami's producing, which is cool. I like to support my friends."

Jay knew what Nash wasn't saying—he was a selfish prick if he didn't do this.

"And remember how much fun we all used to have? You and me and Cami and Ariel. Even Crosby's not so bad."

Of course they'd had fun. Five teenagers spending twelve hours a day, five days a week together. Hormones running high, tons of attention, and the first real money most of them had made as actors. It had been a blast.

Except it hadn't been real. It had been a three-year fantasy. Jay had been living in the real world ever since. He wasn't sure he could face going back.

"I gotta go, man."

"Okay, but think it over. And call me if you need to talk. Or I could come there—should I fly out for a few days?"

"I thought you were in Bulgaria."

"We wrapped a couple of days ago. I'm in Paris doing press, but I could weasel out early."

"No, thanks. I'm good." Jay hadn't expected any of this, but he didn't need Nash to come rescue him for God's sake. He could handle Cami fine on his own.

He just needed to get his head together and remember why signing up to spend time with her wasn't a good idea. No matter how much money was involved.

The rest of the day he functioned on autopilot, trying to stay present for the Harbor Fest meeting but losing track of the conversation until Melba, the semi-retired owner of the diner, touched his arm and threw him a concerned look. He apologized and said he hadn't gotten a great night of sleep. Which was a lie. He'd slept well, but he had a feeling he wouldn't tonight.

They were only barely on budget for this event, and if no one came, it would be a wash. He wanted the Fest to be a success, with plenty of money banked to do it again next year. He would show Cami they didn't need a big Hollywood production coming in to pour money into the local economy. They were doing fine on their own.

"We need to do more promo. What about advertising?"

"Besides the posters and the banner, there's no money in the budget for it," Ray, an accountant who did the books for half the businesses on Main Street, reminded him.

Jay had used his own money to pay the printer. "Well, we can get an article in the paper about it, anyway. Put it in the events section."

"We could try social media," Danica said mildly. She was the manager at The Cove, twenty-five, and never missed an opportunity to make fun of Jay for not being on social media in any way, shape, or form. He'd had a Facebook account in high school, but the minute *Sawyer's Cove* aired, it was inundated with friend requests and sketchy posts. He'd deleted it and never looked back. The town had accounts and put out information that way, to let residents know about storm warnings and city services. He supposed they could use their platforms, too.

"Sure. Whatever. Do it," Jay said.

Danica wrinkled her forehead. "You feeling okay, Jay? You just told me to use social media. I thought Instagram gave you hives?"

He gave her a look. "I'm not a complete Luddite," he answered. "I'm just private."

She rolled her eyes. "And we're trying to get ten thousand people to come to Misty Harbor for this thing. We can't be precious about it."

"I know. I know. That's why I said do it. Jesus."

"What is wrong with you today?" She looked worried rather than annoyed, and he sighed.

"I'm fine. My head's just somewhere else." Twelve years in the past, apparently. Cami's appearance had wrenched the lid off a whole barrel of memories. A few were bad—breaking up with her at the top of that particular list. He still had nightmares sometimes about her stricken expression, the way she'd seemed to literally shrink into herself by the time he was done telling her they were through and he was leaving her in Los Angeles to go back to Misty Harbor.

But some of them were good. Her silk-soft hair bunched in his hands. Her fearlessness in portraying Amy. Her breathless giggle when he'd convince her to sneak off to empty corners of the set to talk or kiss between takes.

Those were the memories that scared him senseless.

"Do you need me to open tonight?" Danica asked.

"No, stick to the schedule. I'll do it." Thursday nights, he always opened. He had a routine, his days were busy and full. He had a life. He *liked* his life. He didn't have room in it to shoot a stupid television show. And he certainly didn't have room in it for Camille Corsair.

Chapter Five

Erika: One thing I love about the show is that it takes place in a tiny coastal Connecticut town, and it looks it.
Jules: That's because they shot it in a tiny coastal Connecticut town.
Erika: Misty Harbor doubles for Cloudy Cove—huh, wonder how they came up with the name?
Jules: Didn't Ryan Saylor grow up there? The executive producer?
Erika: Maybe? Somewhere around there, I think. Anyway, it's super pretty, and they light it so well. It's the quintessential New England town, all that brick. It always feels like fall. You can practically smell the wood stoves and the evergreens.
Jules: Evergreens? It takes place on the ocean. How about the salt air and seagulls?
Erika: What the fuck do seagulls smell like?
Jules: Like the sea, of course!

From *The Sawyer's Cove Rewatch Project Podcast: Pilot*

Cami's corner room at the Misty Harbor Inn had a king-sized bed, attractive writing desk, and two big windows that let in tons of June sunshine. As much as she wanted to draw the blinds and sink into the big claw-foot tub in the oversized bathroom, Cami straightened her shoulders and got to work. If she was going to be a producer, she had shit to take care of.

First, she checked her email and socials, responding to a couple of time-sensitive messages. She posted a picture of her latte from that morning with a generic caffeine addiction caption to keep the social media machine fed, without tagging a location. Her dad hadn't called or emailed recently, but he was copied on an email from her contact at the studio about the reboot. This was her project, but he was still her manager. She needed to call him, but she tried Selena first, to keep her updated on exactly how little progress she'd made so far.

Selena picked up after a single ring. "Hey, that was fast. You got him to sign already?"

"I got him to say no already." She flopped down on the ultra-comfy bed and stared at the eggshell white ceiling. "I ran into him in the lobby and barely got out my pitch before he was turning me down cold."

"He's just playing hard to get." Selena sounded supremely unconcerned. "Does he even have representation anymore?"

"I don't think so." She sighed, longing for the bath. She'd once heard about a famous writer who used to return all their calls from the bathtub on one of those old-fashioned phones. It seemed weirdly intimate to talk to someone while you were naked in the tub, but it wasn't as if they could see you. She rolled her shoulders, cracking her spine in a couple places in the process. Maybe she could find time to get a massage at the inn's spa.

"So let's talk strategy. Did you appeal to his sense of nostalgia?"

"This town is dripping in nostalgia, but apparently Jay is immune, even though he owns a damn bar called The Cove."

"Seriously? How did my research not turn that up? Then he's just holding out for a better offer. Wouldn't a show revival boost his business?"

"He didn't even see the first offer. We never got as far as money. I suck at this."

"Hey, listen to me." Selena's voice was sharp, and Cami sat up instinctively. "You don't suck at this. You're learning, and you're doing an awesome job. No one knows this project better than you. You convinced Nash, didn't you?"

"Nash would do anything for money," Cami said morosely.

"Stop feeling sorry for yourself. Do I need to come out there and knock some self-esteem into you?"

Cami laughed. "I don't think that's how self-esteem works, but thanks."

"All I'm saying is, I know I've been pushing, but this isn't all on you. I can come and help."

That gave Cami pause. So far, she'd been enjoying producing. It was already more satisfying than shooting her last two lackluster movies, and they hadn't even started production.

But Jay was turning out to be her first real test. Was he being difficult just because it was her? Would he have answered differently if Selena had been the one to approach him? No, he'd been the one to end things, way back when. He didn't get to be vindictive, if that's what was fueling his negative response. She wanted this to happen too much to indulge in bitterness over the past. It was a testament to her acting skills that she'd been able to face him down in that lobby and skate nimbly over the decade-old scar of their premature breakup.

Or maybe he really didn't want to be a part of it and it had nothing to do with her. He hadn't acted since *Sawyer's Cove* had ended, after all.

She sighed again. She had to learn how to deal with situations like this if she was going to make it as a producer. And she had to succeed to prove to her dad that she didn't need him holding her hand every step of her career.

"I promise I'll let you know if I need to be rescued. In the meantime, I do have a couple of ideas. I want to go check out his bar, see what the scene is like there."

"Yes, work the bar angle. He's a businessman; appeal to his business sensibility."

Then Selena asked something Cami had been anticipating. Dreading, to be honest.

"Okay, shop talk over. New topic: how did he look?" Selena's voice lost some of its edge as she pivoted from work wife to girlfriend.

Selena knew about their past—everyone who'd worked on *Sawyer's Cove* back in the day had been aware of their relationship. They'd tried to keep it secret for a while, but it was pretty much a lost cause, two horny teenagers constantly surrounded by the rest of the cast and crew had to get creative when they wanted alone time. Looking back, Cami was certain they weren't nearly as subtle as they thought they were. Everyone on the set was probably sick of their puppy love.

"He looked like Jay Orlando, only older."

"Fine, in other words."

"Fine as hell."

"Well, good. I wasn't looking forward to telling him to lose a beer gut."

"No beer gut in sight."

"Whew. I feel like there's something you aren't telling me though."

Cami traced the hem of her skirt, struggling to put her thoughts into words. Life would be so much easier if she could consult a script when she lost her way. "It's just being in Misty Harbor—you know, it feels the same, but nothing is the same. I'm not, anyway. Jay seems different, too."

"You aren't having second thoughts about the show, are you?"

"No. No, that I'm sure is a good idea. But I hate feeling like so much is out of my control."

"That's show business."

She laughed brittlely. One reason she wanted to produce was to feel like she had a modicum of control over her projects, instead of continuing down the safely mediocre path she'd been on for a few years, recycled rom-coms and forgettable horror flicks. Toronto, with its half-baked script and scandal-ridden set, was the last straw. Sure, her bank balance was healthy, and she never lacked for work, but she'd never been in this business for the money.

"On that note, I better go."

"Hey, everything is going to turn out amazing, I promise," Selena said with her usual stark confidence, then hung up before Cami could argue.

Cami knew her friend meant the show, not necessarily her life. She reminded herself that's all she should be worried about. Her career, after all, was basically her life. In the last twelve years, work had taken over until it was pretty much the only thing she had. Even her dad was her manager first, her father second. There would always be a part of her that resented that he couldn't just be her father, that he always put her career before anything else. What would it feel like to make her own decisions and base them on something besides the next project, the next contract, the next job?

Jay had done it. After *Sawyer's Cove*, he could have done almost anything. He'd walked away and chosen the real world over make-believe ones. Clearly it had been the right choice for him, and here she was, trying to pathetically convince him he wanted back in.

Cami tossed her phone down, stalked over to the windows, and gazed out. One side looked over the back of the hotel, the newer ell wings that held the bulk of the rooms. Behind the building, a lawn led to the privately owned woods used by the town for light hiking and dog walking. The other side's view reached all the way to the ocean, glinting gold in the afternoon sunlight.

She'd never been a guest at the inn before. In the old days, Jay had occasionally "borrowed" his mom's keys to sneak onto the pool deck after hours and use the hot tub. Good times. Sneaking around to take a dip in the hot tub was pretty much the most risqué activity her sheltered seventeen-year-old brain could imagine. She didn't drink, she didn't smoke. Making out with her slightly older boyfriend in the hot tub of the hotel where his mom worked—that was as wild as she got.

She'd never been able to afford a wild phase. For one thing, she was too much of a professional to jeopardize any of her jobs with bad behavior. For another, her dad was inevitably hovering nearby. Even when he stopped traveling with her to sets, his voice was in her head, reminding her to be good, to not cause any problems. It wasn't in her to be a diva, but over the years she'd gotten a reputation for being easy to work with, and it was a mixed blessing. She didn't mind being accommodating, but she didn't want to be a pushover. With Selena's help, she was learning to be assertive and ask for more. To demand her due. It was still a work in progress.

A quote from her favorite actress floated into her head. Katharine Hepburn had famously said, "If you always do what interests you, at least one person is pleased." Fuck it. She left the drapes open and retreated to the bathroom to take a damn bath.

Chapter Six

The tub was huge. She always felt guilty taking baths at home in perpetually dry Los Angeles, where every drop of water carried the weight of guilt. But she refused to feel remorse for filling this tub nearly to the brim with steaming hot water. A liberal dose of body wash in lieu of real bubble bath turned the water fragrant and decadently bubbly.

She poured herself a glass of water from the pitcher on her nightstand, brought the portable speakers she traveled with into the bathroom, and pulled up her power playlist on her phone. She twitched her hips in time with the music and dipped her toe in to judge the temperature. She always liked it this side of scalding. Inch by inch, she sank under the water, her peach skin pinking up in the heat.

Seeing Jay with no warning had messed with her head. She'd still had coffee breath and crumbs from her breakfast on her skirt. Next to no makeup. It wasn't as if he hadn't seen her in every stage of makeup and not, clothed and...not. But that was when she'd been a teenager who could stay up all night and still look fresh and lovely for shoots the next day.

No, she wasn't going to think about the old days. She had to focus on the present, on the future. This time next year, if all went well, the new season of *Sawyer's Cove* might already be out. It might have been a big hit. And it would have been partly because of her.

She just had to convince Jay it was in his best interest to be a part of it. She'd struck out once, but she didn't give up that easily.

Jay Orlando. She was a little surprised he looked as good as he did, quite frankly. His job was no longer to be hot and say lines. But he had the same look, the one that had made the casting director pluck him out of a line of dozens of hopefuls and say, "That is the one."

It wasn't his looks that had turned her head on the set of *Sawyer's Cove*. She'd been around thousands of attractive people since she started acting. All the actors on the show were appealing in their own way. Crosby was fair, his light coloring contrasting with his glowering mood, but the angst worked for him. Nash was different, nicer, with a touch of country good-old-boy manners. Cami had always liked him, had rooted for him after the show, because he was both genuinely talented and had a good heart.

But Jay was the one she'd looked at twice, the one who had given her butterflies from nearly day one. Partly it was because he'd never been on a set before. He had to learn everything from zero, and he tried to pretend like he didn't care, but she could tell he did, desperately. He wanted to do a good job, and she admired that. He was kind to everyone. From the assistants to the director, he treated everyone with the same level of respect. Later, when he got more comfortable on set and in the role, out came his playful side, the one that made him such a good fit to play Parker Wild.

Parker was a jokester, a damaged kid who used humor as a coping mechanism to deflect from his pain, to make it invisible to people around him. Jay wasn't as clownish as Parker in real life, but he understood everything Parker did was a choice to protect himself from the world, from people who could affect him, both negatively and positively. He'd always told her life wasn't easy for his single working mom in this small town, but he'd had a pretty great childhood, all the same. If Jay had baggage, he didn't show it, or he used it to make Parker more than just a class clown with a pretty face.

Jay made her laugh. And every time he did, he'd grin, as if he'd won some private challenge with himself.

They were laughing the first time they kissed.

She'd been stressed out over a scene where she'd be fighting with her on-screen mom. She always found scenes between Amy and her mom hard because she felt like she was simply copying someone else's performance. She had never been a teenager with a mom to fight with, after all. That day, Jay had noticed her pacing and nervously going over her dialogue. He'd pulled her outside and put on a fake high voice, flawlessly imitating the actor who played her mom as they ran the lines. She was laughing, and then she tripped in the stupid wedge heels she was wearing for the scene and stumbled forward. Jay caught her. He stopped laughing. And then he kissed her.

She'd had dozens of stage kisses by then, and they had been nothing like that one.

In the steaming hot bath, Cami shivered as she recalled the sensation of that kiss. His soft lips, their teeth bumping together, the brush of his nose against hers.

When they stopped kissing, Jay had the biggest smile on his face, as if she'd made him the happiest guy in the world by falling like a klutz and fumbling through her first real kiss.

Everything happened so easily after that. One moment they were friends and co-workers, after the kiss they were everything to each other.

She shook off the memories and reached for the

body wash. Maybe her issue was that she hadn't so much as kissed anyone, for a role or not, in months. She did the math in her head as she lathered up her arms. Her last relationship had ended when the screenwriter she'd been seeing left her to date a higher-profile actress. At least he'd been honest with her and she hadn't had to see photos of them on social media while she still thought they were exclusive.

That was almost a year ago. Not her longest dry spell, which was a sad enough statistic to give her pause. She'd gotten used to putting her love life at the bottom of the list. Hell, she'd never expected to have it all. A thriving career as an actress was more than most people could hope for. Still, it nagged at her that she had this beautiful hotel room, this big fancy tub, and no one to share it with.

She slid a soapy hand up her leg slowly. She felt restless from remembering what it was like with Jay, how big he was, how she'd cling to his strong shoulders as he kissed the breath out of her. He'd asked her to wait until she was eighteen to have sex. Since there were only a few months to go by the time they got together, she'd agreed to wait, and they did everything but in the meantime.

Her hand traveled farther, tracing her belly and the curve of her breasts as they floated in the water. She remembered how impossible it was to find privacy to do anything physical together. The set was a nightmare—a dozen people were liable to walk in on them at any moment. The apartment where she lived with her dad was a no-go. Jay had it worse—he could have moved out, but with Mimi away at college, he'd decided to stay put, living with his mother in their small condo. He had his own room, and sometimes Deb worked late at the inn, but still.

Their best bet was to take Jay's Land Rover Defender, a monstrosity of a vehicle that he'd bought early in the show's run, out for drives. He'd been driving a beat-up station wagon to and from the set for the first few episodes. Once they started getting paid and it looked like they would be picked up for another season, he showed up one day in the dark gray SUV on steroids. He was so proud of it.

He'd pick her up, and they'd drive over back roads to woodsy turnoffs, listening to music and sharing a giant bag of candy she was pretty sure he'd swiped from craft services. They'd stop and make out, their kisses tasting like chocolate and food coloring, until she'd beg him to touch her. He'd oblige, stroking inside her with blunt fingers. Every time he felt how slippery wet she was, his breath would catch, and he'd squeeze his eyes shut, as if he was concentrating on how she felt, awed and surprised at the evidence of her arousal.

She echoed his technique now, teasing open the folds of her sex, fingers seeking out her slippery channel. She was getting wet just thinking about him and those epic makeout sessions in the backwoods of Connecticut.

As she touched herself she gave in to the urge to picture Jay and his liquid chocolate eyes, his strong, capable fingers. She closed her own eyes, pretending it was him touching her pussy, him kneading against her clit. It felt wrong—a little dirty, in the best possible way —to actively think about someone she normally spent a lot of energy trying not to think about while she did this.

She moved faster, pressed harder, let her legs fall open, the water in the bath making waves over the peaks of her hardened nipples. She felt hot all over, and so, so close. She screwed her eyes tighter, bit her lip, picturing Jay's face, the way his eyelids came down almost to a close when he was really focused on her pleasure, the way he coaxed orgasms out of her with his fingers and his voice, murmuring against her temple or her neck, his breath hot and damp against her sensitive skin as he told her how beautiful she was, how much he wanted her, how good it felt to make her—

She came as his words from so long ago echoed around her head in the voice she'd heard him use just that morning.

She opened her eyes slowly to the late afternoon light streaming through the high window in the bath-room. She shivered again, goosebumps on her skin belying the heat of the water. She felt drowsy after her orgasm. Water had sloshed over the side of the tub, making a puddle on the tile floor. She reached over to knock a towel onto the mess, pressed her hands to her flaming cheeks. If she looked in a mirror, she'd be pink from head to toe.

Well, that was a huge mistake. A fresh orgasm thinking about the man she wanted something very specific from—not sex—was only going to complicate matters.

Still, as she scrubbed herself clean and carefully chose her outfit for tonight's campaign, she couldn't bring herself to truly regret it. What happened in the bath was between her and the tub.

Chapter Seven

JULES: Part of our obsession with this show is that it was about teenagers who were actually played by teenagers. Instead of twenty-five-year-olds playing fifteen-year-olds, they had sixteen-year-olds playing fifteen-year-olds. It made it feel so much more real. Not that the soapy storylines were particularly realistic, but it looked real, so it felt real. You felt like these teenagers were actually going through some shit.

Erika: Four of the five leads were only sixteen when they started production, and Jay Orlando was eighteen, but he'd never acted before.

JULES: Complete unknown.

ERIKA: Should we talk a little bit about the casting process?

JULES: How long is this episode going to be, like four hours?

ERIKA: We can just cut it later.

JULES: You mean I can just cut it later. We don't have an editor.

ERIKA: Fine, you can cut it later, and I'll buy you a cinnamon roll from the place you like.

JULES: Sold. I'm easy.

FROM *THE SAWYER'S COVE REWATCH PROJECT PODCAST: THE DOUBLE DARE*

Jay hadn't worked behind the bar in a while, but the downtown development event had attracted a surprising number of patrons. Until Danica came on shift, the only bartender, Chelsea, was a little swamped, so he threw on an apron, washed his hands, and started pulling pints.

"Nice turnout," Chelsea shouted over the din of Misty Harbor business owners getting mildly buzzed on local brews. Clarence in the kitchen was busy turning out nachos and jalapeño poppers like it was a game night and not a business mixer.

"We should make this a monthly thing," he said. They already had trivia twice a month, and live music at least three nights a week. Danica had suggested they start opening for lunch instead of waiting till happy hour, but he'd resisted. They weren't exactly a gastropub—they had a limited apps menu and a few basic items—burgers, pizza, stuff that came ready-made from the restaurant supply company a single cook could take care of except on the busiest of days. But it was something to think about.

He spotted a non-business owner walk in and snag a spot at the bar. Warner was one of their regulars. Jay had heard him once say he wasn't a professional drunk but was studying hard for the qualifying exam. Warner had the air of someone with a sad backstory, or perhaps just a regular white dude who felt the weight of the world. It wasn't exactly clear what he did for a living, or if he had a job at all, but he always settled his tab, and he tipped well, which was good enough for Jay.

"The usual, Warner?"

"Make it a double."

"I thought your usual was a double."

Warner smiled wryly and saluted. He was dressed like an ordinary thirty-something guy in jeans and a slightly rumpled blue denim button down, but he had the mannerisms of a jaded P.I. in post-war America.

Jay poured him a couple of fingers of bourbon, started a tab, and put in an order for Warner's regular burger without asking. The guy seemed like maybe he'd forgotten to eat today, and Jay didn't want him drinking on an empty stomach.

He looked up when the door opened yet again to see Cami striding into his bar. Of course.

He'd figured their exchange that morning wasn't going to be the end of the story. For one thing, according to what Nash said, if Jay wasn't going to do the project, that meant they weren't going to get greenlit, and there were too many people with money to lose if that happened. He had no illusions Cami or her people would take his initial response as the final answer.

But he hadn't expected her to walk into The Cove looking like *that*.

She stood just inside the entrance, taking a survey of the room. Her expression was neutral; if she was surprised there were so many people in a bar in Misty Harbor on a Thursday evening, she didn't show it. But her stillness allowed Jay to take in every inch of her, from her high-heeled boots to her artfully tousled hair. *Sex hair*, his mind helpfully supplied.

She wasn't dressed up, not formally anyway, but she looked put together, like she had a stylist hidden away in her hotel room. Hell, maybe she did. Maybe she traveled with a whole entourage of assistants and employees and professional friends who were there to make her look good.

Not that she especially needed help with that last part. She had always looked good to Jay, whether she was wearing baggy pajamas or a ball gown.

But if she traveled with an entourage, where were they now? Shouldn't she have some personal security, at the very least? Anyone could come up and do or say anything to her right now, and she'd be completely unprotected. He didn't like the thought of that.

She looked particularly alone, standing in a pool of light from one of the faux-industrial fixtures that kept the ambiance in The Cove inviting. Her black high-waisted trousers ended above the ankle, showing off those chunky heeled boots, and a simple black tank top showcased her slim, pale arms. She carried a black sweater, along with a small black purse. She looked sophisticated, beautiful, and so very out of place.

Warner swiveled his barstool to see what Jay was staring at, whistled low, and turned back around. "Classy dame. Friend of yours?"

Jay narrowed his eyes at Warner. Either he didn't recognize Cami, or he was fucking with him. Jay didn't know how to feel about either option. But even if Warner didn't recognize her, someone else was bound to. Before he could overthink, he was out from behind the bar and striding up to her.

She watched him approach with a smile on her face. Jay had made an extensive catalog of Cami's smiles over the time he'd known her. This one felt fake; she exuded confidence and star power, hell, she was practically glowing, but it seemed forced.

He wanted to take her by the elbow and steer her to the back office, out of sight, where no one could bother her. But touching her seemed like a very bad idea. Instead, he smiled at her tightly. "What are you doing here?"

"Oh, is this a private club? Do I need a password?"

His molars smashed together at her sassy rejoinder. "Look, Amy Green can't just waltz into The Cove. It's like throwing chum to the sharks."

Her smile grew sharper. "Aren't you getting confused? Didn't you just tell me that Misty Harbor isn't Cloudy Cove? That no one cares that Jay Orlando was once Parker Wild? Why should anyone care about me? I'm not Amy Green either."

"I'm not an attraction anymore," he said. "No one gives a shit if they see me on the street."

He felt a pang of guilt at the statement, which wasn't strictly true. Only last week, one of those silly walking tours had turned the corner as he'd been heading to visit Mimi at the library, and he'd had half a dozen twenty-something girls begging for selfies with him, which he'd sheepishly posed for.

"But you—you're actually famous."

"I am?" She blinked her big blue eyes innocently. "What does that have to do with anything, Jay?"

"Because if Camille Corsair and Jay Orlando are in the same place, it—it means something."

"What does it mean?"

He opened his mouth, then closed it. What *did* it mean? Why was he freaking out about this? He felt Warner's jaundiced gaze on them. What did they look like? Two old friends exasperated with each other? Two ex-lovers navigating a surprise encounter? Parker and Amy, more than a decade older, still as much chemistry as ever?

He squeezed his eyes shut. No. They weren't those stupid characters, and if Cami wanted to draw attention to herself, that was her own business.

"Fine. Never mind. You want a drink?"

She glanced down at his apron, then back up to his face. The mischievous smile was back. "What do you have on tap?"

His shoulders relaxed. Maybe he was overreacting. The citizens of Misty Harbor were pretty cool, after all.

He walked back to the bar and trusted her to follow him. She shimmied onto the stool next to Warner, the one closest to the back exit, he noticed. From down the bar, Chelsea threw them a curious glance, but she was busy enough getting orders out and left them alone.

"We have a great lineup of local brews. You want something light or dark?"

"Light," she said. "Not bitter."

"Hefeweizen?"

"Sure."

It occurred to him as he poured that she hadn't even been old enough to drink the last time he'd seen her. He'd missed her twenty-first birthday, and eleven more besides. Regret, which once had dogged his every breath but was now only an occasional visitor, soured his stomach as he grabbed a slice of orange for the rim, slid her glass toward her on a coaster. He wasn't Tom Cruise in *Cocktail*, but he'd do.

The polished copper bar top reflected the overhead lights and let off a warm glow. Cami tasted the beer. Her lips came away glistening, and Jay had trouble looking away.

He finally tore his gaze from her face and collided with Warner's knowing glance. Asshole.

"Shut up," he growled.

Warner's smirk deepened.

"You must be a friend of Jay's," Cami said brightly.

Warner bared his teeth at her, as if he could manage a smirk but a smile was out of his comfort zone. "I'm well-acquainted with his liquor cabinet.

Speaking of which." He tapped his empty glass. "I could use a refill."

"After your food comes out," Jay said. He didn't need six feet of soused Warner to deal with on top of whatever drama Cami was bringing in with her.

Not that she was like that. She wasn't one of those actresses who cultivated drama in her personal life. At least, she hadn't back then.

Shit, this was so annoying. She was keeping him on edge, making him feel like an insecure twenty-year-old when he was on his home turf here. She should be the one out of place, but she appeared perfectly at ease perched on her barstool, downing Hefeweizen like it was her job, pretty and cool all at once.

Of course, it was her job, in a way. She got paid to be cool, or to be scared, or happy, or in love. She had to be able to project confidence, to act like she belonged, if that's what the role required.

Was she playing a role now?

Someone nudged him with an elbow. He turned, but instead of Chelsea, Danica was there, tying on her apron.

"Hi," she said brightly to Cami, "I'm Danica. Did the boss here forget to give you a menu?"

Without waiting for Cami to respond, she grabbed one from behind the counter and slapped it down. "The sweet potato fries are really good. Hey, Jay, can I talk to you for a minute?"

Then she yanked on his arm and pulled him through the swinging door to the kitchen without leaving him time to protest. The odor of grilling meat was strong as Clarence worked the grill behind them.

"So glad you're here; we've been slammed."

His number two ignored him. "What is Camille Corsair doing here?" Danica hissed.

"She's—it's complicated. Why?"

Danica's face cleared. "Oh! This is why you've been moody today."

"Give me a break." He tried to sound casual, as if he had visits from famous actress ex-girlfriends all the time. "She's actually a friend." They had been friends, once upon a time. Maybe enough time had passed since the other stuff that it could be true again. He'd stayed friends with Nash, maybe he could do the same with Cami, and explain to her reasonably, friend to friend, why he wasn't going to do the reboot.

Danica didn't look convinced. "Well, let me know if you need backup."

Why would he need backup? "Sure. Now go help Chelsea. I'll cover Warner and Cami and anything else that comes up."

"Cami, huh?" Danica looked at him with a speculative gleam in her eyes he didn't like. "Well, just don't forget to schmooze your business buddies tonight. You need to make sure they've filled out their sponsorship forms for Harbor Fest."

That was actually good advice, and how he'd planned to spend his evening before Cami walked in and distracted him. It was so much easier to blame her for the way his head had been turned around all day than to admit to himself the idea of revisiting *Sawyer's Cove* held the tiniest sliver of appeal.

Clarence pushed a plated burger onto the pickup counter, and Jay took it. "You help Chelsea. I'm fine." He ignored Danica's eye roll, returned to the bar room, and set the plate down in front of Warner.

Warner was talking to Cami, who had her full attention on him, nodding along with whatever shit he was no doubt spouting, so she didn't see the two college-aged young women approach her with shy smiles and an outstretched cell phone. But Jay did.

He was around the end of the bar and next to Cami in two long strides. The girls probably just wanted a photo, but you never knew. With a swell of nervous irritation, he wondered again why she didn't have someone playing interference for her.

"We're huge fans," the girl with dyed black hair and Doc Martens said. "Could we get a picture with you?"

Cami agreed graciously, leaning her head in so the other girl, who was taller and had longer arms, could take the picture. When they'd snapped the pic, Cami started to make conversation. "Do you live here in Misty Harbor?"

They giggled in unison. The long-armed one said, "No, we're on a post-graduation road trip. We bonded over *Sawyer's Cove* first day of freshman year. We heard about this place and the tour you can go on, and we just had to make it one of our stops. But we never imagined we might see you here, I mean, this is incredible!"

"So you guys like *Sawyer's Cove*, huh?" Cami asked encouragingly.

Jay frowned. What was she doing? He found it hard to believe she needed her ego stroked.

"OMG, it's the absolute best. So much angst. We watch the carnival episode all the time."

Cami smiled. "That's one of my favorites, too."

The girls cooed at that. "You are so pretty. I can't believe we're talking to Amy Green."

"Thanks, it's always nice to hear people still like the show."

"My mom used to watch it when it was on," said Doc Martens, "but I didn't discover it until I was in high school. I couldn't believe it when I got to the last episode. How could they leave it like that?"

"What do you think should have happened?" Cami asked.

"I always imagine that Parker got on a plane and followed her to college. I like to think they were able to stay together," Doc Martens said decisively.

"Parker and Amy are definitely my OTP. I also wish Will and Noah hadn't broken up. They were my second favorite," Long Arms contributed.

Jay couldn't believe Cami was talking to these fans as if they were a test screening audience she was mining for plot ideas.

"Hey, Jay," Cami said, as if she was just now noticing him. "Come meet, uh, what are your names?"

"I'm Tracy," said the girl with the long arms, "and this is Beth. Oh my God, Jay Orlando."

He gave them a practiced smile. "Hey, welcome to The Cove." He raised his eyebrows at Cami. What was she doing?

"So it's true you own this place?" Beth asked. "There's a whole Tumblr thread about it, but I thought it was just speculation."

"Afraid so," he answered.

"Wow, you guys are so nice. My mom is not going to believe this. I have to go text her," Beth said.

"Thank you so much," Tracy added.

The girls resettled at the table they had presumably come from. Warner was hunched over his booze and food, so Jay felt free to ignore him.

Cami, however, would not be ignored.

Chapter Eight

ERIKA: The most interesting casting story is Jay Orlando's, of course. The studio marketing people thought it would drum up interest in the show if they did one of those open casting calls to try to find an unknown. The other four already had Hollywood credits—Camille Corsair was in a few movies, Spencer Crosby had done a bunch of theater, Ariel Tulip had modeled and done a few indie features, and Nash Speedwell had done lots of commercials and a few guest parts on TV, most notably as "boy with mysterious rash" on that doctor show.

JULES: Oh, I love that episode.

ERIKA: I know, he's so good. But the point is, Jay was one of literally hundreds of guys they auditioned in the Northeast. They wanted someone local, someone "authentic" to play the hot bad boy jokester Parker Wild. The casting director said she was drawn to his, quote, appealing features, charming smile, and good nature, end quote. Whatever that means.

JULES: I think it means that he's, like, objectively hot, but he's not a jerk. And for Parker Wild to really work as a character, he has to be both good-looking enough to justify the cockiness and good-natured enough to not completely write him off as an asshole. And Jay Orlando is both of those things...no acting required.

FROM *THE SAWYER'S COVE REWATCH PROJECT PODCAST: THE DOUBLE DARE*

"See, this proves my point."

Jay seemed to slip from polite interest into glower mode as soon as Tracy and Beth left. "What point?"

"That there's still an audience for *Sawyer's Cove*. An audience willing to travel for miles just to visit a place with a tangential connection to it. I mean, for a joint called The Cove, I thought there'd be more to the theme, Jay."

The moment Cami had walked in, she'd instantly taken to the place, with its warm lighting, comfortable-looking chairs, gleaming copper bar top, and intimate stage off to one side that was currently empty. She could imagine that local musicians would bring in crowds on the weekends. But other than the name, there was nothing directly connecting The Cove to *Sawyer's Cove*. Not that she exactly expected framed cast photos or a television playing the show on a loop.

"Why did you call it that, anyway?" she asked.

"I told you, it wasn't my idea," he drawled as he crossed his arms.

Cami held his gaze until he sighed and relented.

"My sister thought it would be a hook that would set it apart. And in the end, I figured it was subtle enough that it wouldn't turn off people who didn't know about the show."

"But you get your share of show-oriented tourists?" she guessed.

He grudgingly nodded.

"Well, it's a great place, Jay. I can see why people would want to come here, stay a while."

He looked around, as if trying to see it through her eyes. "I've tried to make it more than a watering hole. Half the downtown business owners are networking over there. We're the only small live music venue in the area. Misty Harbor needed a downtown nightspot."

Jay spoke like she was a loan officer he needed to convince of the viability of his business. But what came through was how much he cared about contributing something to his community.

Cami wasn't surprised. Jay had always been a cheerleader for Misty Harbor. He wasn't one of those kids who couldn't wait to get out of their hometown. On the contrary, it had been almost impossible to get him to travel outside it. He'd only gone to Los Angeles once because he was contractually obligated to do press there.

Her mind skittered away from that trip, the one that left her brokenhearted and alone while Jay flew back to Misty Harbor for good.

In a flash, Cami realized her approach was all wrong. She'd been emphasizing the show and what it meant to the fans. She needed to explain what it could mean to Misty Harbor. This town was Jay's first love, not her. There was no use in appealing to his nostalgia when obviously the past didn't mean as much to him as the future of the town.

She swiveled on her barstool to face him fully. "Look, I'm going to be honest with you. The studio wanted us to move the production to Canada, but Selena and I pushed for filming back here in Misty Harbor, and we got them to agree. Think about it, Jay. We can handpick the locations we use in town. We could even use The Cove. Think about the location fees, all that crew being put up around town, craft services—we're talking hundreds of thousands of dollars all going directly into the Misty Harbor economy. Not to mention the exposure. All those old fans, all those new ones—some of them are going to want to visit, stay at the inn, drink at The Cove, shop at all the little shops."

Jay looked grumpier than ever, which she decided was a good sign. He could be stubborn about this if he wanted, as long as he signed on the dotted line in the end.

"Let me know when you're ready to see the contract." She slid off the stool, tucked a bill under her pint glass, and headed for the door. She had mastered powerful exits long ago.

She was halfway up the next block when he caught up to her.

"Shouldn't you have someone with you?" he asked disagreeably. He'd lost the denim apron, but his grumpy face hadn't budged.

She took perverse satisfaction in being such a thorn in his side. "What, like a chaperone? I'm not eighteen anymore, Jay."

"Like security. Misty Harbor is safe, but I don't think it's a good idea for you to be walking around at night alone."

"Are you serious right now?" She stopped and looked up at him, because even in her high-heeled boots she was still half a head shorter than him. "It's barely even dark."

"I guess I'm not used to..." He stopped, started walking again without waiting to see if she'd follow. "I'll walk you back to the inn, if that's where you're going."

She wasn't about to let him off the hook and hastily started moving to catch up. "Not used to what?"

"Your dad wouldn't let you go anywhere alone back then. But obviously you can do what you want now."

"The sooner you get that into your head, the better." She declined to share it took years before her dad got the message she was an adult woman who didn't need a keeper. Sometimes he acted like he still didn't believe it. "And I'm hungry. I was going to the diner."

"Melba's?" He sounded surprised.

"You got a better suggestion?"

"There's Antonio's, the Himalayan place, sushi."

"Misty Harbor's gotten cosmopolitan."

"We try. But Melba's is good. I haven't been there in a while."

She couldn't decide if he was angling for an invitation or not. She thought about her trip down memory lane earlier, and her bare arms got goosebumps. Maybe it was a good idea to get more exposure to him—the grumpiness was a turn-off that would erase all those old feelings.

"You want to get a bite with me?" She kept her voice brisk. "I promise I won't talk business."

"Really?" He side-eyed her. "Are you sure you can stop yourself?"

"I'll do my best."

She spent the next two blocks thinking of something to say that didn't have to do with work. She was about to resort to a comment on the weather when they arrived at the diner.

Jay held the door open for her to pass through, smiling at the middle-aged woman in the fifties-style red and white polyester uniform behind the chrome hostess stand. The server's name tag read "Loretta," as if she was right out of central casting. Cami didn't remember her. Loretta knew Jay, though. As she showed them to a booth, she made small talk about the new streetlight being installed in front of the middle school. They had both testified at the public information session apparently. Cami shot a curious look at Jay. What didn't he have a hand in around here?

Loretta laid menus down on the Formica tabletop and took Jay's order for black coffee.

"I'm going to need a minute," Cami said. Loretta nodded genially and bustled off, returning momentarily with Jay's coffee.

She scanned the menu, trying to decide if she should give in to her sudden craving for a chocolate malt. It was probably sacrilegious to eat at a place like this and not order something unhealthy. While she debated, she said, "I forgot you can drink caffeine and not have it keep you up."

"It's a gift and a curse," he said, warming his hands on the mug. "I think I read somewhere it's a genetic thing. Some people just aren't affected by it."

"Is your mom?" she asked.

"She's strictly a morning drinker. Mimi, too."

"Must be—" Cami stopped herself. She'd always found it awkward to acknowledge Jay's father, or lack thereof. But that was then. She was more mature now, wasn't she? "From your dad's side of the family."

He didn't seem bothered by the allusion. "Yeah, I guess."

"So what are you going to get?"

"I already ate, but I could go for some fries."

"Your metabolism hasn't slowed down, then?" Jay had been notorious for eating his way through the catering table on set and asking for more.

"I burn through a lot of calories taking care of this town," he said.

"You're not actually the mayor and someone forgot to tell me, are you? You only act like you own the place, right?"

"Not the mayor. Carl Kurtzman would be very offended if I implied I was after his job. I'm not interested in public office, but I'm a big fan of public-private partnerships. We all have a vested interest in seeing Misty Harbor thrive."

"That's why—" She refrained from launching into her spiel again, put a finger over her lips briefly. "You're trying to get me to break my promise."

"Sorry. I guess I'm as bad as you are. I honestly don't have that much to talk about outside of work stuff."

"The bar, you mean?"

"Yeah, the bar and everything that comes with being a business owner. People depend on me for jobs, and that's a responsibility I take seriously."

"I can see that." It was strange how different he was from the energetic, goofy kid she'd once known. He was still as charismatic as ever, but he'd put all that charisma in service of something real, something that impacted people's lives. She believed in the power of entertainment to heal and make lives better, not to mention it was an important industry that employed a lot of people. But it was also ephemeral. You made a movie, it came out, people tweeted about it for a few days. Sure, it lived on, but sometimes the projects she did felt disposable. Maybe that was why she felt passionate about going back to *Sawyer's Cove* and cementing its legacy. It was a show that had endured, that continued to inspire fans and commentary. It felt nice to be part of something bigger.

But it seemed Jay didn't care about that.

"So tell me about the town, about the people. I've already met some cool folks."

"Misty Harbor's thriving for the most part, but there's always more work to do. Tourism goes up and down, but what I'd really like to see is more people moving here. We lose young people all the time to the bigger cities. That's one of the reasons I offer full benefits and childcare to my employees."

"You pay for your employees' childcare?" That seemed above and beyond, even to her.

He rubbed the back of his neck with his hand, as if reluctant to take credit. "Yeah. I sort of talked the inn into doing it, too. It's a co-op. There are good private daycare and preschool options, but most of the people who work in service industries can't afford those, and they're the ones who need it most. I just thought it would be good if they could do their jobs and not have to worry about finding childcare during their shifts."

Cami could connect the dots between Jay's position on this and the fact that his mother raised him and his sister alone while working full-time at the inn.

"So what'll it be?" Loretta was back and looking at them expectantly.

Cami decided. "I'll have a patty melt and a chocolate malt, please."

"A side of fries," Jay added.

"Mayo and ketchup?" Loretta asked.

"You know it," Jay responded.

Loretta bustled away, and Cami was going to ask what the mayo was for, but then she remembered—Jay liked to mix mayo and ketchup into a kind of sweet-sour sauce for his fries. Weirdo. How could she have forgotten that?

She surveyed Jay and realized she hadn't forgotten anything. She remembered every quirk and every expression and every way being with him made her feel. It was all still there, in the darkest recess of her heart that she'd ruthlessly locked up in order to survive after he left her.

This entire endeavor suddenly seemed like a really bad idea. If she got him to agree to this project, they'd be spending weeks on end together, and there'd be no protection from the inevitable bubbling up of memories. She wanted to make this show, she wanted to produce it, but she was starting to understand exactly what she was signing herself up for. Mild emotional torture at the very least, getting her heart broken all over again at the very worst. That is, if he even said yes.

She felt damned either way.

But maybe her dramatic side was overreacting. Jay could have a girlfriend, making whatever chemistry they still had irrelevant. Any memories they shared could be blasted back to the past, where they belonged.

"Tell me, do you have a better half these days?" Cami asked.

"Excuse me?"

"A significant other," she clarified, doing her best to hold her chin high and not seem like she cared one way or the other about the answer.

"Why do you want to know?" Jay asked.

"Just wondering if there's someone with some sense I could appeal to."

Jay shot her a darkly amused look. "Ha. Well, sorry to disappoint you. I'm single."

Cami's stomach tightened at the focus in his eyes. It was just muscle memory responding to his smolder. She forced lightness into her tone. "I'm surprised. You're such a mother hen, I'd have figured you to settle down with some kids of your own by now."

He didn't answer her at first, which was fair. She shouldn't be pressing like this, but it was hard to remember where the lines were with someone she'd once shared everything with. "Came close with a couple of relationships. But they weren't meant to be."

"Oh." Of course he hadn't been single for the last twelve years. She decided she didn't need to know the details.

"What about you? You must have someone waiting for you back in L.A."

"I'm hardly ever there. And no someone, not for a while." She smiled briefly, unwilling to go into her numerous romantic failures. She'd been hurt, been bored, even occasionally been happy with some of the guys she'd dated over the years, but she'd never loved any of them. Most of the time, she thought not loving them made it easier. Sometimes it made it harder. But as she sat across from the one person she knew she'd truly loved, she was glad she hadn't tried to talk herself into any grand love affairs. They were too world-shattering when they ended.

"Too busy?"

It was sweet, him trying to make excuses for her pathetic love life.

"Not meant to be, as you said." She shrugged. The guys she'd been with weren't looking to find their other half, mostly they were looking for exposure to further their own careers. "I don't want to tie myself to someone who only sees Camille Corsair, B-list actress, when the person they'll end up with at the end of the day is Cami Cosinsky, Valley girl."

Jay's eyes grew even darker, along with his expression, but then Loretta set down their plates, Cami's malt, and two squeeze bottles and hustled off again.

Cami watched in fascination as Jay squirted two mountains of mayo and ketchup respectively on the side of his plate, took a French fry, and swirled the condiments together to make a camellia-pink dip.

"That takes me back." She took a long sip out of her malt. "And so does this. Delicious. The metal straw is new, though."

"We enacted a citywide ban on single-use plastics last year. Disposable straws are now only available on request."

She felt steadier with the food and transition to a new topic. "I love that. Misty Harbor seems to have changed a lot."

"For the better, I hope."

"I always liked it here."

"You did?"

"Sure, it was my home base for three years. I don't

think I've ever lived anywhere for that long, except for our house in the Valley when I was a little girl." She barely remembered her childhood home, could vaguely picture a modest ranch house with an orange tree in the front. Her mom had gotten sick, and after she died, her father had put the house on the market right away. They moved to an apartment closer to the studios to make last-minute auditions easier. Once she started working, she was often traveling.

"I never thought about it like that," Jay said.

He'd finished half his fries, and she'd barely put a dent in her patty melt. It was greasy and salty and amazing, and she probably wouldn't be able to finish half of it. Not when the malt was sitting right in front of her, calling her name.

"So how's Mimi?" She'd always liked Jay's older sister, but since she was away at college most of the time they were shooting, they had never gotten close.

"Mimi is the best librarian on the Eastern seaboard," he said proudly. "We're lucky to have her running the place."

"And what about nieces or nephews?"

"Why are you obsessed with children? You got a little one back at home no one knows about?"

"No, I'm child-free." She tried to make her voice sound cheerful. She'd recently gotten to an age where random babies on the street had stopped being abstractly cute and started to make her heart twinge with longing.

"Mimi is another one who seems allergic to long-term relationships. Maybe the Orlandos are better off single."

"No grandkids for Deb, huh?"

"She swears she's too young to be a grandmother yet, so at least there's no pressure." He licked salt off his fingers, and she smiled despite herself. The teenager she remembered was still in there somewhere, it seemed. "How about you? How's your dad?"

She dropped her gaze to her plate. "He's fine, I guess."

"What do you mean?"

"We haven't been talking much lately. He doesn't think I should—" She cut herself off. "No work talk, remember?"

"He still involved in things?"

By "things," Jay meant everything, the way it had been in the old days.

"He's still formally my manager, but I've been thinking about how to...disentangle our work relationship. So far I've avoided having any of the tough conversations." She would have died before letting anyone know she was considering this, but somehow Jay was different.

Jay's eyebrows came together. "He giving you a hard time?"

"He's just overprotective. Thinks he knows the best thing for me, like I'm still sixteen. I don't think he actually understands I'm an adult now. Selena's been helping me be firm about my boundaries."

"Selena Echeveria, right?"

"Yeah. Is it pathetic that I need help to be independent?" She'd never feel comfortable talking about this with anyone else in her life, but there was something about Jay. With a start, she realized she trusted him. Yeah, he'd hurt her once upon a time, but he was a good guy—then, and now. She knew he hadn't changed that much.

"Family ties can be the tightest. It's okay to get help cutting the cord." His tone was blessedly judgment-free, and she appreciated it.

"Thanks."

"So, are you going to eat the rest of that, or are you just going to leave it there, staring at me?"

She pushed her plate toward him. "I'm filling up on this malt."

He ate the rest of her sandwich in two bites, wiped his mouth on his napkin, and said, "All right, so you're producing this thing. Good for you. I think you'll be a phenomenal producer."

"You do?"

"Sure, you're a careful listener, good problem solver, and you pay attention to details. You understand the entire process, the scope of production. You're a natural."

His easy praise astonished her, but he went on before she could respond. "So here's your job—figure out a way to kill off Parker Wild, or write him out. The studio is bluffing if they say they won't do it without me."

"You might be right," she said. "But you're forgetting one important thing—there is no *Sawyer's Cove* without Parker Wild."

Chapter Nine

Erika: So Sawyer and Parker are heading to the carnival and finally I'm buying them as friends. Their friendship doesn't exactly feel organic in the earliest episodes.
Jules: They are definitely figuring out how to sell this relationship.
Erika: Spencer Crosby looks the part of the clueless rich kid, doesn't he? That curly blond hair and green eyes—he's like a WASP wet dream.
Jules: Gross, but accurate.
Erika: Thank you. Yeah, it takes a few episodes for them to figure out how to make these two guys with such different backgrounds being friends seem realistic. And I get it—Jay Orlando didn't have much acting experience to speak of, and Spencer Crosby was on Broadway at age ten. The actors were from really different backgrounds, too. But they got there eventually.
Jules: It's true. Sawyer and Parker's friendship is one of

the reasons people love the show so much, even when Amy gets in between them.

From *The Sawyer's Cove Rewatch Project Podcast:*
The Carnival

Loretta dropped off the check, and Jay pulled out his wallet to put a couple of bills down on the table.

"I could expense it," Cami offered.

He gave her a hard look, and she held her hands up in defeat. "Never mind. Thanks for dinner."

"Since I ate half of yours, seems fair. Where to?" They walked out to the sidewalk. Main Street was empty but well-lit thanks to the closely spaced old-fashioned street lamps.

Cami started in the direction of the inn, and he fell into step beside her. He wasn't ready to say goodnight. He was still processing what it felt like to be with Cami again, sharing a meal and conversation. Like they were friends. Like no time had passed at all.

"You still don't trust me to walk home alone?" she asked wryly, but he didn't think she was really mad about it.

"I trust you. It's the rest of the world I have issues with."

"You sound like my dad."

Since the last time Jay had exchanged words with her father was the day he'd walked away from Cami for good, he chafed at the comparison. On the other hand,

Barry Cosinsky loved his daughter more than life. He understood where the guy was coming from, mostly.

"I just think maybe you should be more careful," he said as calmly as he could.

"Look, I always have security when I'm at public events, and usually when I'm traveling. But I'm not Angelina Jolie. I can go places and not be recognized."

"Not in Misty Harbor. Everyone here knows who you are."

"I'm beginning to realize that," she said dryly.

"Those girls got awfully close to you before." He was pushing, but he couldn't seem to help himself.

"They're harmless. And they prove there's still a ton of interest in *Sawyer's Cove*."

"What happened to no shop talk?"

"That agreement was only for the length of dinner."

He sighed. "Technicality."

"Anyway, you brought it up. We're not killing off your character. He's the heart of the show."

"What are you talking about? And never let Crosby hear you say that."

"Crosby would be the first to agree with me."

Jay hadn't talked to Spencer Crosby in years, but he remembered a standoffish actor's actor type who was always trying to get the writers to give him big, dramatic monologues. He was born to be a star, the one who carried a show on his Shakespearian-trained shoulders. He was the title character, and he took the job seriously.

But something funny had happened in the middle of season one. The writers picked up on Parker and Amy's off-the-charts chemistry, and even though the show had been envisioned as a slow burn between oblivious rich kid Sawyer and shy, sweet Amy, focus started to be pulled by Parker, initially introduced as comic relief and someone whose fuck-ups would drive action on the show. By the end of the run, Parker and Amy's relationship was the main arc, with Parker getting more screen time than Sawyer in a lot of episodes.

"I doubt that," Jay said. "He probably still resents me for bogarting the—you know what, never mind. This is all ancient history."

"Well, the way Selena and I see it, Parker has been living a full, rich life. So have you, apparently."

"Don't you get it? I don't want to be Parker again. I wasn't any good at it the first time, and I'm not interested in making a fool of myself all over again."

He made it to the inn's driveway before he realized Cami had stopped half a block back. He turned and looked at her, but she was between street lamps, so he couldn't see her expression. "What?"

"You don't think you were good?" She spoke at a normal volume, but since he was a few dozen feet away, she sounded as if she was whispering. She could have been shouting at the top of her lungs with how uncomfortable talking about this made him.

"Come here," he said. The request came out more like an order. He wasn't surprised when she didn't move. He retraced his steps until he was a foot away from her. "Come on, Cami," he said, as if she was being stubborn on purpose instead of just being herself.

"First, tell me something. You really thought you weren't good? At acting, I mean?"

"I didn't know what I was doing half the time. You know I had never even been near a set until that first day."

"I knew you didn't have experience, but acting isn't always about training. You were brilliant at playing Parker because you understood him."

"I was just being myself, and that proves my point. I wasn't an actor. Not like you and Crosby and Ariel and Nash."

He didn't know why he had to explain this to her. She'd been there. He'd covered it up well, but he was terrified half the time they were shooting he'd do something wrong. Forget his lines, trip over a cable, ruin a take. It wasn't until a few episodes in he realized everyone did those things, whether they were veteran actors or newbies like him. After that, he was able to relax a little more, have fun with it.

When he and Cami started having more scenes together, it got even better, because being with her was easy. Their characters fell in love on screen, and to Jay it had been the most natural thing in the world to channel all the affection and admiration he had for the gorgeous, talented, funny Cami, a person who'd become his friend, and transform those feelings into Parker falling for the pretty, smart, witty Amy, the girl his best friend Sawyer was supposed to end up with on paper. But it didn't turn out that way.

"I'm not an actor. I was a kid with a cute smile and an appealing, nonspecific ethnicity."

"I never knew you felt that way." Cami sounded truly puzzled.

"Yeah. Well."

"Is that why you came back here after the show was over? Why you didn't stay in L.A.?"

This was getting too close to old hurts that hadn't entirely scabbed over. Jay had made peace with his short acting career. He'd answered the casting call on a dare from his sister. No one had been more surprised than him when he got the part.

Casting a hometown pretty boy for the part of the ultimate hometown pretty boy had been something of a publicity stunt. It had given the trades and reviewers something to write about. They needed a nod at diversity, too, and Jay had been convinced he'd been cast more for his "ambiguously ethnic features," as the casting director had so charmingly put it at the time, than his acting ability.

Being half-white, half-something else allowed him to appeal to a demographic cross-section. The something else didn't matter, which was convenient because his mom had never offered him anything more than the first name of the tourist who'd knocked her up, and he'd never cared about finding out more than that. He had a family and a home he loved. He wasn't looking for either.

But there was no point in rehashing all of that. "I

didn't stay in L.A. because I hated it there." It wasn't a lie, but it wasn't the whole truth.

He might have been a dumb kid, but he wasn't stupid. Cami had her entire career in front of her. Hollywood was knocking down her door. She had her pick of projects, being both talented and motivated. He was only famous for looking good without a shirt on and stealing Amy away from Sawyer. He'd been in *Teen Beat*. She'd been in *Teen Vogue*.

He was just a guy from a small town who'd gotten a lucky break, made a little money. She was going to be a star. And he had no intention of standing in her way.

The fact that her father hated him and implied he was only going to hold Cami back from her career if he insisted on trying to make things work with her, well, that was almost beside the point. Barry hadn't said anything he hadn't already worked out for himself.

In any event, Cami had gone on to bigger and better things, as predicted, and Jay had gone back to Misty Harbor. He'd tried to be a normal person again, but the first few years were tough. The bar was a fluke—he'd passed the empty storefront one day and realized that end of town needed an anchor, something to draw people in. He'd recently met a local brewer who was looking for a place to test out new products. It took almost a year of harder work than shooting a television show ever was, but The Cove opened strong. He embraced the long, arduous hours. Exhaustion meant he didn't dream. Which was good. Because whenever he did remember snatches of his dreams, he always seemed to be chasing blonde hair, blue eyes, and phantom laughter.

The ghost of teenage Cami had faded over time, but the woman she'd become was standing in front of him, real as life.

"Well, I'm glad you're happy here," she said firmly. "And I get that this is complicated. But I'm determined to do this show. And you're going to be a part of it." She pushed past him, marching all the way to the inn's entrance. He trotted to catch up, but she put up a hand. "I'll be fine from here. Thanks for dinner, Jay. I'll be seeing you soon."

He walked slowly all the way back to The Cove, her words echoing in his brain, a promise and a warning both. Once he was back in the familiar confines of the bar, he realized he'd forgotten to badger the downtown development group into signing their Harbor Fest sponsorship agreements. He'd have to chase them down individually now. Cami had proved to be as distracting as he'd feared, but he still couldn't bring himself to regret spending time with her, no matter how much of a fool that made him.

He was older, but he never claimed to be wiser.

Chapter Ten

ERIKA: This episode is the one people use when trying to prove the point that Lily Fine is "the slutty one." I'm doing air quotes, by the way, since this isn't a visual medium.

JULES: Yeah, I think the listeners get it. Lily Fine, played with sass and panache by Ariel Tulip. Is that her real name?

ERIKA: I've never met anyone with the last name Tulip, but my last name is Rainwater, so I can't really be critical.

JULES: Okay, so Ariel Tulip plays Lily, and she's a way different type, physically, than Amy. She's tall and curvy and bossy and outgoing.

ERIKA: Basically, the inverse of Amy Green.

JULES: We can tell that she's a badass, because she wears a lot of leather.

ERIKA: The costume department must have had so much fun dressing Lily.

JULES: Oh, totally. I mean, who else could pull off a leather miniskirt with Chucks? She's totally hot.

FROM *THE SAWYER'S COVE REWATCH PROJECT PODCAST: THE ROAD TRIP*

Cami woke up with a start to her phone's alarm and rolled onto her back. Damn, this bed was about fifty times more comfortable than the one she'd had in Toronto. She'd slept like a rock, even after all the sugar from the malt. And after her curious conversation with Jay.

It was so strange she'd missed such a big chunk of his life. She felt like an open book—he only had to check IMDb to see what she'd been up to—but learning about his bar, about his role in the Misty Harbor community, that was all news to her. She wasn't surprised Jay had done well, but she had been astonished by his apparent belief that he wasn't an actor, that his success as Parker had been a fluke. She knew different, and she'd have to convince him of it before she could convince him to rejoin the cast.

Her own complicated feelings aside, he deserved to know how good he was. He deserved the chance to bring Parker Wild to life once again.

She contemplated how exactly to do that as she ate her room service breakfast in a cozy armchair while she watched the woods outside her window. It was going to be another gorgeous day. Early June had ripened past spring's bloom, but the air hadn't given over to summer levels of heat and humidity.

She should call her dad. It had been days now; they rarely went so long without talking. But when she reached for her phone, she remembered it was three hours earlier in California. He wasn't a morning person either.

With a sense of guilty relief, she put it off a little longer, ignored the rest of her messages while she dressed in casual jeans and sneakers and an oversized sweater. She threw on some chunky earrings, some makeup, and left her hair down and a little wild. She'd put product in it the night before to make her grand entrance at The Cove, and it still looked decent. Good enough for today's plans, which consisted of walking around Misty Harbor, taking pictures of locations, and ingratiating herself with the locals. There was more to this project than just Jay Orlando, even though he was the main roadblock at the moment.

She took care of some emails and paid some bills. She hadn't had her own full-time assistant in a couple of years. If the reboot went forward, hopefully she'd be busy enough to need one, between acting and producing. Maybe she could get someone local. No point in hiring someone in L.A. when she was there so rarely. She'd only been in Misty Harbor for two days, and it already felt like home. But she couldn't live in a hotel forever. She'd spent enough of her life in one already. And finding a place to live was in her control, something she could make happen for herself without any outside approval.

In the lobby, she stopped to ask the employee behind the desk for a recommendation of a good real estate firm. Max, she quickly came to discover, had a cousin who had the best sales numbers in Eastern Connecticut, and he'd be happy to give Cami her number.

"Thanks, Max," she said warmly.

"I hope this means we'll be seeing more of you in Misty Harbor, Miss Corsair."

"Me, too." She turned, spotted Deb Orlando walking across the lobby, and hesitantly waved when she saw Deb had noticed her.

Jay's mom stopped and waved back stiffly. Cami was determined to win over every single person in Misty Harbor, even if she had to wage individual campaigns with all eight thousand of them to do it.

"Hi, Deb," she said brightly. "Can I talk to you for a minute?"

"Everything okay with your room?" Deb asked courteously, as if Cami was nothing more than a high-profile guest.

"Oh, gosh, yes, it's been wonderful. And the tub in my room is extra luxurious..." Cami trailed off, thinking about what she'd done in the bathtub, then snapped herself back to the present. "Anyway, could you give me Mimi's number? I was hoping to set up a time to see her before I leave town."

"Are you leaving so soon?" Deb's tone indicated she thought that was wonderful news.

"Sorry to disappoint you, but I don't have any definite plans to leave," Cami said easily.

Deb winced. "That was rude, I'm sorry."

Cami would have chalked her apology up to a hotel employee worried about offending a customer, except Deb glanced around to see if anyone was within earshot, then offered Cami a genuine, if small, smile. "It's not that I'm not happy to see you. I honestly can't believe it's been twelve years since you and the other kids were running around town. It feels like yesterday Jay was graduating high school and Mimi was talking him into auditioning for the show. So much has happened since then."

"It feels like a lifetime's worth of things."

"Exactly. But you have to forgive me for being overly defensive when it comes to Jay."

"Jay?" Was she talking about the contract? Did she know about the possibility of the reboot?

"You being here brings back a lot of memories, good ones, of course. But it also reminds me of how difficult things were for him after the show ended and you two broke up. I wouldn't want something to happen to take him back to that place. It was a dark time for him."

Cami was confused. A dark time for Jay? He was the one who'd ended things. She'd been a wreck, barely made it through the shoot on the film she'd taken immediately after the breakup just to take her mind off the devastation of being dumped by the boy she'd loved with her whole heart.

"I don't really know what to say." Nervously, she

flicked the tip of her earring and set it swinging. "I'm not here to hurt Jay, if that's what you're worried about."

"I know, sweetie," Deb said kindly.

Cami wanted to bristle at Deb's tone. But the part of her who still missed her mom every single day leaned into the scrap of mothering like a plant starved for the sun.

"He's a really good guy," Cami said, not that Deb needed to hear it from her. "And I want what's best for him." If he decided not doing the show was going to be best for him, then she'd just have to make it work somehow.

"I'm going to use my mom card to say one thing." Deb smiled self-deprecatingly. "Jay thinks he knows what's best for everyone else, but he can be woefully blind about what's best for him. All he wants is for his family and for this town to be happy and healthy, and sometimes he burns himself out in the process. I wish he would be more selfish sometimes."

"I think I understand," Cami said. She wasn't offended by the implication. She'd worked in Hollywood long enough to know most people didn't have the best interests of anyone but themselves at heart. It was standard practice. She intended to operate differently. "It's not my intention to hurt anyone."

"I think you could hurt him just by being yourself. So please be careful."

"Ouch, Deb," Cami said, stung. "I'm not some femme fatale who's going to use him up and spit him out. His heart might have gotten broken, but he broke mine first."

Deb's mouth made one of those wry twists she'd seen other moms do when they seemed to be aware they weren't going to be able to protect their children from something painful. "Oh, sweetie. It's really so good to see you. Can I—can I give you a hug?"

Cami blinked. Surely, those weren't tears threatening to well up, were they? She didn't cry unless it was required in a scene. It was too dangerous. If she started to cry, then she might not be able to stop. Controlling her emotions was her number one marketable skill.

"Okay?" It came out more of a question than a statement, but Deb took it for consent because she reached out and gathered Cami in like a mother duck folding her duckling under her wing. Deb's synthetic crew neck sweater smelled of laundry detergent, and her skin smelled like cold cream. Cami squeezed her eyes shut as hard as she could, as if she could keep the tears from falling if they had no space through which to flow.

Deb let her go and refrained from remarking on the tightness around Cami's eyes.

"Look, that's all I'm going to say about Jay, because you two are going to have to figure things out on your own. I promise to stay out of it. But if you need anything from me, just say the word, okay? As for Mimi—she and I were supposed to have lunch, but I had to book some interviews over the lunch hour, and I haven't canceled on her yet. You could go in my place and catch up."

"I'd love that."

As Cami recorded the numbers Deb reeled off, she reflected on what she'd said. She couldn't control Jay, she could only be accountable for her own actions. But it was nice to be reminded she could have a relationship with Deb that didn't have anything to do with her son. She had a history in Misty Harbor, and it was up to her to figure out what her future here would be.

Mimi Orlando was almost as tall as her brother, which made her several inches taller than Cami, and her purple hair made her easy to spot waiting outside of the Misty Harbor Library.

She was reading a book, naturally.

Cami quelled unexpected nerves as she tugged at her sweater and approached. Deb's rather cryptic warning still rang in her ears. She and Mimi had never been close, but Cami could only imagine she was disposed to being as protective of Jay as Deb was. And it seemed in their eyes she'd done something egregious to him. Which was not how she remembered it at all.

But as she neared Mimi and remarked, "Portrait of a Librarian on Break," Mimi was all smiles.

"Hi Cami, it's been a while," she said, tucking away her book in a hot pink tote bag that seemed to be doubling as a purse. "Should we hug, or—?"

Cami smiled, nerves gone. Mimi always was direct. "Sure. If we don't start off hugging, then by the time we get to a point where it feels right to hug, it will be awkward to start doing it."

"Very well, then." Mimi hugged her, brief but firm, and when she drew away, she looked Cami up and down. "You look exactly the same."

"I do not, but thanks for the compliment," she said. "I love your hair."

"Oh yes, I never grew out of my rebellious teenage boxed hair dye phase," she said, laughing and touching her curls. "Only now I pay a fortune at the salon and the kids expect it. It's a town pastime to come see what color Miss Mimi's hair is today."

Mimi suggested the Bakeshop for lunch, and Cami readily agreed. Trevor was working behind the counter, and Cami gave him almost as warm a greeting as he gave her.

"Cami! You came back. See, Zelda, I didn't scare her off. Zelda thought I scared you off."

Zelda threw Mimi and Cami a put-upon smile and muttered, "It wouldn't be the first time." She was loading a fresh batch of what looked like salted chocolate chip cookies into the case, and Cami's mouth watered.

"I had to come back for more goodies." She pointed to the cookies. "This place is dangerous."

"I'll make a box for you. And a latte?" Trevor guessed.

Cami nodded, added a panini to her order. "Mimi, what do you want? My treat."

Mimi asked Trevor for a beet salad and black tea and

then disappeared through a curtain in the back of the room.

"Where did she go?" Cami asked him.

"We have a whole seating area back there, beautiful."

"Oh, I didn't realize."

Trevor waved his hand imperiously. "Scoot. I'll bring everything out in a minute."

Lunch from the Bakeshop was every bit as good as breakfast, and Cami inhaled her food while Mimi ate hers at a more sedate pace. Catching Cami up on twelve years of being a small-town librarian took about two minutes. Cami gave her the abbreviated version of her journey, from indie roles to mainstream rom-coms to slasher flicks.

"So that's work, and you're obviously successful. I mean, just being a working actress is a huge accomplishment," Mimi said.

"Thanks." It was a sentiment Cami agreed with but sometimes was too busy to appreciate.

"But what about the rest of your life?" Mimi asked.

Cami smiled ruefully and decided to answer facetiously. "I don't understand the question."

"You know, pets, hobbies, friends. Boyfriends."

"Well, I travel a lot. Don't have it in me to make an animal put up with either being boarded or forced to live in a hotel with me. Hobbies—um. I read a lot on set. Mostly scripts, but sometimes fiction. Friends, well, most of my friends are in the industry."

"And your love life?"

"Nonexistent," Cami said. "You can't have it all,

Mimi." She was beginning to wish for the first time in a long time she could have *more*, though.

"Fair enough," Mimi said lightly.

Cami was silent, waiting for Mimi to make some pointed comment about Jay, but she hadn't mentioned her brother all day. It was kind of nice to connect with her without Jay being the reason for it. "Well, what about you? What do you do when you aren't at the library?"

"Oh, gobs of things. I've been helping book acts for the stage at The Cove. It's really fun. I think in another lifetime I could have been a concert promoter or something."

"It's not too late," Cami said, nibbling on the salted chocolate chip cookie Trevor had delivered with a wink.

"I could never leave the library, but it's a fun side gig. You should come out tonight. This awesome band from Providence is playing. It's going to be a good show."

"I'll think about it." Cami checked her watch. "Listen, you said you were off work for the rest of the day, right? Could I talk you into doing something silly with me?"

"Silly? With Camille Corsair?" Mimi put her hand over her heart, as if she'd never heard of such a thing.

"Yeah. You don't have to if you don't want to."

Mimi grinned. "Of course I do."

"Then let's go, because it starts in ten minutes."

"What does?"

"The *Sawyer's Cove* walking tour."

Chapter Eleven

JULES: This is a tangent, but did you know you can actually go visit some of the places they filmed the show? I heard there's some kind of tour you can take.
ERIKA: I did not know that, and why haven't we done it yet?
JULES: Maybe because we live in Seattle and the show was shot in the middle of Nowhere, Connecticut?
ERIKA: Road trip!
JULES: Totally. Or maybe we fly to New York or Boston or wherever and rent a car?
ERIKA: Plane trip!
JULES: Let's do it.

FROM *THE SAWYER'S COVE REWATCH PROJECT PODCAST: THE SLEEPOVER*

"So do we need tickets for this thing?" Mimi asked curiously as they rounded the corner onto Edward Street. They'd had to rush to get to the meeting place on time.

"I made a reservation online." Cami smiled when she saw where they were—outside the historical society building, a nineteenth century Victorian home-turned-museum that had been used for exterior shots of Sawyer North's house on the show.

A small cluster of people waited on the cement sidewalk outside the black wrought-iron fence that edged the property. She spotted the two young women from the bar last night, Tracy and Beth, plus a skinny teenage boy who was with an older man, probably his father. Last were the two middle-aged women who ran the tour. Cami recognized them from pictures on their Instagram. She thought Maria was the olive-skinned one with gray-shot black hair, which made the freckles-and-cream lady with the short red hair Rhonda. The two of them were consulting a piece of paper when she and Mimi arrived, slightly out of breath from their jog across town.

"Here come our last two guests," Maria said, studying the paper. "Full tour today." When she finally looked up and made eye contact with Cami, her brown eyes widened, and she nudged Rhonda in the side.

"Holy Camille Corsair," Rhonda said when she recognized who had joined the group.

"Hi," Cami said in her best *I'm a celebrity, but you shouldn't treat me any differently than you would anyone else* voice. "I'm Cami," she said, mostly for the benefit of the dad whose face was the only one that hadn't cleared with recognition when she walked up.

"Hi, Cami!" Beth said happily.

"Hi, Beth, Tracy," she said. "This is my friend Mimi."

"Nice to meet you." Mimi waved at the crowd. "Hi, Maria. Nice to see you, Rhonda."

"Well, we're all friends here, it seems," Rhonda said. She turned to the lanky kid and his dad. "Except for the two of you. Want to introduce yourselves?"

The boy hadn't taken his eyes off Cami the entire time, and he turned bright red at being prompted to talk. She immediately took a shine to him. "What's your name?" she asked.

"I'm Joel," he said. "This is my dad."

"Henry," the dad said. "We're on a college trip. Saw Yale yesterday and heading up to Brown tomorrow, but Joel said we absolutely had to stop here in between, so here we are. *Sawyer's Cove* is his favorite, but I've never seen it."

"Well, you are in for a treat, Henry, because we have an actual star of the show with us today. Camille Corsair, who played the one and only Amy Green," Rhonda said, just running with it as if this happened all the time. "Thanks for coming on the tour, Camille."

"Cami, please," she reminded her.

"Trevor at the Bakeshop said you were in town. This is a real honor," Maria said.

"Well, I heard about this tour and just couldn't resist," she said. "So you just go on and do your thing. I'm a fan of the show, too, so yeah. Carry on."

"All right, then." Maria launched into a prepared spiel about the production of the show and Sawyer North's house, giving a surprisingly accurate synopsis of the character and location. That is, Cami assumed Maria had the facts right. She'd long ago realized superfans of the show were much more familiar with the finished product than she was. They'd filmed nearly seventy episodes of *Sawyer's Cove*; she definitely didn't remember details about all of them. But as the small group moved toward the beach, Cami was able to chime in with a few behind-the-scenes anecdotes.

Maria and Rhonda encouraged the tour group to share their own thoughts about the show, and Beth and Tracy had no trouble talking about their favorite moments, which all seemed to revolve around Amy and Parker. The boy, Joel, was quiet. As they moved from the beach back up Main Street, she fell into step beside him.

"So, you're a fan?" she asked.

"Uh, yeah. It's a good show," he said shyly.

"Who's your favorite character?" she asked casually.

"Uh." Joel glanced ahead to his dad, who was a few feet away. "Will, I guess. He has as many problems as the other kids, but he likes who he is, deep down."

"I like how you put that. I always thought that was cool, too."

"He's just like, this is who I am, take it or leave it, and I admire that. I kinda wish I could be like him."

"Why can't you?"

"My dad, uh, he doesn't know. That I'm gay," Joel said

on an exhale. "It's kind of hard to be yourself when the people you're closest to don't understand you."

Cami thought about her own father. About how they had so much in common and yet he didn't understand what she really needed from him.

"I think we all want to live authentically, but it can take some time to figure out what that means." Cami shrugged. "I'm still working on the person I want to be when I'm not playing a part. It's a lifetime work-in-progress kind of thing, I guess."

"Yeah? So I shouldn't feel bad about not living my best life at seventeen?" Joel asked semi-seriously.

Cami laughed. "God, no. You're going to be just fine."

"Thanks. You're really nice."

Cami caught Joel's dad's eye as they approached The Cove, apparently the next stop on the tour. She nodded at him, and he nodded back.

"Good luck with your dad. Maybe you should tell him, give him a chance to understand you. It might make you feel better, anyway."

"Yeah. I've sort of been working up to it," Joel said. "I'll get there."

"I know you will."

"This is The Cove," Rhonda announced. "Now, this bar wasn't a setting of the show, but we point it out because our most famous Misty Harbor resident owns and operates it. Jay Orlando, aka Parker Wild. So you might want to make a stop there later, or in a few years, young man, and try to cross another cast member off your bingo card. Moving on!" Rhonda kept them at a steady march, and Mimi hung back in order to walk next to Cami.

"My feet are killing me. Rhonda is a notorious speed walker," she complained.

"I think it's almost over," Cami whispered.

"Thank the lord," Mimi said. "This has been fun, though. I'll have to tell Jay they're plugging the bar."

"He might not appreciate that," Cami said.

"What are you talking about? He loves anything that brings in business. He's like Mr. Chamber of Commerce."

"Really?" Cami frowned. Then maybe it was just her he had a problem with.

"You've seen him, right?"

"Jay? Yeah. We talked yesterday. And I saw the bar. It's got a great vibe." She left out the shared patty melt at Melba's.

"I'm really glad you reached out to him. He's such a homebody, sometimes I think he forgets there's a world outside of Misty Harbor."

"Yeah, I'm glad, too. I stayed away too long."

"You did. When you go home, it better not be another dozen years before we see you again."

"Home? Oh, L.A.?" Cami debated whether to tell Mimi she was thinking about buying something local. "Don't worry. I really hope I'm going to be spending a lot more time in this town."

"That's what I like to hear."

They ended the tour within sight of the inn, where they shot the prom episode. Cami signed autographs for

Joel, Beth, and Tracy, and Maria and Rhonda, while she was at it. "Wonderful job, ladies, I thoroughly enjoyed myself."

Pictures were taken all around, and then everyone parted ways. She waved at Joel, who waved back cheerfully. He was talking animatedly to Henry as they left.

Mimi cocked her head at Cami. "What did you say to that kid? He was all tongue-tied, now it seems like he has a new lease on life."

"I just told him it was okay if he didn't have everything figured out at seventeen. Something I wish someone had told me at the time."

"I second that." Mimi smiled ruefully. "It's okay if you don't have everything figured out at thirty, either. Or thirty-four."

"Good point," Cami agreed. "Thanks for doing this with your afternoon off."

"It was surprisingly fun. I wasn't around much when *Sawyer's Cove* was filming. There's a lot I don't know about the show. Plus, now you owe me."

"Definitely. What's the tab?"

"Come out to The Cove with me tonight to see the band. I want you to come as my platonic, non-romantic date."

"Aren't platonic and non-romantic redundant?"

"Well, half the town thinks I'm a lesbian, and no matter how many times I tell them I'm not, it hasn't stuck. I just wanted to make it clear. I'd never do that to Jay, anyway."

"Do what to Jay?"

"Date his ex."

"So you do remember. I thought maybe you were pretending it had never happened."

"Why would I do that?"

"Your mom gave me a stern warning earlier today."

Mimi's eyebrows lifted. "My mom? Seriously?"

"She seems to think I broke his heart, when I remember it being the other way around." She wouldn't normally share this with someone she wasn't very close to. Problem was, she wasn't very close to anyone these days, except Selena, and she was on a different coast. Maybe she wanted confirmation it wasn't all in her head.

"It was rough for a while after the show ended. I assumed your breakup was your idea, but he never wanted to talk about it." Mimi's gaze turned thoughtful. "Though it would be like Jay to do something he thought was best for someone else, even if he ended up hurt in the process."

Cami pursed her lips. That lined up with what Deb had said. She didn't know how to feel. Whatever his intention was, they'd both ended up damaged, and that pain was still there, threaded through all their interactions in the present. She had been kidding herself to think she could show up and act like the slate was clean.

"Anyway, the band goes on at nine. Be there, my friend." Mimi backed down the street, waving until she was out of sight.

Cami turned the phrase around in her head. Mimi had said "my friend." Easy as pie. As if she hadn't basically doubled Cami's friend total in one afternoon. She smiled all the way to the inn.

She'd been walking all over town, but she didn't want to return to her room just yet. It occurred to her to explore the inn's grounds while the weather was fine. Then she could get room service and take a disco nap before meeting Mimi at The Cove. It didn't cross her mind once to stand up her platonic, non-romantic date.

Cami followed the signs for the rear exit past the bank of elevators and a conference room, turned the corner down another hallway. She heard voices, then spotted an open door with a colorful sign announcing it as "Kid Care." This must be the daycare operation Jay had mentioned.

She heard giggling and shushing, and she stuck her head in the door to check it out. At a glance she took in the large, brightly lit space. There was a check-in counter and small alcove filled with hooks where she imagined tiny winter coats would be placed in the colder months. On the other side of the counter, she spotted three caregivers and about ten little ones of varying ages. Two were playing with toys on a mat, but the rest were crowded around the feet of a man sitting in a big armchair.

Jay.

He was reading to them from a book called *Reed and Lucy Go to the Zoo*, a title Cami wasn't familiar with. It seemed to have a large cast of characters, because he wasn't just reading to them, he was doing voices, too, making the kids laugh with the range of tones coming out of his mouth.

He didn't notice her right away, so she could freely enjoy watching him perform for a group of toddlers as if he was auditioning for a Scorsese movie, that's how into it he was. She laughed along with the kids when one of the characters ended up inside the monkey enclosure and had to be rescued by his ingenious friend. She let out a chuckle, clapping a hand over her mouth belatedly, but Jay looked right at her. She'd been caught.

"From that day forward, whenever they visited the zoo, Reed and Lucy always visited the monkeys first. The End," Jay finished, with somewhat less enthusiasm than he'd read the rest of the book.

"Thank you, Mr. Jay," one of the caregivers said. "What do we say, friends?"

An uneven chorus of thank yous rose from the crowd of small people at his feet.

"Read more!" one little one demanded.

Jay shook his head. "I wish I could. Next time I'll read two, okay?"

"You don't have to make them promises, Jay," the caregiver said. "You do plenty."

"You know it's the best part of my day, Robin," he said. He made eye contact with Cami and held up a hand for her to wait. She supposed after spying on him she could spare a moment.

He washed his hands at a sink on the wall and said goodbye. Most of the kids were already on to other activities, but a few waved at him with pudgy hands that made Cami's stomach hurt.

Damn, she normally only felt this way when there was a part she really, really wanted. She'd trained herself to mistrust that feeling. Usually, when she wanted a part badly was when she auditioned the worst. She had to pretend to herself she didn't care how she did to do well enough to be in the running.

Jay Orlando being soft with a bunch of adorable little children—well, she had lots of practice pretending she didn't want something. It should be easy for her to press the ball of want down into a hard, stabbing line so tiny it only hurt a little. When she moved, for instance. Or breathed.

But this kind of longing wouldn't go away with the next part or next hit. It could only be assuaged by taking on an entirely different kind of role.

Chapter Twelve

From The Sawyer's Cove Rewatch Project Podcast: The Sleepover

"What's up, Cams?" Jay asked as he came around the counter.

Cami smiled. "You called me 'Cams.'"

Oh, shit. He played it off. It wasn't that he was getting

used to her or anything, slipping into old nicknames like no time had passed. "What are you doing here?"

"Don't you get tired of asking that?" she asked, a little peevishly. He supposed it would be annoying to continually imply she didn't belong. "I was going to go for a walk out back, heard the voices. This place is incredible. And they got a special guest and everything."

Jay looked past her shoulder at the kids and rubbed the back of his neck. "It's just something I do when I have a free minute." He didn't know why he was feeling bashful. He supposed it was different when the audience was a bunch of two-year-olds. Cami was a professional. Then again, he was only reading a picture book. Civilians were allowed to do that. Dramatic readings took on a different dimension once you'd been on TV.

"I'm not making fun of you, Jay. It was amazing. See, this is why I don't get the whole 'I'm not an actor' thing."

"Huh?"

She huffed impatiently. "I'm not saying this because I want you to join the show, I do, but that's not as important as you understanding you actually are good."

"Don't play, Cami."

She let out a little noise of frustration that would have made him smile if he hadn't been so ill at ease.

"Look, I'll prove it to you. Do you have a second to come up to my room?"

"Uh." That seemed like a terrible idea. "Sure."

He followed her to the elevators.

"I just had lunch with your sister," Cami said offhandedly.

"Mimi?"

"Unless you have another sister I'm not aware of."

"God forbid." It was inevitable the two of them would run into each other in a town the size of Misty Harbor, but lunch meant planning and forethought. And talking. He could only imagine what they had talked about. On second thought, he probably couldn't. Over the years, he'd learned that as much as he loved and supported all the women in his life, they were still largely a mystery to him. Maybe it was because he hadn't had any older male role models to let him in on the secrets. Of course, that assumed those men would know anything about women in the first place.

The elevator rose slowly to the fourth floor, and Jay found himself anxious to get out of the enclosed space. They were on opposite sides of the mirrored box, but he fancied he could smell Cami's hair. The scent was herbal, tangy, and fresh. Probably some outrageously expensive product. He held his breath until the doors slid open to avoid the temptation to edge closer and breathe her in.

"My room's got a great view. Two of them, actually."

"Nice. You know, I've never actually stayed here," he said for something to say as the heavy door clicked shut behind them, sealing them away from the eyes of the world.

"Where do you live?" she asked.

"I've got a house on some land a little way outside of town. I just moved there...well, it's been a year already. Feels like I just moved in. Looks like it, too, sadly. I like the quiet. I used to live downtown, but I get enough of people at the bar."

"Must be nice to have a place to get away to." She moved through the tidy room to the desk and pulled out a pink laptop case and from within a silver laptop.

Housekeeping had already come through and made the big bed with its fluffy white bedding. Not that he was looking at the bed. Or thinking about the last time they'd been in a hotel room with a bed. Of course, all hotel rooms had beds. Didn't they? Okay, he needed to focus and stop thinking about beds. "Why am I here again?"

She tapped on her computer keyboard. "I want to show you something."

"It's not a PowerPoint presentation detailing how many jobs I'll be responsible for killing if I decide not to do the show, is it?"

She glanced up from the screen, her big blue eyes wide. "I thought you already decided not to do it?" she said with mock innocence. "So there'd be no point in that, would there?"

He had no comeback, just sat down in the chair she offered him with what he assumed was a petulant air. Because that was how he felt, sulky as a teenager bested by the smart girl who was out of his league.

She turned the screen toward him and hit the spacebar. It took him a minute to place what he was seeing. Cami was on screen—only it wasn't Cami; it was Amy Green. She was sitting on the beach, looking forlornly out over the water. She looked young and vulnerable and angelic. Here came Parker, right on cue, plopping down in the sand next to Amy.

Jay cringed as his character spoke. He'd always hated the way he sounded on tape—a common affliction, but one he'd never gotten used to. He looked young, too, and myopically stupid in that way of all nineteen-year-old boys.

He spoke over his dialogue. "What's the point of this?"

"Watch the scene," Cami whispered.

"You look great."

"Don't watch me. Watch you."

"I don't—"

"Just watch. Please."

He flicked his gaze over to Parker, who was talking about his dad and the summer he left. How Parker had woken up every morning and padded to his parents' room and looked in, hoping his dad had come back in the night, would make him a bowl of cereal, and they'd go to the park to shoot some hoops.

It was a sad scene, full of Parker's pain, compounded by the fact that what they were really talking about was how if Amy gave up everything to be with Parker, he was terrified she'd end up leaving him, just like his dad. It wasn't the most sophisticated storytelling, but it was effective. Amy's heart was breaking for Parker, you could see it all over Cami's face, even though she barely had any lines in the scene.

Jay had to admit, his delivery was pretty good. He

remembered shooting this scene and feeling drained after every take.

The scene ended on a shot of Amy reaching over and taking Parker's hand in hers. The simple act of tenderness meant a lot to Parker, who hadn't experienced much softness in his life.

Cami paused the scene with a tap of a key, freezing on a frame of their hands twined together.

"See?" she asked triumphantly.

"See what? That was a good episode," he allowed cautiously.

"You were really good. You *are* really good. That's top-notch acting right there, Jay Orlando."

"You know all that daddy issues stuff came easily to me." He was being stubborn, but he honestly wasn't sure what she wanted him to say.

"Jay, stop. You're a natural. I've worked with a lot of actors. You're one of the most charismatic I've ever worked with."

"I told you, I just drew on my own personal experience. Absentee father, that's an emotional goldmine, right? Only thing mine ever gave me, and I milked the hell out of it."

"I don't believe you." She wasn't outraged, just matter-of-fact, which hit infinitely harder. "I always envied how easy it was for you. You didn't have any expectations of greatness. You were just great. It was annoying as hell, actually."

"If it was easy, it's because the storylines they gave me weren't a stretch. It was easy to act like I was falling in love with you because I was falling in love with you."

He'd meant it to prove his point, but as it came out of his mouth, he realized he'd revealed something much closer to his heart than he'd ever intended.

Her pink mouth parted, but no sound came out, as if she'd forgotten her line.

"I mean—" What had he meant? What was he even doing here? He made a move to shove out of the chair, but she put a hand up, and he stopped in his tracks.

She shook her head as she apparently recovered her equilibrium. "Parker and Amy were falling in love. Cami and Jay falling in love was something entirely different."

"Was it?" At the time, the two things had been intertwined, and he'd had to really work to believe Cami loved him for him, and not because she'd fallen for his screen avatar.

Cami held his gaze. They were a couple of feet apart, her leaning against the side of the desk and him in the chair. It wouldn't have taken much to grab her hand and pull her down into his lap. He had the sudden urge to bury his nose in her hair and inhale her fancy hair products. Or he could get up and put his hands on the desk, boxing her inside them, lean down and—

"One doesn't have anything to do with the other. And neither of them has anything to do with this."

Her words came out close to a whisper, and he wondered if she could read his mind. He tried to erase the images in his head, just in case. He had no business thinking about touching her, let alone doing it.

"You're right. I shouldn't have said anything," he said roughly. "The point is, your demonstration failed. I'm not that good of an actor."

Her response was immediate and pithy. "Bullshit."

He couldn't help a smile. She was relentless.

"Besides, I'm asking you to reprise Parker. You know him like the back of your hand, clearly."

He shrugged. She had a point, but he wasn't ready to give in. Not yet.

"You're impossible," she finally said. "But I know what I know. You're a good actor. You've got charisma in spades. And you're perfect for this project. But—" She pushed briskly away from the desk and shut the computer with a click. "I'm not here to sell you on it again. I just thought maybe I could get through to you."

"I'm not known for being quick on the uptake," he said, trying to be funny and failing.

"Okay, you're a good actor, but right now you're just being obtuse."

Better she think him obtuse than imagining a reality in which kissing her was an option.

"I better go. And weren't you going to take a walk?"

"Yeah. Maybe I will."

He got up and crossed to the door. Every time he was with her, it got harder to walk away. But their scene together had ended. He found himself wishing this one could last a little longer. That they didn't have the show hanging over their heads. That she didn't only want to be around him because of what she needed from him. He wanted—shit. He wanted her to want to spend time with him. Just Jay. Not Jay Orlando in the role of Parker Wild.

Fuck. When was the last time he had wanted something so unbelievably stupid? Maybe the first time he wanted Cami to want to kiss him as much as he wanted to kiss her. The feeling had apparently never gone away. Maybe it never would.

But he'd learned you didn't always have to act on your feelings.

Before he could think of a smooth exit line, she said, "I'm sorry."

"What for?"

"For thinking that would help. I hope I didn't make you feel bad."

"Why would you think that?"

She touched the skin between her eyebrows. "You've got the groove of despair there."

He smiled despite himself, touched his own forehead in response, as if he could smooth away the line that was slowly etching itself permanently into his skin. He couldn't tell her he was angsting because he was frustrated with himself for wanting more from her than she was there to give.

"Not your fault. Really." And it wasn't. She couldn't help being kissable. Half the men and a good chunk of the women in America probably wanted to kiss her at any given time.

"There's something else I wanted to tell you," she said. Her tone said he wasn't going to like it. Well, what else was new?

"Lay it on me," he said, resigned to his day going from bad to worse.

"Mimi invited me to The Cove tonight to see the band. I won't go if you think it's a bad idea."

"Why would it be a bad idea?" he answered automatically. But as soon as he'd given it two seconds of thought, he realized why it might be a terrible idea. Camille Corsair, at The Cove again. He was usually there on show nights to make sure everything ran smoothly. It would be another chance for photos and gossip. But again, it was a free country.

"No reason," she said carefully. "You're okay with it?"

"Of course," he said, confused about how exactly he'd been maneuvered into giving his endorsement to this plan. "Mimi worked hard to get this band to play. If she wants you to come, that's cool."

"Cool." She flashed a smile. "Thanks."

"Cool," he said again. There was a moment of silence. He realized she was waiting for him to leave. She still had the ability to turn his brain to absolute mush. "Well, I guess I'll see you later, then."

She nodded. "See you, Jay."

He closed the door behind him, then paused long enough to clunk his head against the wall. What the hell was he doing?

Chapter Thirteen

Jules: I love this episode so much, I cannot even tell you.
Erika: Well, you need to try, because that's the entire point of this podcast.
Jules: Oh, right. Well, for one thing, I think this is where the show starts getting into iconic territory.
Erika: Amy and Lily entering the school talent show and lip-synching Britney Spears?
Jules: Iconic.

From *The Sawyer's Cove Rewatch Project Podcast: The Test*

The Cove had a different vibe tonight than it had the night before. It was busier, for one thing. A small crowd of people stood outside, waiting to show a bouncer their IDs before being let in.

Cami adjusted her purse and felt a little overdressed.

The group in front of her, mostly twenty-somethings, wore jeans and T-shirts. A few of the girls were in skirts, but they were dressed very casually overall. Cami's wardrobe options had been limited by what she'd brought with her from Toronto, which in turn had been culled from what she'd brought from California weeks earlier. She could stand to buy some more clothes if she wasn't returning to L.A. soon.

Selena would probably have a fit if she extended her trip again, but unless the studio backed down, there wasn't much more they could do on the show until Jay changed his mind.

So, she'd put on a black dress, pretty tight, and the same heeled boots from last night, piled her hair on top of her head with a few pieces wafting down by her face. Her makeup was simple; she'd thrown on a classic red lipstick for a pop of color. She looked like she should be going to a city nightclub, not a small-town bar. She tugged her dress down over her thighs, flashed a smile and her ID at the bouncer, and strolled in with as much confidence as she could muster.

She needn't have worried. Mimi accosted her almost immediately, engulfing her in a one-armed hug, while holding a glass of clear liquid out of the spill zone. "You came, I'm so happy! The bassist is extremely cute. Let's go ogle him."

Cami laughed. "Are you tipsy already?"

"Never mind that. You need to order so you can catch up."

"This place is slammed, that's great," Cami said. The

band was warming up on the stage, and yes, the bassist was cute if you liked shaggy hair and soulful eyes. Almost every table was full, while the bar itself was two or three bodies deep. Cami had never been good at bars, but she was usually able to talk someone helpful into getting drinks for her.

"Don't worry, I have a table over here." Mimi wove her way through the crowd to a table next to an emergency exit door. Cami followed in her slipstream and took in the people already at the table—a pretty, young woman in a bright blue top and jeans. And Jay.

Which made sense. He owned the place, after all. They'd even talked about it earlier. He knew she was going to be there. He'd given her his blessing.

And he didn't even seem to notice her, not the way he was laughing broadly at whatever the girl in blue was saying. Mimi set her glass down on the table with a clink. "Say hello to Cami," she ordered.

Jay looked up at that, his gaze locking onto her mouth first, for a split second, then sliding up to her eyes. "Hello, Cami," he said dutifully. It was annoying that everything he said sounded sexy.

"Cami, hi, so nice to meet you," the girl in blue said. She had a low voice and artfully cut short black hair only slightly darker than her flawless ebony skin.

Cami pushed aside her brief flare of jealousy, because seriously, she didn't do jealous, and waved to the woman, trying to put a genuine smile on her face. "Hi."

Mimi belatedly made the introduction. "Cami, this is my co-worker at the library, Pauline."

Jay got up from the table. "My break's over," he said. "Can I get you ladies anything?"

"I'm good," Pauline said. She had a bottle of beer in front of her.

"Yes, another vodka tonic, please, little brother," Mimi sing-songed. Cami hoped she wouldn't be holding Mimi's hair back at the end of the night at the rate she was going.

"And for you?" Jay looked right at her. His expression was neutral, none of the sadness he'd been throwing off that afternoon in her hotel room, but he didn't seem nearly as happy to interact with her as he did with Pauline a minute ago.

"I'll have a martini. Olives. Please," she tacked on, remembering her manners.

He raised his eyebrows, and she glared back. She liked martinis, dammit.

"Right away, miss," he said sardonically and then retreated to the bar.

Mimi laughed. "Oh, shit."

"What?" Cami had been here for five minutes, and she felt like she'd made ten mistakes already. She didn't need Mimi rubbing it in. She sat in the chair vacated by Jay, threw her purse on the table, and gave Pauline a half-hearted smile.

"You're going to be my sister-in-law," Mimi said gleefully.

"How much have you had to drink?" Cami asked meanly.

"She's on her second," Pauline answered. "I think. But she's a known lightweight."

"She's wild," Cami said. She didn't know what Mimi thought she saw between her and Jay, but with women like Pauline around, women who could offer him baggage-free attention, there was no reason for Jay to look at Cami twice. She decided to ignore Mimi and get to know the woman who'd made Jay laugh. "So, you're a librarian, too?"

"I am a librarian. Research. We have quite a collection of nineteenth century seafaring logs, as well as the complete papers of Captain Zachariah Bragg, one of the founders of Misty Harbor. I'm writing grant applications to get funding for a permanent Bragg family display."

"Zachariah Bragg, that's who built the house that was turned into the inn, right?"

"Yes. He built the original building in eighteen seventy-one and—"

"Pauline, darling, as happy as I am for you to have someone new to talk to about the captain, the show's going to be starting."

"You're a bossy drunk," Pauline said.

"I'm not drunk," Mimi insisted. "Ahh, thank you! Maybe after this one." She took the glass offered to her by an employee in a T-shirt embroidered with The Cove's logo, not the woman Cami had met the night before.

"Martini?" The smiling server held out the tray, and

Cami took the martini glass. "I'm a big fan," she said quickly, then slipped away before Cami could react.

"Fan?" Pauline asked, with a wrinkle in her brow.

"Cami is an actress," Mimi said.

"For real? That's very impressive."

"Thanks," Cami said. Maybe Pauline wasn't so bad. She didn't know Cami from Adam. Even in Misty Harbor, there were regular people doing regular jobs; not everyone's life revolved around *Sawyer's Cove.*

The band struck up the first notes of a lively song Cami didn't recognize, but a good portion of the audience did. It got loud fast, between the music belting from the stage and the crowd's enthusiastic response. Mimi was up on her feet, hollering and swaying along with the best of them. Cami had to smile. She'd never seen Mimi like this, so loose and uninhibited. It was like the music turned on a part of her, or turned off another one, and she seemed totally in the moment.

Cami, however, was not feeling the effects of her quite good martini just yet. She sat stiffly at the table, like a stick-in-the-mud. She didn't know the band, she didn't know the people, except Mimi, and she felt the uncomfortable sensation that even though Jay wasn't anywhere near her, he might be watching her. Judging her.

Pauline, for her part, seemed merely mildly amused at her co-worker's vodka-fueled enthusiasm. Cami would have liked to talk with her more, but the volume of the place didn't really allow for it.

Pauline seemed willing to try, though. "So, what kind of acting do you do?" she yelled over the din.

"Movies, mostly. Some TV," Cami bellowed back.

"Nice," Pauline answered.

There wasn't anywhere for the conversation to go after that, and Cami didn't want to strain her voice trying to be heard over the music. She drained her martini in two big sips that burned going down and made her eyes water. She always saved her olives for last, and she savored them, crisp and briny and cold, telling herself her world did not need Jay Orlando at its center just because everything in this town seemed to connect back to him. He was like a spider whose web was woven into every aspect of Misty Harbor life. She felt herself caught up in the strands, struggling to escape. Or did she want to get closer to the spider himself?

Okay, maybe the martini was hitting her now.

Cami stood up, leaving her empty glass behind. She joined Mimi on the dance floor and started swaying to the beat. She shook and shimmied, and Mimi screeched her approval. They danced side by side for a couple of songs, making room when Pauline joined them, her dance moves hesitant at first, then more confident.

Cami lost herself in the upbeat indie band's thumping bass and rapid-fire drums. The music crashed into her violently, and in the clarity of being alone with her slightly alcohol-tinged thoughts in a crowded room, she understood she'd come to Misty Harbor under false pretenses.

Oh, she'd come because of *Sawyer's Cove* and Selena

and the unpleasant way her job in Toronto had ended and needing to prove to her dad she could handle her own career. She'd come because she had so much energy; she was bursting at the seams with it. Producing was a way to apply her energy to something lasting, something she'd be proud of.

But she'd been lying to herself every day for twelve years. She'd told herself when Jay flew back to Misty Harbor from Los Angeles, leaving her crying alone in a hotel room, she didn't care. If he didn't want to be with her, that was his loss. She had bigger and better things to move on to, and she did. She had no idea what her career would have looked like if she and Jay had stayed together, but she was pretty proud of everything she'd done. Sure, there had been some clunkers, but for the most part, she liked her body of work.

The lie was that she didn't miss him.

She'd missed him every day of those twelve years. And she was missing him fiercely from twenty feet across the bar, his dark eyes seeming to pay her no attention while he performed his Jay Orlando-humble-barkeep act and treated her like she was just another one of his patrons.

Coming to Misty Harbor had been more dangerous than she realized. It had dredged up old feelings, ones that were threatening to destabilize an already tricky balancing act. Now she was caught between needing to do what was best for the show and what her core was screaming at her to do, which was march over to the bar, lay herself on top of it, and demand Jay do right by her.

But that was never going to happen. The project came first. And she was waiting on him for that, too.

Her impotence made her want to scream. She settled for whistling and clapping hard enough to make her palms red when the song ended. The band announced a break before their second set, and she, Mimi, and Pauline collapsed back into their chairs, sweaty and flushed.

"You two are wicked," Pauline complained. "You know I'm constitutionally opposed to exercise. Dancing counts as exercise."

"You're just too young to understand us thirty-somethings actually need exercise. I'll have you doing hot yoga with me yet, Pauline," Mimi declared. "But I definitely need water."

"I'll get it," Cami surprised herself by saying. There was a predictable surge at the bar as the people who'd been enjoying the show took the opportunity to snag fresh booze, but her blood was up now, and she didn't mind pushing her way through the crowd, bellying up to the shiny copper bar. She caught the eye of the bartender she'd met last night—Danielle? No, Danica. Danica nodded at her as she pulled a pint for someone else, but suddenly Jay was right in front of her, filling up her entire field of vision.

"Enjoying the show?" he asked, as if he had all the time in the world. As if she was the only one waiting for his attention. She liked it, the fact that she could still pull him toward her.

"The band is great," she said, flashing a smile. "And we're thirsty. Can I get three waters?"

"I'll bring them over," Jay said. He nodded in the direction of their table. "You go sit."

She narrowed her eyes. "Is this your protective nonsense again?" Though, when she tuned into it, she did feel eyes on her, and was someone taking a picture? She'd forgotten for a minute she wasn't just a woman with a job and hopeless mess of a love life. She was Camille Corsair, and she was always supposed to be on.

"You want another martini?"

"Better not, but the other girls might want another round."

"You sit," Jay repeated firmly. "Go back to Mimi."

"Okay."

It was more difficult to push her way through the crowd on the way back to the table, maybe because people were starting to recognize her. She imagined she could hear them buzzing about her. Or maybe it was just hard to walk away from Jay.

With relief, she returned to the table. Mimi caught her expression. "Everything okay?"

"I'm fine," she said. "Can I switch places with you, though?" Mimi jumped up from the chair closest to the wall, and Cami sank into it. Now she had Mimi between her and the room, and maybe it was silly, or selfish, but Mimi could take care of herself, and Cami felt a little less vulnerable. A little less on display.

"Jay's bringing the drinks," she said. It was still loud

in the bar, but without the band playing they didn't have to shout to be heard.

"So what's the deal with you and Jay?" Pauline asked. "Are you really engaged?"

"What?" Cami's voice came out embarrassingly close to a shriek.

"Mimi said you were going to be her sister-in-law, and I thought—"

"Pauline, you literal-minded dear, I was—I was tipsy." Mimi looked at Cami anxiously. "Now I've sweated out all the alcohol, and I shouldn't have said that."

"It's okay."

"No, seriously, that was shitty of me." Mimi was still frowning.

Cami knew she'd been making fun, and since they were friends now, Cami was quick to forgive. "It's okay, Mimi," she said sincerely.

"Thanks." Mimi bit her lip as an awkward silence grew. "So, are you glad you came out tonight, or—?"

Cami laughed, and the tension was broken. "I'm glad, really. Otherwise I'd probably be watching HGTV in my room and raiding the minibar."

"Why drink overpriced mini bottles of vodka when you can drink here for free?" Mimi asked.

"For free?"

"What good is being the sister of the owner if you can't get free drinks for your girlfriends?" Mimi asked. "Especially when he owes me for setting up this gig. I should really know better than to volunteer myself for unpaid labor, but it's something I enjoy."

"If we're drinking for free, then I'm having another beer," Pauline said.

"Your wish is my command," Jay said, flourishing a tray carrying three glasses, a pitcher of ice water, and another round for Pauline and Mimi.

"Thank you, little brother," Mimi said, without a trace of sarcasm.

"You ladies doing okay?"

Cami nodded and let the other two chime in.

"Aces," Mimi said, while Pauline added, "Best night out in weeks."

"That's what I like to hear. Cami, you're not going to walk home alone, are you?"

The protective schtick was getting a little old. "I'm not sure how to answer that question."

Jay turned to his sister. "Mimi, can you walk Cami home later, please?"

"Um." Mimi glanced at the stage where the cute bass player was chatting with the drummer.

Cami rescued her. "No one needs to walk me home. I'm not ten."

"How about I drive you all?" Jay said.

"You going to start a taxi company next?" Mimi asked sharply.

"No, I'm just going to worry about you all night if I don't know you have a good plan for getting home."

"Fine, drive us then," Mimi said with a sarcastic huff.

"That's great. Thank you so much."

"You're welcome." The two siblings glared at each other until Jay broke and stalked off to the bar. The band was getting back on stage with their instruments, and Cami suddenly felt exhausted.

"What's that all about?" Pauline asked. "I know I'm an only child, but that seemed weird."

"He's just an overprotective asshole," Mimi said resignedly, as if she'd spent a decade trying to change him and knew it was futile.

"He might be overprotective, but he means well." Cami had no place defending the man. "But honestly, how much trouble could we get into walking home through downtown Misty Harbor on a Friday night?"

"We all live in different directions. He's being extra," Mimi complained. "But I'm not going to let it ruin the rest of my night. Who's with me?"

Cami laughed and huzzahed with Pauline, and as the band started again, something uptempo and fun, she got a second wind.

After what seemed like minutes, but was the better part of an hour later, the wind abruptly left her sails. Her feet hurt, her ears were ringing, and she had to pee after all the water she'd drunk had diluted her one-martini buzz down to nothing.

"I'm going to the restroom!" she yelled into Mimi's ear, who nodded, but her attention was on the stage, or more specifically on the bass player, as the band delved into its encore.

She found the restroom easily and admired the cute herringbone-tiled walls as she washed her hands. A girl waiting in the hallway caught her eye as she exited. Cami gave her a little nod, and the girl's eyes widened and she looked down at her shoes before she practically bolted into the bathroom. Cami had experienced the whole range of people's reactions to her. Seeing someone famous turned some people shy and others into dicks. Or more likely, they were dicks already and felt justified in saying and doing whatever they wanted because they were dealing with a famous person.

Cami was glad when she got back to her table. The band was done, and while there were still a lot of people hanging out, it was less of a crush. Still, she was hot, and tired, and regretting the boots, even though after years of wearing heels, her feet should have been beaten into submission by now.

"Are you ladies ready to go?" she asked.

"So ready," Pauline answered, while Mimi made a pouty face.

"I don't have to work tomorrow," Mimi said pleadingly.

"Yeah, but I do," Pauline said reasonably. She was none the worse for wear for her two beers.

"I—" Cami wasn't sure what she had to do tomorrow. She'd stalled out on her quest to get Jay to sign the contract, Selena had been in meetings all day and they hadn't connected. There were scripts she could read, phone calls she could return. She should woman-up and call her father. Tomorrow was Saturday. What did normal people do on Saturdays?

"If we go home now, all I'll do is stay up too late,

watching British procedurals and eating a whole bag of popcorn," Mimi complained.

"Simple solution," Pauline said. "I'll take Cami where she needs to go, then take myself home. You stay here, and Jay can give you a ride later."

"That is a simple solution, thank you, Pauline," Cami said, trying not to be disappointed at not getting a chance to spend more time with Jay.

"You guys are no fun." Mimi glanced around the room, her eyes lighting on the cute bassist. "I'll just have to make my own fun. And he looks like fun."

"You do that," Pauline said with a good-natured smile. "Goodnight, Mimi."

"Goodnight, my friends," Mimi said, good humor restored. She hugged Pauline, then Cami, and then she went to chat up the bass player.

"I'm parked a block down," Pauline said.

Cami hesitated. "I guess we should tell Jay we don't need his services after all."

"Can't Mimi tell him?"

"Um."

Pauline's eyes narrowed to slits. "I'm missing something, aren't I?"

"You know how sometimes things you know would be terrible ideas by the light of day sort of seem like good ideas late at night?"

"I don't think you're making much sense, but I think you don't need a ride."

"No, I don't think I do."

"Nice to meet you, Cami. Stop by the library sometime and I'll give you a tour of the Captain Bragg collection."

"I'll do that," she said, leaning over and giving Pauline an impulsive hug. "Wait—I should walk you to your car."

Pauline just waved her off. "If you walk me to my car, then you'll be walking back here alone, and it just becomes a weird fox and hen crossing a river kind of situation. Besides, I have pepper spray."

"If you're sure."

Pauline headed out with a wave. Mimi was making out with the bassist in the corner. Cami was truly the last woman standing.

If only her feet didn't hurt so bad.

Chapter Fourteen

Erika: Fun fact about Camille Corsair I discovered
when researching this episode: she doesn't have a
driver's license.

Jules: What, it's expired?

Erika: Let me rephrase: she apparently doesn't know
how to drive.

Jules: Like Jessica Fletcher in *Murder, She Wrote*?

Erika: Exactly like Jessica Fletcher. I wonder if Camille
Corsair solves mysteries on the side.

From *The Sawyer's Cove Rewatch Project Podcast:
The Test*

"Hey, so I need that ride."

Jay looked up from his computer in The Cove's tiny back office. Cami stood in the doorway. Her cheeks were pink, and most of her lipstick had worn off. Earlier her hair had been artfully tousled, now it just looked kind of messy. She leaned against the doorway as if those silly heeled boots were bothering her.

He wanted to kiss her.

Actually, he wanted to pull her onto his lap, shuck off her boots, and give her a foot rub. Which was much, much worse.

"Sure. Give me a second. I'm parked in the back. Want to grab the others?"

"Pauline already left, and your sister is, ah, finding alternate transportation."

He caught her drift. "Oh. Well." It wasn't the first time Mimi had hooked up with someone at his bar. He reminded himself she was an adult and didn't think about it too hard.

"So it's just me," she said in a kind of fake cheery voice. "If you don't mind."

"I offered, didn't I?"

"Forget it, Jay. I'll just call a—"

He was up and out of the chair, pulling his keys out of his pocket, the purchase orders he was compiling to send to his accountant forgotten. "Let's go."

She backed out the doorway far enough for him to see she was limping slightly. He led her through the boiler room and out a side door to the alley behind the bar. His pride and joy was parked where he left it, a dark gray bastion of masculine technology.

"Wait, you still have this?"

He clicked off the locks and opened the passenger door for her. She wasn't a tiny woman, but still, it was a step up, and her heels didn't help. He hovered behind her, just in case, until she'd levered herself into the passenger seat.

"Of course," he said. "I love this beast."

He'd bought the Land Rover Defender when the show had been picked up for a second season and the studio had given them bonuses. He'd been making a decent amount per episode, most of which he saved, but the bonus was more money at once than he'd ever seen. He did the first patently selfish thing he'd ever done—bought himself an oversized, gas-guzzling, luxury European SUV.

The Defender was rugged enough for New England winters, but stylish, too. He loved everything about it, and he'd taken meticulous care of it; it was still running like a top and would for as long as he was alive. Or until fossil fuels ran out. Whichever came first.

This was also the vehicle where he and Cami used to make out, shielded from the eyes of their families, from their co-workers, behind the semi-tinted windows, parked in side streets or out in the woods, the seat racked back as far as it would go to allow room for her to straddle him in the driver's seat, her plush body surrounding him with soft heat while they kissed until their tongues went numb.

Good times.

He didn't know if she was thinking about that as she buckled her seatbelt, holding her purse on her lap in front of her like a tiny beaded shield.

"What are you doing tomorrow?" she asked him out of nowhere once he'd turned the key, the rumble of the engine his comfort sound. It had clearly lulled him into a false sense of security.

"Why?" He couldn't help if his voice sounded suspicious. She'd had an agenda ever since coming here. No question was innocent.

She looked out the window. Downtown wasn't very big, and they were already halfway up the street that paralleled Main looping their way back to the inn. "Jesus, Jay, I'm not trying to trick you into anything. I just wondered what people do around here on the weekends. Do you have the day off?"

He considered the question. "I don't take a lot of days off," he said. Being an entrepreneur and self-appointed town guardian took a lot of hours. "But sometimes I go hiking."

"And what about tomorrow?"

He had just been trying to get through the week and navigate the curveball Cami had thrown him. He'd been battling the steadily growing feeling that not only was he going to be agreeing to do the show before she was through with him, he might try to do something stupid like ask her out or something.

"Errands. Farmer's market. Work."

"Oh." She sounded disappointed, and he hated being the cause.

"Why? Did you want to hang out?" He regretted the juvenile choice of words immediately.

But instead of making fun of him, she smiled. "Yeah, I guess. I want to do something fun."

He drove slowly around the U-shaped driveway and

idled in front of the inn's front entrance. A sleepy-looking doorman waited in a pool of light just outside the doors, waiting to be of service.

"Fun?"

"Yeah, unplug, go someplace maybe?"

"With me?"

She took longer to answer. "Yeah."

It sounded honest but still didn't tell him what he needed to know. Why did she want to hang out with him when they spent half their time together bickering? Did she feel the pull between them the way he did? Was she as intrigued by the tension of what they'd been to each other in the past and what they might be to each other in the future as he was?

He couldn't glean any of that from her one-word answer, so he took his only option. "I'll pick you up at ten, and we'll go do something fun."

Her brilliant smile was brighter than the danger alarm going off inside him at voluntarily agreeing to spend one-on-one time with her. "Okay, great. Thanks for the ride."

She unbuckled and opened the door. The gingerness with which she stepped down to the ground had him grumbling and unbuckling himself. He jogged around the front of the vehicle, scooped her into his arms, walked her the twenty feet to the entrance, and deposited her on a bench next to the sliding doors. The hotel doorman was studiously not looking at them, but he had a faint smile around his lips.

It was all over too quickly to register much more

than the weight of her against his chest and the whiff of her herbal hair products, then he stepped back. She hadn't said anything, perhaps shocked into silence by his audacity.

"Take off those damn shoes," he growled.

"All right."

He didn't look back until he was inside the Land Rover. She'd done as he'd told her, slid the shoes off her feet, and was now holding them as she chatted with the doorman. He trusted her safety between there and her room. His mom ran a tight ship and safe hotel. As he left the driveway, he didn't examine any of what had just happened too closely. He'd have plenty of time to freak out and overanalyze when she went back to California, and he was left on his own in Misty Harbor.

"Do we have a destination in mind, or are you taking me to a secondary location to murder me? Or maybe we're going to drive until we run out of gas on some creepy back road."

"Isn't that the plot of one of your slasher flicks?"

"Probably. How would you know?"

"I've seen a few."

"Really?" Cami had sometimes wondered if Jay ever watched her movies, or if he'd boycotted anything with her on principle. When she'd done that space program movie, in the back of her mind she'd thought it was the kind of thing he'd like.

"Hey, did you ever see that John Glenn biopic I was in?" Was her voice actually coming out casually, or was she kidding herself?

"I did." He sounded as if maybe he was amused at her transparency. Whatever.

"What did you think?"

"I liked it. And you were really good, in case you were looking for a free ego boost."

"Not exactly." She could admit to being pleased at his dry words of praise, but she moved on quickly. "It was interesting to work on. I got to tour Cape Canaveral when we were on location in Florida. You would have loved it."

"Sounds cool. And to answer your earlier question, I do have a destination in mind. It's up to you if we eat first, do the activity second, or the other way around."

"How long will it take to get to the activity?"

They were on the interstate, heading south. He'd picked her up at ten on the dot. She'd been waiting on the bench where he'd left her last night, dressed in practical linen trousers and sneakers to give her abused feet a break. She'd gotten up, had a light breakfast, and beelined for the bench. There was no reason to suspect he'd come up to her room to collect her, but she didn't want to take any chances.

Being in the car together was bad enough. There were memories here, but at least he was occupied with driving. It was when his concentration was on her that she felt the zing of risk. In Misty Harbor, their actions were restrained by the eyes that always seemed to be on them, no matter where they were. Even in her hotel room, the fact that his mom was likely a few floors below had a dampening effect on her imagination.

But this was the wide open world, where they were just Jay and Cami. No one knew them, and no one knew where they were. The freedom was intoxicating. It made her want to be reckless and push. Last night, she'd slipped up and asked him to spend time with her. He didn't owe her anything, and she wasn't sure what she was even free to give, but she'd asked for this anyway. She wouldn't think too hard about why.

The farther they got from Misty Harbor, the more playful he got, and the more she felt like Cami Cosinsky instead of Camille Corsair, buttoned-up leading lady. It was a fantasy, a seductive one. Could she have this, if only for a day? She didn't dare think too hard about the future.

The future could be so good if they let it.

"We'll be there in half an hour. There's a park nearby. I thought we could have a picnic."

"Activity first, then lunch. That way we'll have something to talk about at our picnic."

"I didn't realize we needed material for our picnic conversation."

"Oh, yes. Otherwise, what would one talk about on a picnic?"

"Is it on a picnic or at a picnic?" Jay mused.

"I have no idea. I didn't graduate high school."

"Sure you did."

"Getting my GED isn't the same thing." She wasn't bitter about it; it was just the way it was.

"Well, I graduated high school, and I don't know either."

"Maybe it's personal preference."

"Besides, we could always talk about picnic stuff. Like checkered napkins."

"Wicker baskets."

"Ants."

"Sunburn."

"Speak for yourself."

"Oh, so you never wear sunblock?"

"Of course I do. How else do you think I look as young as I do?" He gestured vaguely to his maddeningly beautiful face.

She stuck her tongue out at him. He did look young. She was two years younger, but she had seen it happen —men in their thirties kept looking youthful, while the difference between thirty and forty for women was a hard slide into fine lines and sagging necks. If one took the cosmetic surgery route, you could put it all off for a few years, but then you started looking shiny and tight. Cami understood why people did it and didn't judge, but she would rather not look in a mirror and be unable to recognize the face looking back.

"So, activity it is," Jay said. "I think you're going to like it."

They passed a garish billboard advertising a hotel with a waterpark. "Are you taking me tubing? I didn't bring my swimsuit."

Jay scowled. "Definitely not. Ever since that place opened, hotel bookings across Misty Harbor have been down. That's one of the reasons we're putting together Harbor Fest."

The groove of despair was back between his eyes. Cami resisted the urge to put her hand on his thigh as she reassured him. "The waterpark is a novelty. Misty Harbor has timeless charm, and Harbor Fest is going to be a smash. Things will balance out." She didn't really know what she was talking about, but the groove eased, and a few minutes later, Jay turned off the freeway.

They drove through the tree-lined streets of Old Saybrook until they reached Main. It took a minute to find a parking spot large enough to accommodate the Land Rover, but once parked, Jay ran around to the passenger door and opened it. "Shall we?" he asked, offering Cami his arm like an old-timey movie character.

"Okay," she answered, unable to help the embarrassingly girlish giggle that escaped as she hopped out of the vehicle and took his arm. "And where on Earth are we going?"

"We are going to the Katharine Hepburn Cultural Arts Center—they have a museum all about Kate."

Cami stopped dead in her tracks. "Seriously?"

"Well, I know she's your favorite. This place opened a little while after we wrapped *Sawyer's Cove*, so I figured you haven't been here."

"She is my favorite, and I haven't been here. This is so amazing."

"I'm pretty sure it's like three rooms and a documentary," Jay said, as if to temper her expectations. She didn't care if it was a child's school project on poster board. He'd planned an excursion tailor-made for her, and it gave her an appallingly warm feeling in the vicinity of her heart.

They spent an hour doing the tour. Cami delighted in it all, and Jay looked like he was enjoying himself, too. Or maybe he was simply enjoying her pleasure.

"She was such a badass," she said reverently as they poked around. "She could do the most serious drama, and she pulled off physical comedy like a queen."

"I remember you showing me *Bringing Up Baby* and being shocked this was the same actress from *Guess Who's Coming to Dinner*."

"You remember that?" Cami had grown up on the classics—both her mom and dad had loved old movies and figured anything that was in black and white was suitable for their daughter. She'd been raised on Cary Grant and Myrna Loy, Barbara Stanwick and Jimmy Stewart. But above all, Katharine Hepburn was her favorite. Outwardly strong and tough but with a complex vulnerability underneath, Cami had been inspired by her. She'd even read one of her *Philadelphia Story* monologues in an audition once.

"I may not have had much of a film education before I met you, but I've caught up. I get TCM."

"What are some of your favorites?"

"I like noir," he said. "It can be kind of depressing, but all those macho guys are fun to watch. Humphrey Bogart is magnetic."

"I would have figured you for a Westerns kind of guy."

"Some of them are good. I don't love the ones where the Indians are the bad guys."

"No, those storylines haven't aged well."

Jay turned to her. She looked into his brown eyes, marveling again that he'd brought her here. "Well, have you gotten your fill of Miss Kate?"

"I suppose so. This has been wonderful, thank you so much for thinking of it."

"You're welcome, Cams."

There was that nickname again, giving her optimism that things might just work out, for the show at least, if not for the two of them.

A girl could hope.

Chapter Fifteen

ERIKA: We made it. It's the season finale of season one.

JULES: It's been a wild ride.

ERIKA: And this episode has one of my favorite all-time moments in the show.

JULES: Let me guess—when Sawyer's mom drops the plate of spaghetti in her cheating boyfriend's lap?

ERIKA: Okay, that's my second favorite moment. You know the one I'm talking about. The kiss.

JULES: Oh, the epic, life-altering first kiss between Parker and Amy? That kiss?

ERIKA: That's the one.

FROM *THE SAWYER'S COVE REWATCH PROJECT PODCAST: THE DINNER PARTY*

They returned to the Land Rover to retrieve a large zippered soft-sided cooler. Jay hoisted it as if it weighed nothing, also grabbing a plaid microfleece blanket, which he handed to Cami.

"I don't think I'm pulling my weight," she said, laughing at their disproportionate burdens.

"You're perfect," Jay said as he led them down the block to the town green. She knew he didn't mean that literally, but the easy warmth in his voice gave her a corresponding warmth all over. The green was empty except for a couple of people eating lunch on a bench. Cami spread out the blanket in the shade thrown by a lush-leafed maple.

"I hit up the farmer's market before I picked you up. We have a selection of Misty Harbor's finest," Jay announced. He unzipped the cooler and started bringing out container after container of food.

Cami shook her head. "Jay, you might have overestimated how much I can eat."

"It'll keep. This thing is full of cold packs. Here." He handed her a sourdough boule wrapped in brown paper.

She held it to her nose and inhaled the yeasty scent. "Is that from the Bakeshop?"

"Of course. Zelda's bread is the best. Not to mention everything else she makes."

"The first time I lived in Misty Harbor, the only bakery to speak of was that crummy donut place."

"That's still there. Still crummy."

"One thing you can say about L.A.—they make superior doughnuts."

"I'll have to tell Zelda you said that. She can't resist a challenge. And what do you mean the first time?"

Cami found a bread knife and cute miniature wood cutting board tucked into the side of the cooler—this impromptu picnic was surprisingly well-appointed—and paused as she sliced the boule, wondering how to respond. She internally shrugged. There was no point in keeping this from him. "If the show goes ahead, I'll be spending a lot of time here. I want somewhere permanent to stay. I have a meeting with a realtor on Monday."

"Wait—really?" Jay snapped the lid off a small container. She could smell the mouthwatering pesto, but she couldn't read his expression.

"Yes, really. I can't live at the inn, and I told you before, I have really good memories in Misty Harbor. I like the idea of having an address there."

He said nothing, buried his head in the cooler for a minute. He came up with a bottle. "I have sparkling water, or this." He showed her a split of champagne.

"Ooh, yummy." So he wasn't going to say anything about her possibly moving. She didn't need his approval, and the day was too fine to ruin with an argument.

He laid his hands on two plastic tumblers. "The glasses aren't right," he said, vaguely apologetic.

"They're great." She clapped in celebration at the cork's audible pop, then glanced around to see if anyone else had reacted to the sound, but they were alone. "We're probably not supposed to have alcohol in a city park."

"I'll hide the bottle." He poured generously and set her cup carefully in her hand.

She raised her tumbler high. "What should we toast to?"

"How about to Kate?"

"To Kate," Cami agreed. "And to a wonderful day. Thanks for this, Jay."

He smiled back at her, touched the rim of his glass to hers gently. "You're welcome."

They ate until Cami was stuffed. She lay back on the blanket, the green leaves of the tree above letting through dappled sunlight like a lace handkerchief draped over a lamp. She was sated and content and a little buzzy from the wine.

"Don't forget about dessert," Jay said, breaking into her thoughtless reverie.

She propped herself up on her elbows to peer at him. "I didn't forget about dessert. I thought you had, though. What do we have?"

"Bakeshop cupcakes. If you have room."

"Rue the day I don't have room for a cupcake," she answered. He handed her the box of two iced cupcakes. They sparkled with fine decorating sugar like fairy princess skirts. She selected the vanilla on vanilla one, while he took the chocolate on chocolate.

"You don't want chocolate?" he asked after taking an enormous bite of his. He had a swipe of brown frosting on the corner of his mouth.

Later she could blame the champagne or the perfect non-date-date they were on. Or she could be honest and tell herself she did it because she wanted to. Cami scooted forward on the blanket, her own cupcake forgotten, and kissed him on the corner of his mouth.

It wasn't a very good kiss, as kisses went. He didn't even particularly kiss her back. She licked at the smear of chocolate. He tasted sweet. It suddenly shook her, the intimacy, the memory of other kisses they'd shared, all combining to have her springing back. She ran her tongue over her lips instinctively, chasing the flavor of him. Then she realized what she'd done.

"Shit. I'm sorry."

He looked at her hard, his gaze indecipherable. "If you wanted the chocolate that bad, you should have taken it for yourself."

"That was inappropriate," she said quickly. "I wasn't thinking."

He didn't rush to tell her it was okay, which she appreciated. She'd gotten enough unwanted physical advances over the years to know how important consent was, and she'd leaned over and kissed him without asking. The lunch sat heavy in her gut.

"Really. I'm sorry."

"Apology accepted," he finally said. "Should we go?"

Cami put her uneaten cupcake back in the box, her appetite for sweets gone. She helped clean up the picnic, pouring the dregs of her champagne into the grass.

"Hey, come on, you look like you found out your movie bombed on opening weekend. It wasn't that bad, Cams," he said, zipping up the cooler swiftly.

"We were having a nice time, and I ruined it."

"How did you ruin it?"

"I kissed you without asking."

She watched his eyelashes sweep down and up as he blinked slowly, as if he was processing. He finally said, "Is that what you're worried about—that you didn't ask first?"

"Yes!" she wailed.

"Okay, so ask this time."

"What?"

"Ask this time," he repeated.

Was that a trick question? She felt her eyebrows come together in confusion. "You want me to ask if I can kiss you?"

"Yeah."

She didn't know what point he was trying to make, but she found herself instinctively following his direction. "Jay, can I kiss you?"

"Yes, you can kiss me."

The way he said it wasn't flippant or coy. It wasn't teasing or flirtatious. He sounded serious, as if he'd thought about it, weighed the pros and cons, and made a decision. Maybe there would be consequences to his decision, but he'd made up his mind nonetheless.

But the solemnity of his tone sunk its claws into her, and she froze. He might have given her permission, she might have wanted to do it, but she was aware of the downside now. This wasn't a spur-of-the-moment impulse she could chalk up to lunchtime bubbly. This was an action they'd be taking with intention.

She swallowed. This was a big deal. And she was choking like it was her first day on set.

His tone softened. "Hey, it's okay. Let's just go—"

Before he could finish the sentence, she closed the distance between them and tried again. The Jay and Cami kiss, take two.

This time, she landed squarely on his mouth with hers, and after a few seconds she felt him open up to her. She was surprised at how warm he was; he still tasted a little like chocolate.

He patiently let her lead the kiss, but when she sucked gently on the tip of his tongue, he seemed to break. He surged up against her like high tide in the harbor during a nor'easter. Their exploratory kiss turned hot and heavy, as if they were teenagers desperate to chase their desire the only way they knew how. But they weren't teenagers anymore.

Cami pressed her entire body to his, craving his strength, needing him to prop her up lest she liquify into a puddle of want on this picnic blanket in the middle of the Old Saybrook town green.

Oh, shit. They were very much in public. Very much making out. And she didn't necessarily think paparazzi lurked around the charming white wooden gazebo or behind the rose bushes, but that didn't mean a passerby with a cell phone wouldn't recognize them.

She pulled away from the kiss with effort, her entire body begging her to dive back in, possible PR fiasco and public decency laws be damned.

He looked dazed, too, color in his cheeks, his lips

pouty and wet, leaning toward her like she was his life source. "Well," he said, voice a growl. He cleared his throat and went on, "That happened."

"It certainly did," she agreed. "Think we could go somewhere else more private and let it happen again?"

"Shit, Cams, I don't know."

With all of her years as an actress, she should have been used to the unique blend of disappointment, shame, anger, and sadness that made up rejection.

"Oh."

"It's just, kissing you feels like foreplay, and if we're someplace private...we won't have a reason to stop."

So not a rejection, not exactly. She felt a little better. "Is that what you want?" Sex with Jay hadn't exactly been on her agenda for the day, but her body was certainly on board. Her panties were damp between her legs, and her breasts tingled with the need to be touched.

"Hey, don't get me wrong, I'd be a fool not to want you. But things are confusing. You're talking about moving back to Misty Harbor, and you want me to do the show, and if we slept together, wouldn't that just complicate everything?"

"You think I'd sleep with you to try to get you to sign the contract?" Cami shouldn't have been surprised. It's not like sex hadn't been a negotiating tactic in Hollywood since the silent era.

"Jesus, of course not," he said hotly.

The thing is, she believed him. That's not what he'd

meant, because he wasn't Hollywood, and that's one of the things she lo—she *liked* about him.

He was right. Things were already delicate, and she had no business adding sex to the mix. They might be working together again soon, and they didn't need to add another layer of complication. But it still hurt to think if she'd come back through town with no strings, he might have been interested in hooking up, but the fact that they might be seeing each other regularly had him putting on the brakes.

Not that she had a better scenario in mind. This was more evidence of how bad she was at relationships. It was sad that her most successful relationship had been with the man in front of her when they were both too young to know all the things they were doing wrong.

Clearly she had learned nothing in the last twelve years. She couldn't control Jay's feelings, but she could go back to what she did best—work. The show was her life now. She was going to be the most amazing producer/actor ever, and no one would be able to say she was a failure as a human being, even if she didn't have someone to share her life with.

"You're right. I'm sorry."

"Don't apologize, Cams." He stood, reached down with his hand as if to pull her up, but she ignored the gesture and pushed to her feet without his help. He shouldered the bag, she picked up the blanket, and they walked back to the Land Rover in silence.

Chapter Sixteen

ERIKA: The cliffhanger at the end of this episode makes me scream every time.

JULES: Do you remember what it was like having to wait months to see the next episode?

ERIKA: Vaguely.

JULES: I can't tell if I'm envious of or sad for people who can just binge the next episode right away.

ERIKA: The will-they-or-won't-they question. I kind of liked having all summer to stew about it. But you, dear listener, and I still can't quite believe we have listeners, don't have to wait. Our recap of season two, episode one, tantalizingly titled "The Night After," is coming to your feed in one short week.

FROM *THE SAWYER'S COVE REWATCH PROJECT PODCAST: THE DINNER PARTY*

Cami didn't say much on their drive back to Misty Harbor, and Jay was grateful. He didn't think he could keep his mind on idle conversation. He was still processing the two bombshells Cami had dropped during their lunch. The first was that she was considering making a permanent, or perhaps semi-permanent, move to Misty Harbor. That changed everything.

He had found it difficult enough to keep her at arm's length when he knew she'd be leaving in a few days. But if she was actually part of the community? That created a situation too tempting to contemplate. He could all too easily see himself unable to stay away.

Cami had this energy about her, a sort of glow she carried around with her wherever she was. When they were younger, it had been a bright, vibrant light, her natural charm combined with her dewy innocent looks. The combination of her inner strength and outer delicacy was deadly; he wasn't the only guy who wanted to be with someone so objectively beautiful and so inherently earnest and kind. As she'd matured, the glow had, too. It was golden now, burnished and strong.

The longer he spent with her, the more he craved time in her glow.

She was assertive when it came to work, but there was still a fragility about her that seemed to stem partly from the assholes she'd dated after him. What had she told herself to justify their behavior toward her? He wanted to erase every shitty guy since him and tell her she deserved much, much better.

If she lived in Misty Harbor, he'd be tempted to spend the rest of his life trying to be what she deserved. And that way lay madness. She might think she wanted time out to live somewhere bucolic for a while, but she'd get tired of it eventually. Plus, that would mean admitting he had feelings for her, when all she professed to want from him was a kiss and his signature on a contract.

That was the other thing. The kiss. It had twisted him up so fast, his heart was still beating overtime from the sensation of her cherry-plump lips and champagne-sweetened tongue.

He'd wanted so much more. He'd wanted all of her.

They'd been right to stop, though. It was too complicated. How could they leap into bed together when so much was left unresolved?

Namely, the contract and terrible, alluring idea of being Parker Wild again.

Walking around the museum with her, getting out of town, rewatching some episodes of *Sawyer's Cove*—he'd been building up to a yes. Not because putting on Parker Wild's persona was something he'd ever seen himself doing again or didn't fill him with trepidation, but because he kind of wanted to see if he could do it. It would be a challenge. He'd proven a lot to himself these last years. He'd built a business. He'd helped his mom and sister the best way he knew how. He'd strengthened this town. Harbor Fest, fingers crossed, would be successful. Bringing television production back to the area would be a boon, economically and professionally.

Signing the contract meant getting to spend weeks with Cami, on screen and off. But signing the contract meant they shouldn't let their relationship get physical.

He supposed they could be friends.

He sighed audibly.

"Penny for your thoughts?" she said.

"Just thinking about timing."

"Ours has been pretty bad, hasn't it?"

"Look, Cams, I don't want you to think I haven't enjoyed seeing you this week. I have. You're amazing. But if I've learned anything in the last twelve years, and I grant you, that is highly debatable, but let's just suppose I have, it's that business and pleasure don't mix."

"Okay."

"Okay?"

"Okay. If we're going to be working together, you're right. We shouldn't be confusing the issue with...other things."

"To make sure we're on the same page, other things like kissing, right?" He needed them to be clear about boundaries for once in his life.

"Kissing, romantic picnics, sex." Cami listed the items like she was making a grocery run and didn't want to forget the milk.

"Right." He glanced over. She was biting her bottom lip with even white teeth. He wondered if she had any regrets or was just glad he was no longer parroting "no" to the offer.

Why was it as soon as they agreed sex would be a bad idea, it was all he could think about? He could chalk it up to a long drought in that department. Prospects had been thin on the ground, and he'd yet to give in to the potentially humiliating prospect of dating apps.

"All right, so we're in agreement." He sighed again. Here went nothing. "And I guess I'm going to need a copy of that contract to read."

She turned her head sharply. "Really?"

"I'll read it," he said firmly. "That's all I'm agreeing to."

Her smile was so bright, he might have steered off the road if he hadn't driven it a thousand and one times before.

"I'll email it to you when I get home. What's your email address?"

Jay shifted in his seat to get his wallet out of his jeans pocket. He slipped his business card out of the billfold and passed it to Cami, who took it and tucked it carefully into her bag.

"Any questions at all, just call me. Or have your lawyer call me."

"I have a lawyer I use for The Cove business, but I don't think he knows anything about entertainment contracts," Jay admitted.

"I could set you up with mine, but that might be a conflict of interest."

"Honey, this business is so tangled up, everything is a conflict of interest."

"But that doesn't mean it's not going to be a success. Oh, this is great, I think you'll be pleased with the terms.

We are going to have so much fun, Jay, seriously." She sounded as if she'd been let loose in Disneyland after consuming a pound of gummy worms.

"You really want this, don't you?" She was going to be a fantastic producer, and this was a worthy project to cut her teeth on, sure, but it was more than that. She'd been nothing but enthusiastic and positive about the show, about their experience of making it, and about Misty Harbor, too.

"I really do."

"I can't believe you're thinking of buying a house here."

They were about ten minutes from the inn. Ten minutes from dropping her off and going home to consider signing up for the torment that would be spending days at a time working closely with her, while not being able to touch.

"Why not? It's a great town, Jay. You should be proud."

"What do you mean?"

"Misty Harbor. It's thriving, and I think a lot of that is down to you. And I'm glad. You should be proud," she repeated. Then she said the most extraordinary thing he'd ever heard her say. "I'm proud of you."

"What?"

"I'm proud of you, Jay," she repeated. "Your life here, it's impressive. You've built something lasting, a community, a way of life. You've made people's lives better. I think you're wonderful."

He felt his cheeks get hot. "Look, you don't have to butter me up. I told you I'll look at the contract."

"Is that what you think I'm doing?" Her shoulders slumped, all of her infectious excitement gone. She looked out the window. "You don't trust me, do you?"

He suddenly realized he'd acted like she had a hidden agenda since she'd walked back into his life. His silence seemed to answer her question.

"Look, I know the industry is really fucked up sometimes, but some of us are professionals. And I've never, ever wanted anything for you but the best. You were the one who—"

She broke off, and he instinctively slowed the car as they approached the turnoff for the inn, as if he could delay the inevitable if they never got to their destination.

"I was the one..." he prompted her.

"I wasn't going to do this, you know. I thought enough time had passed that I could just pretend we were old co-workers and not everything else, and I must have done a pretty good number on myself if I thought that could be true. I'm going to say something, and if it means you won't sign the contract, well, I guess I'll just deal."

She turned back to him, folded her arms across her chest, face pinched and closed off. "I hate this. Hate feeling like I'm not in control of my own destiny, which is astounding since as a working actress, almost everything is out of my control. Anyway—you don't trust me because I'm full Hollywood. But why should I trust you, Jay? You broke my heart."

He'd what now?

"I loved you so much, and you left me. I thought I'd done something wrong, or you hated the idea of living with me, but now I understand." She gestured to the world outside the Land Rover. "You left me for Misty Harbor, didn't you? You love it way more than you ever loved me."

Jay couldn't process that and keep driving. He pulled over to the side of the road and turned to her. Her cheeks were wet. He hadn't heard her start to cry, and his chest felt like she'd reached in and rearranged some vital organs.

"I didn't know that's what I was doing, Cams. I didn't, I swear. You're right, I was a complete dick to you. At the time, I thought it was the best thing for you. Because you called it. I loved you so much, but I didn't want to stay in L.A. I didn't want to keep acting or be the weird semi-famous guy taking community college classes. I didn't want to be Camille Corsair's live-in boyfriend. But I also didn't want *you* to have to choose. You had your entire career unfolding in front of you. You had so many offers. You didn't need me and my insecurities messing you up, weighing you down. Your dad—"

"What about my dad?" she broke in sharply.

"He never liked me, Cams, but he had good reason. He knew if I stuck around, your career would suffer. And he was right. Look what you've been able to do. I would have—"

"Don't you dare say you would have held me back."

He opened his mouth but couldn't make himself deny it.

"I can't believe this." She scrubbed the tears from her face angrily, her face turning blotchy red. "You and my dad decided what was best for me? You thought I couldn't handle a career and a boyfriend at the same time, so you just figured you'd save me the trouble?"

"Don't blame him. It was my decision. But didn't I do the right thing? Your career took off, didn't it?" An acute stab of pain shot through him; he put a hand to his breastbone, as if he could rub it away. "Please tell me I did the right thing."

She was crying again, big wet sobs, and he felt a corresponding pricking behind his eyes. "No, you jerk. My career has nothing to do with how much I loved you and wanted you in my life. You broke both of our hearts."

He closed his eyes. Shit. She was right. He'd taken comfort in knowing he'd done the best thing for her, even as he moped around for a year afterward. But he'd been wrong. He'd watched her go from one success to another and taken a small slice of satisfaction that as much as he was suffering, she was succeeding. It had all been a lie he'd told himself. It had all been hubris.

In the end, he was just another asshole who'd treated her badly.

He had no idea how to make it up to her, but before he could start with an apology, he felt her against his body. He opened his eyes; she'd thrown herself across the seat and put her arms around his waist, tucked her golden head under his chin. She was still crying, the hitch of her breath and sobs rumbling into his chest, heart-wrenching evidence of the hurt he'd caused her. That he'd caused them both.

She cried, the tears piercing through the self-righteous armor he'd built up, dissolving twelve years of longing, until he felt his desire for her as freshly as if he was twenty, in love with the most beautiful woman on the planet, the luckiest bastard in the world because she somehow loved him back.

He encircled her with his arms, cradling her, being there the way he should have been for the past dozen years.

"I'm so sorry, sweetheart," he murmured into her hair. He was finally close enough to sip the scent of her through his nose. He inhaled the sharp botanical fragrance of her shampoo. He smelled her tears, too, metallic, like blood. Or maybe that was just his heart, torn out of his chest, bloody and slashed to ribbons all over the interior of the Land Rover.

He rubbed her back and whispered nonsense until her sobs slowed to shuddering gasps. His shirt was wet, soaked through to the skin by the time she pulled her head back slightly. He didn't care. She could use him as a literal tissue, and he wouldn't mind. He wanted her to make him grovel and pay and atone.

She kept her head tipped forward as she groped for her bag. He reached into the side door pocket and came up with a handful of brown napkins from the Bakeshop and thrust them at her. "Here."

She took them and blotted her face. "I'm a mess," she said, her voice scratchy and thick.

Her face was mottled red, and her eyes were puffy, her hair had half-fallen out of its bun and hung over the left side of her face. "There is no version of you that wouldn't be lovely," he said with complete sincerity.

She snorted, then cried a little again, and then calmed. "I'm not usually so emotional. I try to save it for work."

"It's okay. I deserve it. Do you feel better now?"

She tied her hair back again, looked at him full-on for the first time. Her gaze dropped to his chest, and she reached out a finger, touching him lightly. "I got you all wet."

"I'm honored you would cry on me."

Her finger lingered there, a single point of contact between them. "I do feel better. I guess I needed that. Closure, or whatever."

The stabbing feeling was back. "Closure. Right."

"You know, you haven't signed the contract yet."

"True."

"So we're sort of in an in-between space."

His heart leapt with what she could mean. "So we are," he agreed cautiously, not wanting to hope for too much.

"Would you come back to my room?"

"Do you want me to?"

"I do."

"It's probably a bad idea." It was certainly a terrible idea. But when he'd tried to do the right thing, he'd ended up hurting her. Maybe doing the wrong thing would make things better. And maybe he was just desperate enough not to care.

"We're all entitled to a few mistakes," she said, and she sounded as if she was looking forward to making some. With him.

"Then yes."

Chapter Seventeen

ERIKA: One thing I loved was how they show quite a bit during sex scenes. Not just, like, fading out, but, like, body parts. Horny teenage viewers need that!
JULES: Oh my God, yes, I loved that, too, but it got awkward whenever my mom would randomly decide to watch the show with me that week.
ERIKA: Yikes. Okay. Yes. I've met your mom, and she's not exactly super comfy with sex.
JULES: No, she's terribly repressed. But in a cute way.
ERIKA: So how did you handle it?
JULES: Usually by making jokes. Like you do. And then I'd go back and watch the TiVo recording when she wasn't around. God, the Parker and Amy scenes are so fucking hot. And they aren't even going all the way.
ERIKA: Going all the way? Are you still fourteen?
JULES: I'm using the parlance of the day. There's that scene where it's heavily implied he's going down on her.

Erika: That scene is burned into my brain forever. I'll be thinking about that scene on my deathbed.
Jules: Same, E. Same.

From *The Sawyer's Cove Rewatch Project Podcast: The Night After*

Jay parked in the inn's lot, and they walked halfway to the entrance before Cami remembered their leftovers.

"What about all that food? I wouldn't want to waste it," she said.

"You go in, I'll get the bag. Snacks for later."

"Or now. I'm starving again." Crying always made her hungry.

"Oh yeah, I remember, crying always made you hungry."

She smiled. If she had doubts about whether or not sleeping with him was a good idea, and, to be honest, she had many, it was a moment like this that made her realize it didn't matter if it was a good idea or not. It was something she wanted to do, damn the consequences. Jay had always been the only person who could get her to risk her good-girl reputation.

"I'll meet you at the room," she said. A minute alone would give her time to compose herself. And make sure she had condoms. "You remember the number?"

He nodded and winked at her, and she practically skipped the rest of the way, digging her room key out of her bag so she'd have maximum freshening up time.

She felt light—lighter than she'd felt in years. Crying and telling him something she'd wanted to tell him for more than a decade had freed her, lifted a weight she hadn't been fully aware she was carrying.

He'd listened, and he'd apologized, and he'd held her without judgment. She couldn't ask anything more of him, and yet it seemed he wanted to give more.

She felt too wonderful to worry.

And then she noticed the man sitting in the lobby chair near the bank of elevators.

"Dad?"

"Camille, there you are." Her father rose from the chair, walked over, and gave her a hug she was too stunned to return. He looked much the same as he ever did—he wasn't much taller than her, but he held himself with confidence. His light brown hair was only beginning to gray, and a few lines marked his otherwise still youthful face. He was trim and dressed in tan slacks and a crisp white button down. Brown loafers. He looked like the ex-husband in a Nancy Meyers movie.

He slipped his phone into his pocket. "I was about to call you. Are you okay? You look a little—" He gestured to his face vaguely.

She ignored his unwelcome comment on her appearance. "What are you doing here?"

"I haven't seen you in weeks, and we keep missing each other's calls. I decided to come see you. Besides, there are some things I need to do in New York next week, and I thought you might like to join me. I figured we could drive down together. I booked a couple of rooms at the Four Seasons."

She held up a hand. "Wait. You flew all the way across the country because we were playing phone tag?"

"I missed you," he said. "And I figured you could use some company in this tiny town." His gaze flicked behind her, back to her, then behind her again. "Although it seems you already have a companion. Jay, good to see you."

Cami closed her eyes, took a deep breath, and opened them again. She turned around, and Jay was standing there, her tears still drying on his shirt, the soft-sided cooler hanging from his shoulder. His face was stone as he nodded at her father.

"Barry."

"Jay and I just had a picnic," she said, wondering why she felt the need to explain herself as if she was a truant high schooler. To Jay she said, "And my dad just showed up out of nowhere."

"A family trait, I guess," Jay said.

She winced. "Well, he's here now," she said, inanely. What was supposed to happen next? She felt trapped between two men she cared about and who had both proven untrustworthy when it came to letting her make her own decisions.

"I can see you're busy," Barry said. "How about dinner in a bit? I can make a reservation somewhere. You're welcome to join us, Jay, of course."

She grimaced. Did her dad always sound so officious? One reason she'd come to Misty Harbor without him was to get away from his habit of making decisions for her and acting like that was what she wanted all along. It was especially annoying because he was usually right.

"Dad, I don't know if I can make dinner," she said, giving him an apologetic glance. "What about breakfast tomorrow?"

Her dad looked taken aback, but he smiled. "Breakfast sounds great, Ladybug."

She warmed a little at the nickname. He didn't call her that often anymore, but she liked it. It made her feel less like his client and more like his daughter.

"I'll just head up and get some work done, then," Barry said.

"Up?"

"To my room. I'm on the fourth floor, north wing."

Her heart sank. "Oh. Me, too." Her vision of ravishing Jay Orlando in her big comfy bed, or maybe the oversized bathtub, or both, was suddenly out. She couldn't relax knowing her father was in the same wing. She looked at Jay, who hadn't moved through the entire exchange, as if he was a bellman waiting for instructions from a hotel guest. Shit.

"So, breakfast," she repeated, trying to be firm. She turned to Jay. "Do you—" She was about to ask if he wanted to head upstairs anyway, but he interrupted her.

"You take the snacks, Cams," he said. She wondered if the use of his own nickname for her was intentional. "I think I'll go check on Danica, get some work done myself."

He shifted the cooler off his shoulder and passed it to her. She looked at the bag, then back to him. His expression softened, as if he understood the position she was in and didn't want to make it harder for her. But that was the problem. Why should this be awkward in the first place?

"Then maybe dinner works after all," Barry said. "We could talk about some business that's come up."

"What business?" Cami's voice shrank, and she hated it. She hated everything that was happening right now. Her dad being here, dictating the rules of the game by his mere presence. Jay, trying to help but only making assumptions. The fact that instead of getting laid with the hottest guy in New England, she was going to have to sit through a working dinner with her overbearing father.

"It can wait," he said, glancing at Jay.

Suddenly, her legs felt weak. If she didn't sit soon, she might pass out.

"Bye, Jay," she said tiredly. She clutched the bag as if it was the only thing holding her up.

His expression turned worried for half a second before it cleared and he nodded. "Bye, Cami. Barry."

"Jay." Barry nodded curtly.

He walked away, and Cami's exhaustion warred with frustration. The frustration gave her the energy to walk to the elevators and punch the call button.

"Hey, I'll ride up with you. What do you want for dinner? Italian?" her dad asked, stepping into the elevator with her.

"I don't care." She smashed the button for four.

"Is something wrong?"

She resisted the overwhelming urge to roll her eyes. "Yes, Dad, something is wrong."

"What is it, Ladybug?"

"What do you think, Dad? Why are you here? And don't say you missed me."

He chuckled a little uncertainly. "I did miss you. And there's some business, but nothing urgent."

"Then what, you have a sixth sense that tells you when I might be starting to be happy and you have to come interrupt things?"

He looked truly shocked, and she felt a stab of regret for bursting out with that. She took a deep breath to steady herself. "Look, I'm sorry. I'm tired and hungry." The elevator opened onto their floor, and she pushed her way out.

"Then let's have an early dinner so you can go to bed early. I'm not sure what nefarious agenda you think I have, but I'm not here to make things difficult, Camille, I swear. I'm here to spend some time with you. I haven't seen you since before you left for Toronto, I barely heard how the shoot there went, and I was worried."

"I can take care of myself. I'm thirty. Almost thirty-one!"

He winced. "I know. Come on, Camille. Dinner?"

"I'm going to change. Give me an hour." She let

herself into her room and took slight satisfaction in leaving her father standing speechless in the hallway.

Barry had rented a car to get him to Misty Harbor from the airport, but when he told her where he'd made their dinner reservation, she realized it would be faster to walk the half-dozen blocks to Antonio's than retrieve his car from the inn's parking lot.

The old-school Italian restaurant, complete with dim lighting and red leather booths, smelled appetizingly of onions and garlic. Cami's stomach rumbled; she'd never gotten her post-cry snack, and she was famished.

"Charming place," Barry said as they settled into their booth and looked over the menus. "I don't remember it, but it doesn't seem new."

"Misty Harbor has a lot of charm. It always did," Cami said tightly. She was still kind of mad about being cock-blocked this afternoon. Could she get cock-blocked? Whatever. She ordered a glass of chianti and the creamiest, most carb-laden pasta dish on the menu.

Barry ordered fish and launched into business right away. "We have to get back to Mirabel about the rom-com remake, and Pia is hinting at progress on a deal for another *Forest* sequel. But I'm not sure that's the right move for you. You don't want to get too locked into horror. So I'll tell her no—"

"Stop, Dad, please." She couldn't let him take over the conversation the way he always did. "I don't want you to tell her no. I don't want you to tell her yes. I want you to let me decide, okay?"

"What do you mean?"

"I mean that I'm frustrated with you running my career. It's not that you don't do it well—you've been the best manager I could ask for. But don't you ever wish you were just my dad instead of my business partner? That we could sit and have dinner and not talk about work? You said you missed me. I miss you, too. I feel like I've missed you for a long time." She hadn't meant to launch into a monologue, but once she started, she couldn't seem to stop.

"I want my dad back. We're practically the only family we have, and I don't want to feel like we only talk because of work. Besides, producing *Sawyer's Cove*—that's something I really want to do on my own."

She slammed her mouth shut before she could ask for his approval. The whole point was that she didn't need his approval. Sue her if she wanted it anyway.

Barry frowned and studied his daughter's face. Eventually he said, "I didn't know you felt this way."

She let out the breath she'd been holding. "Well, now you do."

"Am I being fired, Ladybug?"

She chose her words carefully. "I'm grateful for everything you've done for me. We've made a great team. But I think I'm ready to go it alone for a while."

"I see." Barry fiddled with the stem of his wine glass, and Cami experienced a brief flash of regret. Was she making a huge mistake? Maybe she couldn't do this on her own. But then her dad looked up and raised his glass of chianti. "Camille, you're the most talented, the most capable, the most professional person I know. If this is what you want, I know you'll succeed."

The lump in her throat made it difficult to speak, but she raised her own glass, clinked it against her father's. "Thanks, Dad."

"Maybe it's time I took on some new clients, anyway," Barry said as the moment passed and the server came by with their meals. "Remember Lauren Jayne, who played your little sister in *Stay Out of the Forest*? I heard she was looking for a new manager."

She'd encouraged her father to think about adding to his roster of one several times over the years. "She's a darling girl with a great work ethic. I think she'd be a great fit for you."

"So..." He seemed to struggle with what to say next. "I want to know about your life outside of work, Ladybug. I hope you know I'd love you even if you had never gotten a single part, if you had never become Camille Corsair."

Her chest tightened. She did know. But it was nice to hear it out loud. "Thanks, Dad." She sighed. "The problem is, I don't have a life outside of work to share. But I'm working on it."

"With Jay?" he asked lightly.

She didn't really want to talk about Jay with her dad. Not after their raw conversation this afternoon. She figured her dad had partly influenced Jay's decision to leave her, but that was all so long ago, it seemed unnecessary to dredge up his role in it when they were trying to get on solid footing.

"Partly," she agreed. "Jay—it's complicated. He's been reluctant to consider doing the reboot. It would be so fantastic if he said yes. But he's built up a life here—a real life, with his business and the community, and I envy that. My job is so scattered, always moving around, always working with different people. I guess I'm getting to an age where I want to be more settled."

"That's understandable. You've been on the go since you were twelve." Barry smiled wryly. "My fault, I suppose."

"Not your fault, Dad. It was my choice, too. And I'm not saying I never want to act again. I just want to take some time to think about the future. I want to focus on *Sawyer's Cove*. I want to produce this project, and I want to do it on my own."

"Well, you've certainly earned your shot. I know this project is going to be a success. And I know you don't need my help—but if you want it, all you have to do is say the word."

"Thanks." She beamed. "So, what about you? What's going on in your life?"

Barry shrugged. "I was going to meet with some producers in New York next week, but now that I don't have any clients, I guess I'll cancel. Maybe I'll go see some shows instead."

Cami winced, but her dad didn't seem upset. She decided to focus on the part that didn't have to do with her firing him. "You should definitely go see some theater. I went to the Katharine Hepburn Cultural Arts Center today, and it made me realize it's been too long since I've seen anything new."

"Katharine Hepburn was your mom's favorite," he said with a soft smile. "Tell me about it."

So Cami did.

Chapter Eighteen

JULES: I think they handle teenage drinking really well in this episode.

ERIKA: I, for one, was definitely scared off by the sheer misery Parker seemed to be in the morning after getting drunk at the football game.

JULES: He forgot the first rule of binge drinking—hydrate.

FROM *THE SAWYER'S COVE REWATCH PROJECT PODCAST: THE HANGOVER*

When Jay got to the bar after making a pit stop at home to change, he put in an order for a burger, then pulled himself a pint of his favorite local lager. The first pint went down easy. The second went down even easier.

He poured the third as the burger came out of the kitchen. He hunched over it at the end of the bar. It was crowded again tonight. They generally reserved Saturday nights for local musicians, and tonight was a folk duo doing a bunch of sixties covers. The audience seemed mellow. Danica and her crew had everything under control.

He ate in silence, sensing Danica's concerned gaze on him periodically, but she was too busy working to talk to her grumpy boss, and for that he was grateful. He would have stayed home and wallowed, but that would have been too much like the days after he'd left Cami in Los Angeles. That entire year after had been lost to depression and second-guessing. He knew now he should have third-guessed himself and gone right back to her. But then what would have happened? He wouldn't have this place. He wouldn't have Misty Harbor. This time when Cami went away, as she inevitably would, he'd still have those things.

She was already pulling away, was with her dad-slash-manager right now, doing the business of being a movie star.

Barry Cosinsky had been wary of him from day one. Twelve years hadn't seemed to change his attitude, if his hard glances in the lobby of the inn were any indication. It would have been easy to imagine him as a controlling Svengali, or at least an overprotective father. But he wasn't a bad dude. He probably didn't like any of the ambitious assholes she dated. Which made two of them. He hated that he and Barry had anything in common when it came to Cami. It made him itch to be different, to do things differently this time.

He sighed. He needed to stop pretending he didn't desperately want there to be a "this time." And he could have sworn that this afternoon Cami wanted there to be one, too.

But both of them wanting it didn't make it smart.

Then again, after three beers, he was beginning to loosen up about what constituted smart.

Warner wandered in around nine and plonked into the seat next to Jay.

"What's got you down, Orlando?" Warner asked.

"Who says I'm down?" Jay cringed at the sour note in his voice.

"Ah, woman troubles." Warner nodded sagely. "Whatever you did, you should probably apologize."

Jay considered that. It wasn't as if he and Cami were on the outs. They'd just been derailed by her father, and it was too much like the old days for comfort. Then again, she'd tried to put Barry off, and Jay had bailed at the first sign of trouble. He slapped his palm to his forehead. "Shit. You're right, I do need to apologize."

Warner grinned. "I'm always right, my friend."

Jay got to his feet. He wasn't exactly drunk, but the walk to the inn would sober him up. If she was even there. Barry had said something about Italian food. Which meant pizza from one of the three pizza places in town, or Antonio's, the bistro on Bragg Street right off Main that had been there forever and a day. He could walk by on his way, see if they were there.

Or he could just text her, like a grownup.

He thumbed open his phone.

Great, that sounded like a booty call if he ever heard one.

Of course, he kind of wanted it to be a booty call, so there was that.

While he was waiting to see if Cami would respond, he left a tip for Danica, bussed his own plate, and grunted goodbye to Warner. The air hit him hard when he went outside. The temperature had dropped, reminding him that the official first day of summer was still a couple of weeks away. By the time July and Harbor Fest arrived, the night air would stay muggy and warm, but now he shivered as the sea breeze pushed cold salty air up his nose. His eyes watered, and he turned away from the water, toward Antonio's.

He warmed up as he walked, and by the time he reached the restaurant, his head had cleared. Cami hadn't texted, though. He peered through the front window of the restaurant. The interior was dimly lit, and half-full of patrons, but none of them was Cami or her dad. Dejected, he kept going in the direction of the inn.

He could see himself taking Cami to Antonio's sometime for an intimate supper. He'd eaten there lots of times with his mom and sister, with friends, even alone. He'd never been there on a date.

He and Cami hadn't actually gone on many dates back when they were, for lack of a better word, dating. Teenage Jay wished he could take her out to fancy dinners like he saw in the movies, but it utterly eluded him how to accomplish that. He didn't exactly have a lot of role models. His high school friends sometimes took girls out for burgers and bowling. Kid stuff. He could count the times his mom had gone out on dates on one hand, and Mimi was off at college. Cami, by comparison, was sophisticated, having grown up on sets and backlots. But in a lot of ways, she was still young. She didn't even have a driver's license. He'd once offered to teach her, but she'd never taken him up on it.

She had her license now, didn't she? He could have sworn she'd driven in one of her movies. He'd ask her. If he ever saw her again, that is.

In his mind, he'd built Barry into a gatekeeper, a dragon separating him from his maiden, but he was just a man. And Cami was a thirty-year-old woman who could make her own choices.

Still, it was with the air of a prince girding his loins to rescue his princess that he approached the inn on foot.

He nodded to the doorman, considered taking the elevator, but felt the stairs were more romantic, with less chance of running into Barry. Perhaps Cami's radio silence was because she didn't want her dad to know the extent of their relationship.

He took the stairs two at a time, for the first two floors anyway, slowing down on the third flight. Huffing, he made a note to add more cardio to his workout routine. When he got to the fourth-floor landing, he opened the heavy fire door slowly and silently. Was this stalker behavior? Wasn't one person's romantic gesture another person's harassment? He shook it off, saw the coast was clear, and walked to Cami's door.

He checked his phone one more time. No answer, but then he heard voices on the other side of the door. Cami and Barry. Shit. He ran back to the stairwell. This was such a dumb idea. He thumbed open the message app on his phone. He was about to type in *So I decided to come rescue you,* but the space next to Cami's name started dancing with dots before he could. He waited for her to send.

> We're back from dinner FYI. I'm still up, but my dad's driving me crazy.

He smiled and typed a quick reply.

> That makes two of us.

She took a minute to write back.

> I'm about to kick him out. I'd invite you over, but he's literally in the room next to mine.

Shit.

> That is extremely unfortunate. I'll have to have a word with the hotel staff.

> Yeah. Can you get them to tell him there's a bedbug problem and he has to move to the first floor?

> LOL

> Don't actually do that.

Jay smiled to himself and typed back.

> Tempting.

There was a pause. Jay wondered how mad his mom would get if he did figure out a way to make Barry move rooms. Probably pretty pissed if he was doing it just so he could have sex in her hotel.

> Okay, he's leaving. What's up?

Jay pressed his ear against the door and indeed heard a door open, then close, then a second one open and close, presumably Barry now safely inside his room.

Jay checked his phone. After ten. He thought about their options. Neither of them would feel comfortable initiating something physical with Barry right next door. He certainly didn't want to give the man any more reason to despise him. But there was someplace they could go where they'd have privacy.

> I'm actually in the fourth-floor stairwell.
> Up for a soak in the hot tub?

He held his breath while he waited for her to write back.

> Like old times?

> You remember?

Of course.

He grinned like a fool.

> So put on your suit and meet me on the
> stairs.

Give me five minutes.

He'd waited twelve years to see Cami in a bathing suit again. What was five more minutes?

As the son of a longtime employee, he knew every secret the old place had. Including the employee passcode for the pool area, which had replaced the old-fashioned key system years ago. The pool closed at ten and was a camera-free zone, so if they didn't make a lot of noise, they'd have virtually complete privacy.

If they couldn't get in, his plan C was just to get his own room, *not* on the fourth floor. But that might send Cami the wrong impression. He didn't only want to have sex with her. He wanted to be with her, whatever that meant, whatever form that took.

The opportunity to see her in a bathing suit was just a bonus.

He leaned back against the cold concrete wall of the stairwell, hands in his pockets. She was so...sensational. Being with her made him feel alive and young and full of a selfish kind of happiness. He took pride in what he did for the town because it was important work, and he could see the results every day. But being with Cami—that was just for him. And he was a selfish bastard, because he wanted her all to himself.

The door opened a second later, jolting him out of his repose. Cami stuck her head through the gap in the fire door, her blonde hair twisted into a knot on the top of her head.

Her face relaxed when she saw him. "Oh good, I thought maybe I was being lured to my death by someone who'd stolen your cell phone."

"You've been in too many scary movies if that's where your mind goes."

"Says the man lurking in the stairwell until the pretty girl comes stumbling into his trap."

"Fair." He held out his hand, and she took it. "You are very pretty."

She was wearing a pair of loose gray sweatpants, an oversized plain white T-shirt, and flip-flops. No towel. She had a tiny little shoulder bag that clinked when she walked.

"Did you bring beverages?" he asked as they started down the stairs. He kept his voice hushed. Not like they didn't have every right to be together. This wasn't *Romeo and Juliet,* for fuck's sake. But still, there was something appealingly transgressive about sneaking her out of her hotel room under her dad's nose.

"And snacks," she confirmed, squeezing his hand.

"Where did you have dinner?"

"Antonio's. The carbonara was unreal. But I might have room for something sweet."

He took a deep breath. "I'm sorry I bailed on you earlier, by the way. It was shitty of me."

She glanced up at him. "Thanks." She sighed. "It was a weird moment. I guess my dad has a way of making me feel like a kid no matter how old I get."

"Did you have a productive business meeting, at least?"

"Actually—" She stopped herself, then said, "I don't want to talk about it."

"Okay." It was her business. He was just the person she had cried on this afternoon. Of course, she'd been crying because of him, so he supposed he should be happy she was still talking to him at all.

They reached the main floor and didn't spot a single soul as they walked through the back corridor to the pool deck. "To tell the truth," she whispered, "I do want to talk about it. But I'm not used to having someone to talk with."

It made him sad she didn't have anyone in her life she could trust to share these things with. He punched the code into the keypad, and a tiny red light turned green. The air in the pool area was warm and humid compared to the air-conditioned hallway.

They passed by the deserted pool, lit up a glowing aqua by the lights at the bottom, and found the screened-in hot tub. It had been upgraded since they were last here, classy tiling giving it a contemporary look, a few nice deck chairs clustered around the edge. The hotel used some expensive cleaning solution, so it didn't even smell of chlorine, just pleasantly marine. He grabbed two towels from the cart on the wall and set them nearby, hit the button to start the water churning with bubbles.

She set her bag down by the side of the hot tub, stepped out of her sandals, then stopped.

"You don't have a suit," she said.

"I'll be okay."

She hesitated. "You first."

Chapter Nineteen

Erika: Do you think Jay Orlando and Camille Corsair were already together in real life when they filmed this episode?

Jules: Not sure. They never officially confirmed their relationship, but apparently it was the worst-kept secret on the set.

Erika: Their chemistry is so explosive here. They seem so comfortable together.

Jules: Agreed. When you watch them together, the screen burns up. Contrast that with Amy and Sawyer's scenes, and you're wondering who in their right mind ever saw the potential there?

Erika: For a supposedly epic love triangle, it's obvious who we're supposed to be rooting for.

From *The Sawyer's Cove Rewatch Project Podcast: The Hangover*

"Okay," he said easily. Everything with him was suddenly easy. It was as if he'd flipped a switch since she'd finally told him how much he'd hurt her. Maybe he was trying to make up for something, but she liked this Jay, who was fun and flirty and not suspicious of her motives.

He shed his shirt in one swift motion. He'd changed clothes since the afternoon. Probably because she'd gotten snot all over his other shirt. She didn't have room to feel embarrassed about that because she was too preoccupied with his chest. "Jesus, Jay, what happened? Did you start eating spinach or something?"

He glanced down at himself as he unbuckled his belt. "Huh?"

"I don't remember you being quite this—solid."

"Oh." He smiled. "Turns out I still had some growing to do. Bulked up a little. Just the aging process, I guess."

"Right. I guess." Her aging process involved worrying about cellulite and figuring out how to fit in another session with her trainer, not rolling out of bed with the physique of a Hemsworth.

Jay was beautiful as ever. The prettiness of his face matched the masculine elegance of his toned body, with its classical proportions and always-sun-burnished complexion. He pushed his jeans down, and she was met by the vision of form-fitting black boxer briefs covering him from below his navel to partway down his thick, muscular thighs. Okay. He had it covered. Barely.

She tore her gaze from his crotch and decided the only way to fight fire was with fire. She whipped her T-shirt over her head, dropped it onto a chair, then wriggled out of her sweatpants.

Cami felt confident about the way she looked in her bathing suit, a simple black two-piece she'd bought the last time she was in Europe. It for sure made her boobs look good. Her stomach wasn't model-flat, but then again, she wasn't a model. She was strong, slim, and she watched her figure, because that was part of her job, for better and for worse.

But she wished her dress size wasn't always a factor in whether she got a job or not. If she was a producer, that wouldn't matter anymore. If she had a baby, for instance, her body would never quite be the same again. Sometimes she looked at the money she'd saved and calculated how long she could afford not to work if she decided to take time off and have a baby, regardless of the fact that she wasn't in a relationship and had no plans to be.

Her hormones must have been in overdrive if she was contemplating babies while sticking her toes in a hot tub with her ex-boyfriend and possible future lover by her side wearing nothing more than his underwear.

"Too hot?" he asked when she continued to test the water instead of getting in.

"No, I can handle it," she said. She grabbed the rail and proceeded to stumble on the first step. Jay's hand flashed out and grabbed her upper arm to steady her. "Thanks."

He let her go, and she stepped down the three hot tub steps carefully. The memory of his touch burned hotter than the roiling water she sank into. He followed her in, sitting kitty corner from her, not too close. Not too far. She wondered if he pulled this after-hours hot tub shit with other girls.

So she asked him. "You bring all the lucky ladies of Misty Harbor here?"

He laughed. "Yeah, I love romancing them under my mom's nose."

"Oh, I forgot about that. I guess we're both a little overly close to our parents sometimes."

"So does your dad want to murder me?"

She laughed. "I don't think so?"

"You don't sound real certain about that, Cams."

"He's trying." And he was. The ironic part of the whole evening was, once she'd gotten him talking about non-work stuff, he didn't seem to want to stop. They spent the rest of dinner talking about old movies and memories she had of watching them with her mom as a little girl, and he'd kept the conversation going all the way back to the inn and to her room. She'd wanted her dad back, and he'd taken her at her word. She was happy about it, truly. But she wasn't sure how much of that she should share with Jay. She'd spent so long on her own, it didn't come easily to let him in.

She reminded herself they were just starting to know each other again. Maybe now that they'd made some peace with the past, they could start to be real friends again.

Of course, it was hard to be merely friends with

someone whose flat brown nipples peeking out of the water made her want to lean over and lick.

"What are you thinking about right now?" he asked.

She hoped he'd read the red on her cheeks as simply a result of simmering in the steamy water, rather than chagrin from the direction her thoughts had been headed.

"Why?" she said to buy time, since she couldn't remember what she was supposed to be thinking about.

"Your mouth just did this little pouty thing, and I was wondering why," he said. "I'm trying to be better about asking instead of just assuming I know what you're thinking."

That shocked her. "Seriously?"

"Seriously."

"Wow. That's so...adult of you."

"I told you. I actually have managed to grow up a bit."

"So I see."

"And don't think I didn't notice you didn't answer the question," he said, leaning back against the lip of the tub, his arms propped on the sides. "But if I'm being an adult about it, then you're entitled to your privacy and don't have to answer."

She was suddenly overly conscious of what her mouth was doing. The bubbles swirled, and steam filled up the air between them. Jay looked relaxed and unconcerned, completely at ease. She wasn't exactly nervous, but she'd been on edge all day, ever since the kiss, which had flung them into uncharted territory, and it was all her fault. He could afford to be blasé when she'd made all the first moves so far.

Her impulse to go over to him quelled. She shifted so instead of being hidden under the surface of the water, her boobs bobbed to the top, twin curves like those of a regency heroine in a Jane Austen adaptation, reminding him she had—what, breasts? *Pretty sure he already knew that.*

It had been a while since she'd tried to seduce anyone without a script telling her what to do.

"I was thinking about our snacks," she lied. "Want to see what I brought?"

"Sure." He smiled lazily at her, and that was just unfair. He was so effortlessly gorgeous, she lost her train of thought for a moment. He needed to shave. She wanted those bristles rough over her skin. Ugh.

She reached into her bag and pulled out two glass bottles of Coke. They had been in the minibar and probably cost five dollars each, but she'd found herself reaching for them instead of anything alcoholic. She'd brought a can of Pringles, too, and the cupcakes from their picnic.

"Coke?"

"I don't normally drink soda," she said. "But since we're reenacting our glory days, I thought it was fitting."

"Me either," he said. "Give it here."

She passed him the still-cold bottle. He twisted off the cap. She imagined she could hear the hiss of carbonation over the sound of the churning water. They'd drunk a lot of soda on the set of *Sawyer's Cove* before they got old enough to realize how awful it was for you.

She mirrored him, taking a sip of hers. The bubbles were huge, tickling her nose, and the drink was sticky sweet. She wasn't used to the concentration of sugar, and her eyes watered a little. "Whew. Strong."

He chuckled. "Lightweight. What's more your style these days? Green tea? Kombucha?"

She wrinkled her nose. "No, thanks. Can't stand the stuff. I suppose I'm more of a water drinker once I've had my coffee quota."

"Rebel." He took another sip. "What's with the Pringles?"

"Oh, it was the only thing that looked appetizing in the snack bin."

"Hmmm. I'll have to pass your notes on to the manager. I'm sure my mom would love to hear your review of the minibar contents."

She lifted her foot and found the side of his leg, pushed. "Don't you dare."

He laughed and captured her foot with his hand, keeping her there, forcing her to scoot a little closer. She liked it. His hand swept circles around her ankle. Despite the heat of the water, she shivered.

"The cupcakes are because I didn't get dessert earlier."

"You know I'm always going to associate Bakeshop cupcakes with kissing you, now."

"Are you?" She wanted to continue their playful

banter, but her words came out more seriously than she intended.

He nodded.

"Then kiss me." So much for waiting for him to make the first move.

"Are you trying to condition me or something?"

"I'm trying to kiss you," she said impatiently.

He tugged on her ankle. The water felt thick as molasses as she moved slowly toward him. When she got there, she could have snuggled up to his side, but she chose option number two and simply straddled him, her legs bracketing his thighs, knees resting on the rough hot tub seat.

They were chest-to-chest. Face-to-face. Then they were mouth-to-mouth as he kissed her, his hands wrapping firmly around her ass, pulling her closer to him.

Her breasts were squashed against the hard muscles of his chest, and the vee of her legs was slotted right over his pelvis. She could feel him, a hardening bulge in the wet cotton of his makeshift bathing suit. He felt divine.

She looped her arms around his neck, and they made out furiously, kissing hard and fast, like the hard, fast bubbles spouting around them. He tasted sticky sweet like the soda, his mouth warm, his expert tongue licking into her.

They were connected from head to toe, and she only wanted to get closer. She rocked against him, making little waves in the water as she rubbed her clit against the thick line of him.

"Fuck, Cams. You're so hot."

"Well, we are in a hot tub," she murmured against his mouth. She was hot, all over, especially between her legs, where she felt aching and needy as she continued to rock against him, building the friction. She realized she could probably come from kissing and frotting like this. She wondered if he could do the same.

"I wish we were in my hot tub," he said, squeezing her ass firmly.

"What? You have a hot tub?"

"Yeah, on my back deck."

"Shit. I wish we were in your hot tub, too."

"I didn't think this through."

She went back to kissing him; she didn't like where his line of thinking was going. It sounded like he wasn't going to ravish her in this hot tub. Which was understandable, considering this was still his mom's domain. Deb would probably forgive him for sneaking in a girl for an after-hours soak, but not for coming in the hot tub. That was just unsanitary.

"Damn," he muttered as he seemed to come to the same conclusion.

"Yeah. Can I just—" She sped up her rocking motion, and he helped her along from behind, his hands cupping her ass so tightly and in control that she almost came just from his vise-like grip.

"Do it, Cams," he said.

She tightened her hold on him, seeking out the pressure she needed, undulating against him furiously as he kissed her again, hard, forcing her to open for him. She was so close, so close, and then he started sucking on her tongue like he'd suck on her clit, and that was enough for pleasure to burst through her like a firework, a shower of sparks behind her eyes, through her body, her pussy clenching around nothing, but still enough to satisfy her. For the moment.

"Did you get there, sweetheart?" he asked, nipping kisses along her jaw, kneading her ass as she slowed to a halt.

"Yes. Thanks." She was exhausted, bone-deep weary, now that her orgasm was dissipating. She always felt the urge to go to sleep after coming.

"Anytime," he whispered.

She stifled a yawn and became aware the timer had run out on the bubbles and water was calming around them. It was a lot less noisy, too, and she was mortified for a minute about how loud she must have been, caught up in the moment and sensation of bringing herself off against his flawless body.

What now? "Um."

"Hey, that was hot," he said, stroking her cheek with one water-warmed hand.

"What about you?"

"I'm good."

She shifted her hips. He was still hard and fat between her legs. "You sure about that?"

"I'm dying, but I'll survive."

"It's kind of ridiculous that I have a room right upstairs and we can't—" Why did she have to be the kind of person who was bothered by her dad being in the next room to her? "You probably think it's stupid."

"Not stupid at all, Cams. And it's fine, really."

She believed him, but that didn't mean she didn't feel cheated out of getting to feel him inside her. She stroked the fine hairs at the nape of his neck. He always kept his hair so short. "You ever think about growing your hair out?"

"Sometimes. It would be extremely curly."

"So?"

"It's just easier this way. It's my look."

"Looks evolve. Remember when we started the show and they made Nash frost his tips?"

"Of course."

"I was lucky they didn't turn me into a bleached blonde or something."

"No, you've always been perfect."

She wanted to deflect, to demure. But she said, "You think so?" She was curious. Was that just a figure of speech?

"Elegant. Fun. Professional. Strong. Irresistible." He spouted off the adjectives effortlessly.

She sighed. "I wish I had you in my head at auditions."

"You still audition?" He looked surprised.

"Sometimes. It depends. It's tough out there, Jay. Another reason I want to start producing."

"You'll be dynamite."

"Thanks. Now, I better get out before I turn into a prune."

He kissed her one more time and helped her out of the hot tub. She dried off as best she could with the thin terry cloth towel. Jay got out and did the same. She admired him from the rear this time as he dried off, the muscles in his back giving her ideas. She imagined him hovering over her, her hands playing along the ridges of his muscles. "Seriously. Maybe you should take me back to your house."

He paused in the act of rubbing down his arms. "Right now?"

"Yeah. I'm still horny, Jay."

His laugh had a hint of desperation. "Well. That's not what I thought you were going to say."

"See, we're communicating better. We need to ask for what we want. And I want you to fuck me."

"And I want to fuck you. But it's getting late. And you have breakfast with your dad tomorrow, right?"

She scowled at the reminder of real life. She liked pretending she was eighteen again. "I could cancel."

"He's only here for a little while. But yeah, you could cancel."

"I guess I'm afraid if we don't do this right now, something's going to happen, and we won't do it at all."

"Hey, I'm not going anywhere."

She wanted to be able to say the same thing. But even if she bought a house on the spot Monday and sold her other place and somehow everything magically worked out, she'd still have to travel for work, and her dad would still be in her life. She'd still have her insecurities and her baggage, and fucking Jay Orlando wouldn't fix any of that.

Though it might make her feel better for a little while.

Jay went behind the screen to strip off his wet underwear and put his jeans on commando, which didn't help either one of their libidos calm down. He stepped out damp, but dressed, and asked, "You want to come over to my place tomorrow? I could give you a tour."

She smiled. "Including the bedroom?"

"First stop on the tour, of course."

"Sure, I'll come by after breakfast."

"Call me if you need anything."

"Thanks, Jay." She reached up and kissed his cheek. "It's kind of unbelievable how nice you are."

His mouth tightened. "Nice shouldn't be where the bar is, Cams. Come on, I'll walk you back to your room."

Chapter Twenty

ERIKA: This episode is so sad.

JULES: Tears for days.

ERIKA: I mean, this arc with Amy's half-sister is really kind of tragic from start to finish. We're just starting to get to know and like Tabitha, and then she ups and marries an Army Ranger—random—and ditches Amy just when they were starting to bond.

JULES: No wonder Amy has abandonment issues. Pass the tissues.

FROM *THE SAWYER'S COVE REWATCH PROJECT PODCAST: THE WEDDING*

Cami slept hard but not very long by the time she'd showered and turned in after their jaunt to the hot tub. She groggily turned off her alarm, then flipped open her computer to check her email and froze when she realized she'd forgotten to send the contract to Jay the way she'd said she would yesterday.

Her dad showing up, her and Jay's quicksand relationship, it was all messing with her head and distracting her. She felt like she was already failing. She could hear Selena's voice in her head. *The most important thing is the show. We need that signature. Then we have the studio where we want them.* God. Maybe she wasn't cut out to be a producer.

No. That was pre-caffeine Cami talking. She was a professional. She could do this.

She made a cup of coffee using the in-room machine. After the first few life-giving sips, she sent the contract to the email address on Jay's business card, keeping her intro short and to the point. Then she texted Selena an update and clicked on an email from the realtor she was meeting with tomorrow. She'd sent her four listings, all houses with about five times more square footage than her L.A. bungalow, at less than half the price. She'd known her money would go farther outside of the out-of-control Southern California real estate market, but she hadn't realized how much farther.

She checked the weather and saw they were in a warming trend. She dressed with care in a summery dress, comfortable flats, threw on some makeup and brushed her hair back into a simple ponytail. She stuck a few necessities in her purse, drained her coffee, and went to rap on her father's door.

He opened up at her knock, barely greeting her, leaving it open for her to step through on her own.

"Good morning to you, too," she said archly.

He yawned. "Sorry, Ladybug. I'm still on California time."

"We could have planned to meet later," she said, annoyed he'd made her get up early on a Sunday when she could have been in bed with Jay.

She longed for the simple pleasure of spending a lazy Sunday morning in bed with a friend and lover. Because Jay was both at this point, and it was almost too wonderful to believe their reconnection was really happening.

"No, this is good. I might head out to New York today instead of tomorrow."

Cami's relief mixed with sadness. He'd only just gotten there, and yes, she hadn't been expecting him, but it wasn't as if she didn't like having him nearby. Sort of. "I want to take you to this amazing bakery. They have great everything."

"Sure."

"We're walking again, if you're up for it."

"Lead the way."

The air outside the inn was fresh and clean. Cami felt better every step along the way. "Isn't it pretty here?"

"It's very New England-y," her dad said. "And walking is novel."

"I like it. Everything's so close together, and everyone knows everyone else, but in a good way."

"I remember that from when we were living here. I was glad there wasn't much excitement to distract you from the show."

"You were?"

"Of course, that was before you and Jay started up."

"We were in love, Dad," she said.

"Were you?" he said mildly. "You were kids."

"Both things can be true."

It was still early, but there were plenty of people inside Misty Harbor Bakeshop. Cami hoped they could get a table. Trevor was behind the counter—did he live there?—looking put together in neutral lipstick and rainbow eye makeup. He lit up when he saw her and waved her over. "Cami, hey!"

"Hi Trevor, this is my dad. We were hoping for a table."

"Sure. There's room on the back patio if you don't mind a little sun."

"Sounds great. Could I get a latte?"

"Of course, my darling," he said. "And for Mr. Corsair?"

"Americano, please," her dad said politely. She gave him points for at least pretending to be cool with the whole boy-wearing-makeup thing.

Trevor gave them a little wooden number, two menus, and a smile. "Just walk back and take whatever's free."

"Thanks, Trevor."

"Anything for you, my love," he said dramatically. "Next!"

They got settled, and it was only a couple of minutes later when Zelda herself brought them their drinks.

"We're short-staffed today," the owner said by way of explanation. "You want the special?"

Cami had seen the quiche and salad combo on the way in and instantly agreed.

"I'll have the same," Barry said.

Zelda nodded and bustled away, their menus in tow.

"This place is great," her dad said, surprising her. "It kind of reminds me of that cafe we like in Atwater Village."

"You're right." She smiled. This was the kind of brunch she wanted to have with her dad. Easy and light and not bogged down by work.

Of course, work having been all they shared for so many years, she was coming up empty on new topics of conversation. They could only talk about old movies for so long without repeating themselves.

Her phone buzzed with a text, and she gratefully took the distraction. It was a message from the real estate agent confirming the location of their first showing Monday. She typed back a reply.

"Is that Jay?" Barry asked.

"No. Realtor. I'm looking at some properties tomorrow."

Barry's eyebrows shot up. "Where?"

"Here."

"You can't be serious, Ladybug."

Her good mood deflated, Cami blew on her latte, moving the thin layer of foam around. She took a sip as she considered how to respond. "I am serious. I'm thinking about selling my place in L.A. and getting a house here."

"I suppose that has something to do with Jay?"

Cami considered that. She'd had the idea to get a place before she'd fully understood she still wanted Jay. And that he, apparently, wanted her. But he was obviously a factor. "Something, but not everything," she allowed.

"I know I'm no longer invited to make comments about your professional life, but—"

"Come on, Dad. I thought we understood each other last night." Was his "I'm proud of you, daughter" speech just an act?

"No, you're right. I'm sorry. It's a big change for me. You've been at the center of my life from the moment your mother died. It's going to take time to get used to not being involved."

She softened. "I get that. I do. So maybe you could try to understand. I really like it here. Misty Harbor has some incredible things going on. Next month, there's a big festival Jay's helping to stage, and did you know he started a co-op daycare so his employees have access to childcare?"

"Remarkable," Barry said, as if it was anything but.

Cami gritted her teeth. She loved her dad, but he was kind of an asshole sometimes.

"He cares about this town. And he cares about me." If she was sure of anything, it was that Jay's heart was bigger and more beautiful than anything else about him.

"Don't you think it seems a little convenient? You and

him starting up again right when you need him to do the reboot?"

"Dad, Jesus. I can't tell if you're insulting him or me."

"All I'm saying is, what if you can't have both? What if you can have the show and your career is stronger than ever, but you can't keep Jay, because he's never going to leave Misty Harbor? Would you give it up for him? Which one is more important?"

"I don't buy into that binary bullshit that I can only have one, Dad. Having to choose between a guy and my career feels super retro, and not in a cute, trendy way."

"I want everything for you, Camille. I want happiness, success, love. But I know from experience you can't have it all." Barry sounded sorrowful, as if he regretted having to tell his daughter about the true way of the world.

"What do you mean?"

"Your mother. I lost your mother, and I put everything I had into work. Into your career. I had nothing left." Barry fiddled with the wooden number on their table, his face downcast.

Her heart ached for him. She missed her mother all the time, but she'd been gone so long, she missed having a mother sometimes more than she missed the woman herself. But her mom and dad had been together for ten years before Cami was born, and then another eight after that. He'd lost the love of his life.

He'd had friends over the years, people he went to movies with, dinners, parties, but he'd never come close to a romantic affair, as far as she knew. He'd simply taken that off the table. Maybe that's where she'd gotten her aversion to serious relationships.

Well, she was done with that.

"I'm sorry you lost Mom, and I appreciate everything you did for me. But I want a life and a career, and I'm determined to have both."

Zelda brought their food, and they ate in tense silence. Even the melt-in-your-mouth quiche couldn't bring back her good mood.

"I think we shouldn't talk for a while," she said after minutes had passed without a word between them. "You go to New York. I'll be in touch soon. But I need to do things on my own right now."

Barry looked unhappy. "If that's what you want."

"I want you to believe that I'm not going to screw up my life the second you're not running it. That's what I want."

Her father sighed. She couldn't tell if he was regretful or resigned. "You're not going to screw up your life, Ladybug."

She stood up from the table. "No. I'm going to live it."

Chapter Twenty-One

Jay half-watched for Cami from his living room window as he contemplated finally hanging some of the art he'd had leaning against the walls since the movers left nearly a year ago. His house was situated on the rise of a hill, woods on three sides, a wide meadow-style lawn running from the front of the house all the way down to the road below, so he had a clear view of the rather steep driveway. The incline wasn't great on icy winter days, though he'd never had trouble in the Land Rover.

Today was as far from winter as you could get—crystal blue sky, cotton ball clouds, and a warm summer breeze to chase away the last chill of spring. Here, several miles from the ocean, it got a little warmer in the summer and cooler in the winter than the marine microclimate of downtown. He liked the privacy and quiet, though he didn't take advantage of either that much. He spent so much time in town and at the bar that he still hadn't fully unpacked.

Last night he'd fallen into an uneasy sleep, sexually frustrated and wondering how big of a mistake he was making by starting something physical with Cami when he was still partially reeling from finding out how devastated she'd been by their breakup. He wasn't sure he'd ever be able to forgive himself for hurting her back then, and he still wasn't convinced they weren't making the same mistakes all over again. Waking up to her email with the contract had made everything so much more real. He'd shut his laptop with a click before reading the document. Business could wait; he had a girl coming over.

He made coffee and scrambled eggs, changed the sheets on his bed, and put on a load of laundry while he was at it. The bar opened at three on Sundays, so he usually spent the morning taking care of personal stuff. He'd double-checked the schedule to make sure he didn't need to be at the bar at all today. Not that he wouldn't show up if necessary, but it was nice to know if he could convince Cami they should stay in bed all day, he was free to make good on his promise.

When an anonymous silver sedan crested the hill, he dropped the framed watercolor he'd been trying on various walls and watched Cami emerge from the car, which backed carefully down the drive and drove away.

She seemed subdued as she took in the exterior of the house. The place had nice curb appeal, the dark brown shingles blending in with the woodsy setting. He usually kept his Land Rover in the garage, but he'd been too tired to park it inside last night, and it stood like a sentry at the top of the drive.

He opened the side door off the living room, called down to her, "You found it."

She caught sight of him and smiled. In her yellow sundress, she was a lovely wildflower, a spot of color blooming on the mossy forest floor.

"It's a beautiful spot, Jay." She climbed the wooden stairs to join him on the little deck. It felt natural to step close and plant a kiss on her cheek. Her scent wafted around him as she looked up and smiled, pink and pleased.

His throat thickened with emotion. She was here. The woman he'd longed for every day since he left her. It seemed she was giving him a second chance. Who knew what the universe had in store for them, but for right now she was there, in his arms, in his home. Well, almost. He ushered her through the door.

He broke down and asked her the question that had been on his mind for days. "What's that scent?"

"What scent?"

"The smell of your shampoo or hair products or whatever."

She touched her simple ponytail. "Oh, I think it's eucalyptus."

He made a plan to track down a candle or something with the scent so he could torture himself with the memory of her smell after she'd gone. "I like it." His voice was throaty.

"Thanks." They looked at each other in the little mudroom just inside the door, the one he entered through when he was coming back from a tromp through the woods. It was an unremarkable space. His rain boots were on the floor, the coat pegs half-full with various jackets of his. It smelled vaguely of rubber and cleaning products.

Heedless of their surroundings, they surged toward each other, as if no time had passed since they'd made out in the hot tub at the hotel. She tasted like Bakeshop coffee. He licked her mouth clean, his jeans tightening over his crotch with every stroke of his tongue.

She gave as good as she got, pressing her breasts against his chest, her purse dropping to the floor so her hands were free to roam his back, until they finally landed on his ass, pulling him snugly toward her. Shit. She'd never done anything like that when they dated before.

Neither of them had been particularly experienced, or particularly confident. What Jay mostly remembered from their teenage encounters was hormone-fueled fumbling, epic make-out sessions, and cautious, if romantic, sex, on the occasions they could find enough privacy to do it. In the intervening years, it made sense they'd both become more comfortable with initiating sex, but this version of Cami as a woman who knew what she wanted and how to get it was still blowing his mind.

"Bedroom," he managed to get out between kisses. He tugged her toward the center of the house.

"What about the tour?" she asked breathlessly.

"Living room." He pointed over her shoulder. "Kitchen." He pointed in the other direction. "Back deck. Hot tub." By then, they were at the base of the stairs.

"Got it," she said. She glanced up. His arms were still around her. He found he couldn't let her go. "Bedroom?"

"Bedroom," he confirmed, then he leaned down and picked her up, bridal-style, in one smooth move. She squeaked and laughed into his shoulder, making him feel ten feet tall. He carried her upstairs, thankful for every painful CrossFit session he'd ever endured. He got to the top and kept right on going until they got to his bed. He laid her out on the hunter green plaid comforter, her light skin standing out against the dark background. She glowed.

"You are so beautiful," he said softly, looking down at her.

She smiled, the bow of her top lip flattening out. "So are you."

"Yeah?" He'd been called beautiful plenty of times before. He remembered one article that had labeled him the "beautiful bad boy." He'd rolled his eyes, always embarrassed by the attention more than anything. But with her, he didn't mind beautiful. She could call him whatever she wanted.

"I used to think you were pretty. Prettier than me, anyway," she said with a half-laugh. "But now you're breathtaking, Jay. You're a beautiful man. Outside and in."

He'd spent most of his life feeling like only his family could see beyond the surface with him. His looks seemed to distract people from wondering what was going on inside, and that worked for him during the show's run. The focus on the superficial meant random strangers weren't trying to pry into his head. But after, when he was going through the painful process of figuring out who he was and what he wanted after the three-year dream of *Sawyer's Cove*, it would have been nice to be able to shed his skin, to slough off his looks, to disconnect from Parker Wild and start fresh.

Cami had had another role to move on to, other parts to play. He'd always been associated with Parker Wild and only Parker Wild. He probably always would be. And if he did the reboot, all of that would come back, would only reinforce the notion that he was a one-trick pony, cast as a stunt, the literal townie playing pretend with the real actors.

But when he looked down at Cami, he liked that she knew him both as Parker and Jay. It didn't matter how many years had passed, that stupid show was still a part of him. She was still part of him. He'd tried lying about that, but with her so close, there was no longer a filter between his head and his heart.

He was already barefoot, so he got on the bed in his jeans and tee. She rolled toward him, and they clung to each other. He touched a finger to her sweet, kiss-swollen lips.

"I remember being with you made me feel as beautiful as everyone told me I was," he said.

Her eyes darkened. "I think when we're together we make something pretty beautiful."

She pushed him onto his back, straddled his waist. Her skirt bunched up around her middle, and she reached behind herself in a parody of a yoga move to remove her strappy sandals. They made twin clunks as they hit the wood floor.

She pulled her dress over her head, leaving her in a sand-colored lace bra and matching panties. He could see her nipples through the flimsy material. She'd had less on last night, when she'd been in that teeny bikini, but she was even more stunning by the light of day streaming through the big picture windows on the east side of the room than the artificial light of the pool deck. Her yellow hair gleamed like something Rumpelstiltskin would covet, her skin unmarked except for a few moles that dotted her like punctuation marks. He wanted to taste each one.

He flashed back to the previous night, when she'd brought herself off just by rubbing her sweet body against him. He'd been hard as nails and a hairsbreadth from coming before she'd finished, her cries echoing against the tile walls.

They could make all the noise they wanted here.

He snaked his hands up the sides of her thighs. A thumb found the top of her sex, pressed. She jerked; her hands flew to her tits. She rubbed her nipples through her bra, and he groaned.

"Jesus Christ, Cams, you are so hot."

She looked down at him, lids lowered, mouth in a pout. "I'm already wet."

He felt his way along the hem of her panties. She shifted up to allow him access, and he dipped a finger into her folds. Christ. She was dripping. He was in danger of blowing in his jeans.

He hated to stop touching her, but clothes were just getting in the way. He lifted her up and set her down next to him. He was out of his shirt, jeans, and underwear in record time. Cami stared at his cock, then back at him. She hadn't moved. "Um." She licked her lips. His cock twitched as if joined to her tongue by a thread. "Is it bigger?"

He laughed. "Than what?"

"Than twelve years ago. It looks bigger."

"Is that a good thing?" He suddenly worried she was going to be put off by his equipment. He had grown after they split, up and out, and maybe down there, too. He hadn't exactly been keeping track by measuring his dick with pencil marks on the wall.

"That remains to be seen," she said, a bit grimly. "I just don't remember it being…"

He looked down at the familiar sight of his own uncut cock, the head peeking out from the foreskin. The shaft was dark, the blood making his chestnut skin darker yet. He had wiry black curls at the base. He kept them trimmed—an aspect of grooming he hadn't had the hang of at twenty. Maybe that made it look bigger?

"We'll go slow," he suggested. "Or—"

"Or?"

"I don't have to be inside you," he said. "There's other stuff we could do."

Her eyes widened. She leaned forward, kissed him. "You are the sweetest man. You mean that, don't you?"

A distinctly caveman part of him was wondering why he didn't already have his cock buried deep into her drenched pussy, but yeah, he meant it. He wanted to be with her. Everything else was mechanics. "Whatever you want, Cams."

She wrapped a hand around him. She couldn't make her thumb and middle finger meet, but it felt like heaven, the smooth skin of her palm gently stroking his erection. She added her other hand. "Can I lick you?"

His cock twitched again, violently, and his balls drew up. "Sure." He kept his eyes open so he could record the sight of her with her head bent over his cock, her tongue softly licking at the head of it, in his permanent file under the heading "most erotic moments of my life."

She gradually took more and more of him, her hands wrapped around the base. The combined pressure of her mouth and hands had him grasping at the comforter beneath him, struggling for control.

"Cams, that feels so good. You want to stop?"

She pulled off and looked up at him, her hair falling out of its ponytail and making her look like a debauched cheerleader. He was two seconds from coming all over her candy pink lips.

"Why would I want to stop?"

"Because I'm going to come," he said weakly.

"Oh." She released him. He nearly whimpered in frustration. This was sweet torture. But then she said, "I want you to come inside me," and he nearly lost it all over again.

"You do?" he said, cursing his gentlemanly streak. "What about it being too big?"

"I never said it was too big," Cami said. "I have condoms, but maybe we should use yours. Mine are downstairs in my purse."

"Then let's definitely use mine." He rolled over, pulled open the side table drawer, threw an entire carton of them down on the bed.

She picked it up, struggled to tear open the cardboard. "New box?"

"It's been a while."

"Me, too."

"Then for the love of God, please let me." He took the box from her, practically tearing it in half to get at the prize inside. She scooted back, and he rolled the condom on with shaking hands. He could see a thatch of dark blonde hair at the vee of her legs though the lace panties. Fuck, she was sexy.

He assumed she would lay down on her back after

that, but instead she shuffled over on bent knees, strad-dling him again. "Okay?" she asked.

"Whatever you want," he said again.

She grasped him with both hands, positioned him at her entrance. So close, he could practically already feel her wet heat surrounding him.

Then she let him go. His cock smacked his stomach, the lube from the latex smearing on his belly. He did whimper then. "Cams, you're killing me."

"Sorry, I just wanted—" She leaned down to kiss him.

He chased her mouth with his, the sweetness of the kiss belying the heat between them, the scent of sex in the air, the throbbing between his legs, the erotic sweep of her nipples grazing his chest, the lace both rough and silky on his oversensitive skin.

The kiss deepened, and it didn't matter that he wasn't technically inside her. He felt like she was a part of him already.

They were fused together at the mouth, and he was so focused on the way she tasted that he was blindsided as his tip breached her—she'd squirmed around while they were kissing and slid onto him. She clenched around him, and even through the condom it felt wickedly good.

"Ahhh," he groaned into her open mouth when he was fully seated, or so he thought. She sat up and slid down another inch on a breathless gasp. Her ass nestled against his balls, her thighs gripping his hips tightly.

She was still wearing her panties, had just pushed

them aside to give him access. As she started moving, he could feel the drag of fabric adding to the sensations. Her hands slid all over his chest. She was doing most of the work, so he added his strength to the mix, helping her bounce up and down on his length with his hands on her hips.

"That's good," she said.

"Yeah?" he ground out. "Not too big?"

Flushed and sweaty, her thighs trembling, she laughed lightly. "I'll get back to you on that. But yeah, good. Full."

"That's right." He wanted to fill her up. He wanted her to be full of him, to crave it, to need it, to come back for it again and again. "Take it all, sweetheart."

"Jay," she moaned, her hands stiffening as she gripped his pecs, his ribs, anywhere she could for purchase. "Touch me."

He thumbed that hard little nub he'd found earlier. "There?"

"Harder."

He pressed down on it, rubbing in circles, his hips instinctively arching up to drive his cock into her in a hard, fast rhythm, no relief from the pressure and pace. She didn't seem to mind; she kept taking everything he was giving her.

"More," she sobbed. He growled and flipped them without pulling out. He only had one arm to hold himself up, but something told him his strength wouldn't need to last for long. He strummed her clit ruthlessly as he drove into her, watching her mouth open on a silent scream as she went taut as a bowstring as she came.

"Fuck, Cams, I'm coming." His orgasm hit him like an express train, brutally hard and nearly endless. As he gave his final thrusts, Cami went lax, her eyes shut, her entire body a boneless puddle underneath him. He pulled out, careful to discard the condom, then flopped down on the bed next to her.

Her skin was warm and pink all over. She was still wearing her underwear. She was the most gorgeous creature he'd ever seen.

She also hadn't opened her eyes or said anything since they'd finished.

"You okay, Cams?" He brushed some hair out of her face. The room smelled like sex, and it made him want to take her all over again as soon possible.

"Mmmm." She burrowed her head into his shoulder like a newborn cat looking for its mother's milk.

He stroked her shoulder and agreed, "Mmmm." She was quiet and still, and he was fairly certain she'd fallen asleep.

He closed his eyes, the smell of her in his nostrils, the feel of her, sweaty and real next to him, their sticky skin pressed together, the sun gilding everything gold. He listened to her breathe and let the rhythmic sound lead him down into sleep.

Chapter Twenty-Two

Jules: It's so sweet that our five main characters get to spend Christmas Eve together.

Erika: It reminds you that no matter what they've been through, they're still friends.

Jules: It's a little unbelievable, because when you consider all the different pairings of them who've made out with each other, they honestly maybe shouldn't still be friends, but—

Erika: Chalk it up to a Christmas miracle.

From *The Sawyer's Cove Rewatch Project Podcast: The Mistletoe*

Cami had no idea where she was when she woke up. She was in a strange bed, in what seemed to be a treehouse, what with the leafy green forest just beyond the big picture window she could see from her spot on the bed. There was a bear sleeping with her apparently, judging by the volume of the snores and the weight of the body at her back. She craned her neck over her shoulder. Not a bear. Just Jay, passed out, fully naked. Snoring.

She clapped a hand over her mouth to stop herself from letting out a laugh loud enough to wake him. He looked supremely comfortable, one of his arms tucked under his head like a centerfold. The other arm was pressed against Cami's back, his hand loosely resting against her ass.

Shuffling forward slightly so she could get a better look, she peered at his penis. Now soft, it lay against the crease of his thigh with surprising heft. She'd managed to take it all and wanted more. Maybe she had an undiscovered size kink. Hmmm.

She was faintly sore, but she wasn't complaining. Sex with Jay was hot, all-consuming, satisfying in every way. He kissed like a champ, he got her hot, he didn't leave her to fend for herself in the orgasm department like some of the guys she'd been with. In fact, she'd come so ferociously hard that it had been all she could do not to succumb to her sudden, bone-deep sleepiness right that very moment.

But it seemed they both needed a cat nap.

Her eyes found a clock on the dresser, and she was shocked to find it was early afternoon. They'd slept over two hours.

Jay let out another snore. That was new, too. Maybe he had a deviated septum. It was kind of cute, the incongruity of a real-life heartthrob snoring like a grandpa.

She got off the bed carefully, feeling sticky in her lacy underthings. She found a gray flannel shirt slung over the back of a chair that smelled clean, so she put it on and tiptoed down the stairs to retrieve her purse.

On the way in, she'd been too busy sticking her tongue down Jay's throat to take in the floor plan, which was mostly one big room, made even bigger by its lack of furniture, a huge fireplace set into the one wall that wasn't dominated by windows, and a nice-sized kitchen. A few doors on the other side of the staircase indicated guest rooms or office space, perhaps. She liked the honey wood interiors combined with the copious windows that let in lots of June sunlight, even with the trees on three sides feeling quite close. They were secluded, and yet the space felt open and airy, not an easy feat.

The house seemed new—it had modern fittings and looked as though it had been recently painted. But there wasn't much of *Jay* in it—at least not in the public areas. His room felt homey, but that was about it. She stuck her head in the gleaming, empty kitchen. She'd be surprised if he did much cooking. He seemed like the type to want to support downtown businesses by ordering lots of takeout.

She found a cute powder room under the stairs, but since her clothes were upstairs, she returned to Jay's room. He was still passed out. She wanted to climb back in bed, pull the covers up over their heads, and forget about the rest of the world indefinitely.

The sharp vibration coming from her bag

announcing a text killed her dreams of playing hooky. She quietly gathered her dress and stole into the master bath.

She was about to freshen up but reconsidered. If she was only going to try to convince Jay to ravish her again, and she couldn't imagine it would take much convincing, she might as well stay in his shirt instead of getting her dress dirty. She hung it up on a hook in the bathroom, washed her face and hands, and found a perch on the edge of the tub.

This room, too, had a stunning view out over the woods. She assumed he didn't have any nearby neighbors who would be scandalized by the uncovered window right next to the bathtub. The deep, modern tub had jets and would be a lovely place for a long hot soak.

She dragged her purse over and closed her hand around her phone, wishing she wasn't such a Girl Scout. It vibrated with another message before she could even look at her notifications.

That message and the next half dozen were all from Selena. That didn't bode well. She read the most recent one.

Call me.

Cami hit the call button with trepidation. Selena answered on the second ring.

"Oh, thank God, I was beginning to think I might have to call Barry to get ahold of you."

"Why? What's wrong?"

"Didn't you read my messages? Why are you whispering? Are you in a library or something?"

"No. I'm—" Cami looked around the oversized bathroom. "Never mind. What's going on?"

"The studio wants us to come in first thing in the morning for an emergency meeting. Both of us. Can you get a flight out tonight? I'll pick you up at the airport, and we can plan our strategy on the way to the studio."

Cami's stomach knotted into a pretzel. "Tomorrow morning? Why the rush?" She'd have to hustle to get from Misty Harbor to L.A. in eighteen hours.

"I don't know, but they made it seem pretty urgent. Besides, if we don't get them in writing soon, we could lose our holding deals with Nash and Ariel, and who knows if or when we'll be able to schedule this thing. It's now or never."

"Okay, I get it." All things considered, this wasn't that bad. She and Selena had all their ducks in a row. Except for one.

"I don't have Jay on board yet," Cami said. "Is that going to be a problem?"

"I'm not letting one dude be the reason we can't get this done. Whether he signs or he doesn't, we still have to get the studio to release the money. I need you here for that, Cami. Get on a plane, please."

"Yes, I will. I'll let you know which flight."

"Thanks. We can do this." Selena sounded completely certain, but Cami was fairly sure she was trying to convince herself as much as Cami.

"We can," she agreed, and she believed it. She just

wished she didn't have to rush out of here. Then again, this kind of thing was what she had signed up for. She'd spent the last few days being Cami Cosinsky, but she was still Camille Corsair.

She tapped on her airline app and found a flight out of Boston she could make if she left in a couple of hours. It would take her that long to shower, change, and pack.

She sighed, looking forlornly at Jay's shirt. There went her plans for more sex. She had to believe there would be other opportunities for them to spend lazy Sundays in bed. Someday.

She finalized her ticket on her phone, then started when a knock sounded on the door. "Cami?"

"Come in," she called.

Jay cracked the door open and stuck his head in. His eyes were slightly sleep puffy, and he had pillowcase creases on one cheek. He was adorable. Her heart tumbled.

"Everything okay?"

"You can come in," she said. "Or, I guess it makes more sense for me to come out." She stood up and moved past him into his room. He, thankfully, was wearing underwear, and his jeans were on but unbuttoned. The clothes didn't really help with her wanting to jump his bones, though. He still looked like a sex god.

"Nice shirt," he said, brushing his fingers over the soft fabric on her arm.

"Thanks. Sorry. I just—"

"It's okay, Cami. It looks good on you. What's

wrong?" He sat on the end of his bed and pulled her toward him.

She slotted herself between his legs, desperately wanting to sink into him, to wrap her arms around him and never let go. Instead, she was about to fly away from him. Every inch of her protested. But she had never made life decisions because of a guy, not since he'd taken that off the table twelve years ago. It would be disastrous to start doing it now.

She took a deep breath—better to rip off the Band-Aid. "I have to leave. Selena called me and we have a meeting with the studio first thing tomorrow. I have to go to L.A. tonight."

"I see." His hands fell from her hips.

She wanted to cry. He was moving away from her already, and it killed her that she was doing it to them, she was the reason it was happening.

It killed her that her dad might be right.

She sucked in air, tried to keep her voice level. "I'll miss my appointment with the realtor. But I'll get things sorted with the studio, and maybe we'll even have a timeline for production ironed out by the time I get back."

He quirked an eyebrow at her. "Yeah? You think you'll be coming back?"

"Of course I will." Cami wanted to be pissed at his outright skepticism, but she shared his fear. "I'll be a few days, tops. It's not a sign or anything." She cringed at the defensive note in her voice. Katharine Hepburn had once said, "Never complain. Never explain." She needed to channel Kate.

His face softened out of its disbelieving mask. "It's okay. It's your job, right? You need to do your job."

"Thanks." Okay. He understood.

Why didn't that make her feel better?

"So you probably want an answer on the contract," he said.

She didn't know what to say. It felt weird to talk business when they were both half-naked. She was conscious of her still-sticky underwear and her sex hair, and the memory of him on top of her was fresh in her mind.

But the worst part of all wasn't just that they'd fucked.

She loved him.

She was in love with him. All over again. Still.

She was in love with Jay Orlando, and she knew in her heart that she'd walk away from the show if it meant she could keep him. If it meant he could love her back. She'd walk away from everything she'd built, her entire career. She'd tend bar and wash dishes at The Cove every day if it meant she could sleep with Jay in this bed every night for the rest of their lives.

"Did you read the contract?" she finally asked, when she realized she couldn't say any of that to him. If she did, he'd no doubt pack her up and put her on the plane to California himself.

"Not yet."

She tried not to read into that.

"When do you have to go?"

"Pretty soon. I have to order a car to take me to the airport."

His eyes narrowed. "I'll take you."

"I can't ask you to do that. All the way to Logan on your day off? What a nightmare."

"I'm not letting you sit with a stranger in a taxi for three hours."

"Are you sure?"

"I'm sure. We can talk on the way."

She blinked at him. Talk? Jay Orlando? Okay. "If you're going to give me a ride, I probably have some wiggle room."

"Wiggle room, huh?" He smirked at her. The mood suddenly felt ten tons lighter. Maybe this work-life balance thing was possible after all.

She shimmied her hips to demonstrate her best wiggle. "We could save time and take a shower together."

"I like the way you think. Efficient. Great trait in a producer."

She rubbed him through the open fly of his jeans, over the smooth cotton of his underwear. His cock twitched under her hand. "Oh yeah, I'm all about efficiency."

The glassed-in, cedar-walled shower, complete with bench and ceiling-mounted shower head, fit both of them comfortably. She'd barely noticed it earlier in her admiration of the freestanding bathtub.

"I really like your bathroom," she said breathlessly.

The water beat down on Jay's back as he kneeled on the floor of the shower, his head between her legs. She sat on the bench, benefiting from the warm steam rising around them, her entire body singing with every lap of Jay's tongue. It was as muscular and firm as the rest of him, and as talented, too.

She scrabbled to grab the edge of the bench, until Jay reached up and placed her hands on the back of his head. She moaned and worked her fingers through the short hair there, pressing him against her harder. That seemed to do it for both of them, because suddenly he was tonguing her clit so intensely, she saw stars, and he reached down to touch himself.

She was deliciously trapped between the unyielding wooden bench and unrelenting pressure of his mouth. She came before she knew what was happening, an explosion that made her entire body go rigid as the pleasure spiked through her. Then she went limp, pushing Jay's head away with weak hands. He left her with a final, gentle swipe of his tongue that still felt like sandpaper on her overstimulated nerves. His cheeks were flushed from exertion and the shower's heat.

"And you have unbelievable water pressure," she panted.

He licked his lips and curled them into a grin. "Thanks. It's a tankless water heater. Never runs out."

"Genius."

He leaned back on his haunches, his fist lazily stripping his erection. Fuck. It wasn't any smaller this time.

She leaned against the shower wall, happily prepared to never move again, but she gestured vaguely. "Can I help?"

He rose to standing while he slowly stroked himself. "Orgasms really take it out of you, huh?"

"Only when they're mind-blowing," she said.

He bent over to kiss her. His cock bobbed distractingly in the corner of her vision. He whispered in her ear, easily heard over the gush of water. "Honey, they should all be mind-blowing."

She didn't say what was in her head. That every time with him was the best time she'd ever had.

He stood up and with one long arm reached to the corner of the shower where a small collection of bottles sat. He squirted something onto his hand and used it for lube.

She watched in fascination as he jerked off in front of her, proud and strong, his smooth skin beaded with water. She wasn't exactly a porn connoisseur, but she would have bet money a number of people in her acquaintance would have killed for an up-close-and-personal show of Jay Orlando masturbating in a shower.

His lotion or whatever seemed to be unscented, because she could only smell him, and herself, still wet between her legs, and the cedar wood. She was getting turned on all over again, taking notes on the way he touched himself, how his thumb circled the head, how he tugged lightly on his balls with his other hand.

"Jay, you look really hot right now," she said, half in wonderment, half in praise.

"You want to touch yourself?"

She squirmed, suddenly embarrassed. No one she'd been with had ever asked her to do that before. She had a fresh wave of sadness, of frustration, for the past twelve years of her pathetically stilted romantic life, especially if she potentially could have been having this the entire time. He looked at her steadily; she slowly dragged her hand down her chest, cupping her breasts.

His gaze was glued to them; the hand on his cock sped up. She stroked her nipples, fresh waves of arousal breaking over her as she plucked them into hard nubs.

"That's good," he praised.

Cami was very much aware of him looming over her while she continued to sprawl on the bench. She didn't mind it, though, feeling small compared to him. She kind of liked it. The shower was spacious, but not huge. She could reach out and touch him if she wanted to, but there was something hot about them just watching each other, lost in their own separate but intertwined desires.

She slipped one hand from her breasts down between her legs. She gasped; her clit was still engorged from him going down on her. She stroked over it lightly, too sensitive to do much more than that.

"Are you wet?" he asked.

She let her fingers wander lower and rubbed against the slippery slick there, pushed one finger inside. "You know I am. You made me wet."

He groaned. "Yeah. You tasted so good, Cams. Sweet like sugar."

She started stroking herself in time with him,

keeping one hand on her breasts to play with her nipples in turn. "You want me to come again?"

"Can you?"

"I think so." She shifted, kept the pace up. He looked like he was close, his thighs tense, his hand practically a blur as it flew along his exceptional cock.

"Yeah, do it," he said, just as he had the night before in the hot tub. His gentle command sent her over the edge, and she came for the second time within ten minutes.

"Now you," she said, forcing herself to keep her eyes open. She didn't want to miss a second of his release. "Come here."

He shuffled close. "I'm, I'm going to—"

"Yeah. Come on me, Jay." She tipped her face up to him, opening her eyes wide. She wanted to feel him splash on her, hot and wet. "Please?"

"Cams." He made a few more strokes and then obeyed, shooting out ropes of his release, and they landed right where she'd hoped they would, in stripes on her chest, on the tops of her breasts. He was breathing hard and groaning, and she took in everything from his screwed shut eyes and famous eyelashes to his abs, contracting beautifully, to his messy cock, dripping from the tip as he collapsed onto the bench next to her.

He looked at her with unfocused eyes. "Hey."

"Hey."

He reached out and touched the cooling substance on her skin. "That was—wow. Thank you."

She giggled at the understatement. "You're welcome."

They sat in companionable silence for a second. All too soon, he pushed away from the wall, hauled her to her feet. "Let's get you cleaned up. You have a plane to catch."

It was as if cold water had suddenly started cascading out of the shower head. She shivered, nodded. "Okay." But she didn't move.

He seemed to sense her hesitance and positioned her under the spray himself. Then he grabbed another bottle and soaped her up with a squirt of the contents. He ran his hands over her chest, gently scrubbing away the evidence of his orgasm. After a moment of reveling in the feeling of his hands on her, strong and capable and full of care, she started helping. She got clean enough, didn't bother with her hair, stuck her face under the spray while he quickly washed himself.

When they shut the water off, it became deafeningly silent.

"I don't really want to go," she whispered, the closest she could get to sharing how she really felt.

"I don't want you to go." He smiled at her sadly. "But you'll be back, right?"

"Right."

Why didn't either of them sound very certain about that?

Chapter Twenty-Three

*From The Sawyer's Cove Rewatch Project Podcast:
The New Year's Resolution*

Driving Cami to the airport was an exercise in self-control. He forced himself to keep the Land Rover pointed north, toward the plane that would take her away from him, when everything in his soul wanted to turn around, to take her back to Misty Harbor, to his home, his bed, and keep her there until they were both old and gray.

He told himself it was good she'd been called away for work. He needed the cold reminder of her priorities. But still, she seemed reluctant to leave. If she was waiting for him to give her an ultimatum—him or the show—she'd be waiting forever. He would never do that to her. Moreover, he could never let her choose him over her career. Better she left now, so he could return to the life he had built in Misty Harbor without her.

He supposed the trouble was he'd started thinking of her as part of his life there.

There was little traffic until they hit the ring around Boston. Then they were stop-and-go until the airport signs started coming with more frequency. They'd stayed away from sensitive topics of conversation on the drive, chatting mostly about what people they both knew had been up to since the show. They listened to music, and Jay tried not to read an elegy for the love affair they'd only just begun into every song lyric.

"Is this Nash's band?" Cami asked when they were three songs into The Nash Speedwell Experience debut album, a cross-genre alt-rock-country blend.

"It is."

"Huh. I really like this," she said. "It's poppy, but with soul."

"That's Nash. He's surprisingly deep, for a pretty boy."

"You should know a little something about that," she said lightly.

Jay snorted and didn't respond.

Nash had a smooth voice, to which he added plenty of country twang. Jay had been one of the first he'd sent his demos to. Jay didn't know much about the music industry, but he'd been able to give his friend his honest opinion—that the songs were actually good. He'd offered him an open pass to play at The Cove, but Nash had declined.

"Recordings only," Nash had said. "No live shows."

"What are you talking about? You could fill seats with that face of yours."

"Yeah. With my face and my name. Not with my voice. Or my songwriting."

"Well, you have to get them in the door, then you sell them the rest."

But Nash had been adamant that the album would be a one-off. Stubborn bastard.

Jay supposed they all had their issues.

And his was the push-pull he felt for the woman sitting beside him. He wanted to believe they could explore how they felt about each other without letting the complication of the *Sawyer's Cove* reboot matter, but that was naive. Cami clearly wanted the show to work, and he wanted that for her. He'd always wanted more for her than he'd ever claim to want for himself.

Besides, he'd fucked up by ending things twelve years ago, and he hadn't done enough penance to deserve a true do-over. Cami was smart. She knew better than to make the same mistake twice, no matter how good it might feel in the moment.

"What terminal?" he asked as they got in the stream of cars leading into Logan.

She told him a number, and all too soon they were parked at the departures curb. He grabbed the suitcase she'd hastily packed when they finally made it back to the inn. He'd waited in the lobby both to give her privacy and avoid temptation.

"Well." She bit her lip. "Should I text you when I get there?"

He puzzled over her phrasing. "Should you?" Then he got it. She was asking if she should bother. If he'd be thinking about her. Wondering about her.

There was no way to put into words everything that was swirling around inside him before the airport police cited him for idling too long in the drop-off zone. He settled for answering, "Yes."

It seemed to be the right thing to say, because she smiled bright, her blue eyes twinkling with what might have been unshed tears. "I will, then."

He gathered her close, taking one last whiff of her eucalyptus hair. He kissed the crown of her head. "Be safe, Cams."

"I will. And thanks for the ride."

He stepped away, leaving her on the sidewalk, hand on her suitcase handle. He almost said, "Anytime," but that would imply this was a pattern they'd be falling into. Her flying away from him, him tethered to the ground. "Bye," he said instead.

She blinked rapidly. And then she turned and walked into the terminal.

He found himself on the road south on autopilot. He didn't realize how long he'd been driving in silence, without even Nash's twang for company, until he passed from Rhode Island into Connecticut and saw the big blue "Welcome" sign.

He'd been thinking about love. About how love was a tremendous gift. But it wasn't always enough.

He hadn't gotten any emergency calls from the bar, so he could have gone straight home, but he was starving, and his cupboards were perpetually bare. He'd skipped lunch in favor of fucking Cami, then in the rush to get her to the airport, he'd missed dinner, too. He hoped she was getting fed in first class, but he needed food now. At least whatever he'd find to eat would be a damn sight better than airplane food. He tried to be grateful for that minor boon and steered toward downtown.

He parked in front of a small block of apartments, got out his phone.

You home?

Yep. I can see you idling like a creep outside. Come in and stop scaring my neighbors.

Jay didn't bother responding, just shut off the Land Rover and made his way to Mimi's door, trying to look as upstanding as possible. He had to admit it was a tiny bit problematic he'd thrown on a leather jacket over his black T-shirt in his haste to get dressed after the epic shower sex.

Mimi opened her door and shook her head at him. "Mom," she called, "did you order a greaser?"

"Hilarious," he said flatly as he followed her into her cozy apartment. "I'm not allowed to look cool?"

"Cool, yes, but the jacket is a bit much."

His mom came out of the kitchen. "Oh, it's just you, Jay."

"Thanks for the warm welcome, Mom." He took the jacket off and hung it on the back of one of Mimi's chairs.

"Sorry. We ordered Thai. Should be enough for you, if you want."

"Thank God. I'm starving."

"I made some sangria," Deb said, bringing a pitcher and glasses out from the kitchen. They gathered around Mimi's little dining room table stuck in the corner of her living room. The whole place wasn't much bigger than a college dorm setup, but Mimi had lived there for years and seemed happy enough despite Jay's offers to help her buy a bigger place.

"Sangria and Thai food?"

"You got a problem with that, you can find your own dinner."

"No, no problem. Why so salty today, sis?"

Mimi sighed and flopped down on the couch. "I'm just tired. I had a late night Friday, so I slept in yesterday, which meant I didn't feel like going to bed last night, and

I stayed up bingeing British police procedurals and over-slept this morning. It's a vicious cycle."

Jay poured himself some sangria and took a sip, then coughed involuntarily. "Um, Mom, how much brandy did you put in this?"

His mom said, "It's been a long week," and took a healthy swig of hers.

"We're a fine trio," he said grumpily.

"What do you have to complain about?" Mimi asked.

"Does it have anything to do with the fact that Camille Corsair checked out of the inn today?" Deb asked carefully.

Mimi sat up. "She did?" She looked at Jay with concern. "Are you okay?"

He winced. "Yes, I'm okay. She had to go back to L.A. for work. I drove her to the airport, actually. I missed dinner. And lunch."

On cue, the doorbell rang and Mimi took a paper bag off the delivery guy's hands.

Deb distributed plates, and they went to work dividing up the noodles, rice, and curries.

"Good thing I showed up—there's a ton of food here," he said, gulping down a fried dumpling.

"Oh yes, thank you, little brother, for rescuing me from having leftovers to take to work tomorrow," Mimi said dryly.

"How about we meet for lunch instead? I'll buy."

"Deal." She paused. "You're really okay with her leaving? We had a great time at the bar Friday night. She's a hoot."

Jay shook his head at the memory of his sister and Cami dancing like nobody was watching. "It's complicated."

"Obviously. So, is she coming back?"

Jay realized even though Mimi had spent most of Friday with Cami, she still didn't know about the show. There were probably confidentiality issues, but he could trust Mimi if he needed to talk it out.

"She says she is," he said. "I'd like her to. I also know her work is really important to her, and she can't be Camille Corsair living in Misty Harbor."

"Yeah, but her career is changing. She's going to be doing more producing, she said. That could mean less travel."

"Maybe," he said doubtfully.

"Well, I for one think we should have a little faith in her. She told me the other day she was hoping to spend a lot more time in Misty Harbor."

"I heard she was looking at properties to buy," Deb added. "Not that I'd ever gossip about a guest."

"Your integrity is intact, Mom," Jay said. "She told me the same thing."

"Why doesn't she just move in with you?" Mimi asked.

Jay choked on his pad see ew. "Excuse me?" he said hoarsely, then took a mouthful of sangria to try to clear his throat before he remembered it was potent as fuck. His eyes watered as he tried to swallow through the burning.

"Honey, are you okay?" His mom made clucking

noises as he suffered through another bout of coughing. Mimi grabbed a handful of cheap paper napkins and thrust them in his face.

When he got his breathing under control, he repeated his question. "What the hell, Mimi?"

"Sorry, I didn't realize it was such a touchy subject. But why doesn't she just move in with you? You've got that big, lovely, *empty* house. You're obviously still into her. She probably feels the same way, if how she couldn't stop looking at you the other night is any indication." She looked at their mom and then at Jay. "What? I'm just saying what we're all thinking."

"I wasn't thinking that," he said indignantly. Except now he was, imagining her moving in, taking up half his closet with her clothes. She could have the downstairs office he'd never gotten around to setting up, and they could spend every night curled up together in his—their—bed. He'd make room for her eucalyptus tree products in the bathroom. They could take extended erotic showers like the one they had today. His water bill would go up, but he'd happily pay it to see her fall asleep with post-orgasm exhaustion.

"Sorry, forget I said anything," Mimi said irritably.

He glared at her. "Yeah, I'll just go back in time, and that will fix everything."

"Well, I do hope she comes back to town. It's nice to see people wanting to move into Misty Harbor rather than move out," Deb said. "We could use new blood."

"Can we change the subject?" His emotions were feeling as raw as his throat.

"Fine, Grumpy. I've designed a really cool booth for Harbor Fest."

Jay listened with one ear to his sister's enthusiastic explanation of the display of books by local authors she was putting together, while thinking about Cami and airplanes and contracts and the mess he found himself in less than a week after her appearing in his life again. She'd blown up his orderly little world, expanded it in only a few short days. What she was offering him, both of herself, and with the show, scared him. The stakes were too high for him to take either one lightly.

Later, he thanked his mom and sister for the impromptu dinner, ignored their not-so-subtle concerned glances, and then he went to his dark, unfinished house. He left the Land Rover at the top of the drive, unlocked the door Cami had walked through not even twelve hours earlier. He didn't turn on any lights, just scooped his laptop off the kitchen counter and took it upstairs.

His bedroom was stuffy, overlaid with the scent of sex. He eyed the rumpled sheets. Feeling monumentally lonely, he unlaced his boots, shucked his jeans and his jacket, and crawled into bed in his boxers and tee. He imagined he could smell her eucalyptus scent on his pillow and opened his computer.

He had a contract to read.

Chapter Twenty-Four

JULES: Sidebar—did you see on Twitter that some girls went to Misty Harbor and visited this bar called The Cove and they swear up and down they met Jay Orlando AND Camille Corsair and that Jay Orlando apparently owns the bar?

ERIKA: It sounds made up, but sometimes truth is stranger than fiction, listeners.

JULES: My question is, so Jay Orlando owns the bar, fine. But what on Earth was Camille Corsair doing there? Are they friends? Are they back together? What is happening?

ERIKA: Inquiring minds need to know!

FROM *THE SAWYER'S COVE REWATCH PROJECT PODCAST: THE NEW YEAR'S RESOLUTION*

I *'m too old for red eyes*, Cami thought as she wobbled through LAX, sunglasses on, face averted from the crowd. She'd tried to sleep on the plane, but even first class seats couldn't get the look on Jay's face when he dropped her off out her head. He'd been so...stoic, as if she was going to war and he was preparing himself to never see her again.

Admittedly, Los Angeles International Airport was a bit of a battleground. She pushed her way to the curb, as she'd arrived to a flurry of texts from Selena instructing her to go to the pick-up area and look for a red Mercedes convertible.

"There you are!" Selena said, sticking her head out the driver's window of a sporty two-seater. "I'll pop the trunk."

Cami put her bag in the trunk as ordered and got in the passenger side. She hugged her friend and was enveloped in a cloud of black curly hair and minty fresh breath. Selena chewed mints like gum.

"I'm so happy to see you." She blinked away the wave of emotion. God, she was giving herself whiplash.

Selena laughed and jetted out into the flow of cars leaving LAX. "What's gotten into you? I thought you were having a good time in Connecticut."

"I'm all turned around. I didn't want to leave, but it's good to see you. I need to work to remind myself what I'm doing it all for." Then she burst into tears. Crying twice in three days—so not like her.

Selena clucked and accelerated to leap in front of a Porsche on the onramp to the 405. "Did you not sleep on the plane? We're going straight to the studio, but I brought you coffee." She gestured to a paper cup in the drink holder. "Caffeinate. We'll sort all of this out. Traffic is murder, so hang on."

Cami sipped her coffee dutifully, sternly wiping tears off her cheeks. She refused to be sad the coffee wasn't as good as the Bakeshop's lattes. She couldn't be homesick for a town she'd spent less than a week in, could she?

But that was how fast Misty Harbor had started to feel like home. After their prickly start, being with Jay had been as natural as breathing. But it scared her, too, now that she knew what she was feeling was truly love. None of her other relationships had come anywhere close to the contentment she'd had sharing a picnic blanket and a kiss with Jay Orlando, let alone the life-altering sex they conjured up between them.

So what was she doing here, again? Los Angeles looked gray and dirty on this June-gloom morning. Selena was chattering away, full of life and energy. Cami felt more than ever that she was an impostor merely playing at this producer role when she had no idea what she was doing.

Half an hour of Selena's darting and weaving through Monday morning rush-hour traffic, and they were parked at the studio lot where Selena had a temporary office. Cami grabbed her bag so she could change out of her travel-weary clothes before their meeting.

"I talked to Brad last night." Selena filled her in on the walk. "And it seems like it's all coming down to timing. They have a hole in the winter schedule, which is perfect for us if we can start production this fall."

"Wait, that's like two months away."

"I've been looking at the calendar and yes, it's soon, but there are at least three weeks when all the principles' availability overlaps, which means we can really get into the story and have some dynamic group scenes. You know that's what people love—when all five of them are together and chaos ensues."

"Teenage chaos. Are we sure people are going to want to see thirty-something chaos?"

"They will when those storylines are intercut with the fresh teen cast members we'll add."

"Of course. How's casting coming with that?"

"Good. We haven't extended any contracts of course, until we get the final okay. Speaking of contracts..."

"Jay hasn't signed. Yet. Oh, shit!" Cami had been overwhelmed and didn't text him when she landed. She pulled out her phone and scanned her notifications. Nothing from him.

Selena picked up her own phone. "I'm texting Becca to pick up food. Breakfast burrito?"

Cami still felt nauseous from her nighttime plane trip and Selena's exuberant driving, but maybe a meal would settle her. "Sure. Jay said he'd read the contract, but I haven't heard from him. I told him I'd text him when I arrived."

Selena frowned. "Maybe you could just call him? Get his answer now."

"Call him. Right." She bit her lip, mentally

rehearsing what she was going to say. Not blurting out "I love you" seemed to be job one.

Selena snapped her fingers in Cami's face. "Hey, girl, wake up. We're in work mode here, kiddo. You turned him from a hard no into a maybe. You can do this."

Cami squared her shoulders. Right. Work mode. She cleared her throat. "Thanks. I'll call him now. He should have had time to at least look at the contract—it's almost noon there."

"Great. Go ahead."

"Is there somewhere I could have privacy?"

Selena threw her a single worried glance, then gathered up her phone and computer. "Sure. You can have the office. I'll go work outside for a bit."

"Thanks."

When Selena was gone, Cami channeled the Great Kate. She squared her jaw and covered her vulnerability with brash confidence. The phone rang so many times, she was beginning to think he wasn't going to pick up.

"Hi." Jay's voice flooded her ears.

"Hi. It's Cami. I was wondering if you had a chance to look at the contract. Are there any questions I can answer for you?"

Silence on the other end of the line.

Cami squeezed her eyes shut. She might have overdone it on the professionalism front.

"Wait—let me start over. Hi. It's Cami. I made it to L.A. How are you?" Better. Not great, but better.

Jay answered slowly. "I'm glad you made it safe. I did read the contract."

"And?"

"And I've decided to do it. You can tell the studio Parker Wild is coming back to Cloudy Cove."

Cami took a beat to be sure she'd heard him correctly. "Seriously?"

"Seriously."

She couldn't read his tone, but she was caught up in her own mix of excitement and relief. He was going to do it. She hadn't screwed up. The show was going to happen—she knew it in her bones. And it was going to be amazing, because he was amazing and he—*they*— were going to make *Sawyer's Cove* as electric as it ever was.

"Oh my God, Jay, this is so great." She let her enthusiasm bleed into her voice. "You're sure? Because it's going to be so incredible, I promise. You won't regret it."

He chuckled lightly. "I know you're going to do a fantastic job, Cami."

There was something about the way he said it that chilled her excitement slightly. "You aren't doing this only because I want you to, right?" She didn't want him to do it solely as a favor to her, the icky implications of them having had sex making her queasiness return.

When he responded, his tone held nothing but calm professionalism. "As a producer, you were very persuasive. You were right, the production will be good for the town. And being Parker Wild again—I think that could be good for me. See if I still have it." He sounded, if not enthusiastic, at least open to the possibility of success. She'd take it.

She felt a huge smile blossom on her face. "We're going to have so much fun working together, Jay. You have no idea. I can't wait to share some of the storylines Selena's working on. We could start production as soon as early fall if today's meeting goes well."

"Wow, that's soon."

"I'm excited because it's finally happening, but it's going to be a marathon between now and then."

"Totally. You'll need to focus on the show."

"Yeah, but there's a lot I can do from Misty Harbor. A lot I'll need to do, once the shoot gets closer."

"For now, though, it sounds like you need to be there."

"I guess. I miss you." She laughed with the relief of telling him the truth. "I miss Misty Harbor, too. It's all gloomy and plastic here. Once we get the schedule and the budget sorted out, I should be able to fly back—"

"I think you should stay," Jay broke in. "It might be better."

"What do you mean?"

"You need to focus on the show. And now that I'm involved, I don't think we should be."

"What?"

"You deserve this, Cams. You're going to see it through, without distractions."

Goosebumps broke out on her arms at the finality in his voice. "And I suppose we're a distraction." She was aware they hadn't talked about being a "we," but she was too anxious to beat around the bush.

"You said yourself we shouldn't confuse work with other things."

She remembered saying that, but that was before she'd let herself entertain the idea that their relationship could be for keeps. But clearly, he hadn't had the same notion. "I think we both crossed that line when we went to bed together."

"Well, I'm uncrossing it."

He seemed so certain this was what he wanted. What happened to the Jay who'd cleared his schedule for her, who took her on a pilgrimage to her favorite actress's home, who made love to her as if she was something precious?

"I don't understand. You can't tell me you aren't going to miss what we have."

"Of course I'll miss it. But what else is new? I've been missing you for the past twelve years. I can live with missing you. What I can't live with is you messing up your career because I miss you."

The penny dropped, and with it the anger started bubbling up. "You're doing it again. You think you know what I want, what I need, so you're breaking up with me for my own good. I can't believe this."

"That's not what I'm doing. The issue is, we're not compatible. I'll always be a townie with one credit on my IMDb page. You'll always be jetting off to the next location, to the next shoot."

"But we're not kids anymore, Jay. We know how to make this work—a little flexibility, a little compromise."

"I don't know that either of us is capable of that

much flexibility, Cams. I've been doing my own thing for too long. You're just starting out with this new phase of your career."

"So, what, you don't even want to try? Stop making my decisions for me."

"You make your own decisions," he said. "And I make mine."

Everything ached. She'd let him in again, hoped they'd have a different outcome. She had the show, she had her career. And she didn't have Jay. She wasn't allowed to have it all, apparently.

Her voice trembled, but she had to say one more thing. "I'm deciding right now to tell you something, Jay. My cab could get T-boned on Hollywood Boulevard or, I don't know, I could be run over by one of those electric scooter things. So I need you to know that I love you. I love you, and I want the show, and I want you, too. Just for the record."

There was a pause.

"Don't get run over by an electric scooter. Do your job," he said shakily. "I'll get you the signed contract. And I'll see you around, Cams."

He hung up before she could break down in tears.

Selena found her a few minutes later curled into a ball in her office chair.

"Oh, girl, what happened? He said no?"

Cami lifted her head tiredly. "We've got Parker Wild."

"For real? That's great news, isn't it?" Selena looked at her uncertainly. "Shit. You and Jay...something happened, didn't it?"

Cami attempted a smile. "Whatever it was, it's over. And it's okay. I still have work. Work is good."

"You're great at the work," Selena agreed, patting Cami slightly awkwardly on the shoulder. "But you also have me, work or no work. Okay?"

Cami reached for Selena's hand, gave it a light squeeze. "Okay. Thanks." She took a deep, cleansing breath. "Let's go. We need to seal this deal."

Chapter Twenty-Five

ERIKA: Red Alert! We have photo evidence that Jay Orlando and Camille Corsair were in the same place at the same time.

JULES: Looks like they were in a bar—Jay Orlando's bar? And they were looking at each other.

ERIKA: And it was hot.

JULES: What does it mean?

ERIKA: It probably means nothing, but man, it's fun to dream.

JULES: All I want for Christmas is new *Sawyer's Cove* content, even if it's just the actors hanging out together on social media.

FROM *THE SAWYER'S COVE REWATCH PROJECT PODCAST: SPECIAL DROP—THAT PHOTO!*

The funny thing about Hollywood was that you could go weeks, months, even years with nothing happening on a script or a treatment or a project, and then suddenly someone in an office somewhere realizes they want what you're selling and they need it tomorrow, and that means drop everything and make it happen. Like, yesterday.

That's how Cami felt when she got out of the meeting with Selena and Brad and the other folks at the production company and studio.

Rather than having to go in with a hard sell and justify why they should take a spot on the winter schedule, Krista, one of the suits, started off the meeting by waving her phone around.

"This photo of you and Jay Orlando at his bar has over fifty thousand likes on Instagram alone. First some *Sawyer's Cove* podcast that's apparently really popular reblogged it, then it got picked up on all the major celebrity sites. A *Cove* fanatic turned it into a viral TikTok. Everyone's speculating about you and Jay and the possibility of more *Sawyer's Cove*. We need to move fast to capitalize on all the buzz."

"Of course we do," Selena said, as if she was personally responsible for the hype.

Cami opened her own phone, searched the tag of her name on Instagram, and wondered how she'd missed this. The photo was from Friday night. A simpler time, before she'd done the stupidest thing imaginable and fallen back in love with someone who'd continuously proven her love wasn't enough to keep him.

At least she looked good in the candid shot. Jay looked like Jay, looming over her from his side of the bar. They were both smiling slightly, and no wonder people were gossiping. Jay looked like he was about to eat her, and she looked like she was about to put herself in his mouth.

"Where are we with scheduling?" Brad asked.

"Spencer Crosby and Nash Speedwell are good for six weeks from September first. Ariel Tulip is free starting September tenth. Camille, of course, has open availability."

"What about Parker—I mean Jay? He kind of disappeared off the face of the Earth, but clearly the interest is still there if this photo is anything to go by," Krista said.

"He's on board," Cami said calmly. "Parker Wild is coming back to Cloudy Cove."

The suits looked relieved.

"Excellent. Then we're going to finalize the budget, and you should plan for a late August start date. How soon can we get a finished draft of the first couple of scripts?"

Selena and Cami exchanged a glance. They had most of the first episode written, and some notes on the entire ten-episode arc, but not much down on paper for the second episode.

"Friday," Selena said with confidence.

Cami inwardly shuddered. She wasn't a writer, but she thought that sounded awfully soon.

"You two are killing it," Brad said as he ushered them

out. "We're really looking forward to working with you on this project."

Cami allowed herself to enjoy the praise for the length of the walk back to Selena's office.

"This is awesome." Selena started reeling off to-dos while her assistant took notes. "Let's order lunch in. Get a few of those big salads I like, Becca. We need to polish the first episode and dig into the second. See if Neicy and Emmet are available for some writing sessions this week, maybe even today, and coordinate with the production company about location scouting. We need to get permits going if we're going to be shooting in two months. Two months! Cami, this is really happening."

Cami wished she felt anything but numb from the emotional roller coaster of the past few days. "I feel like we should celebrate, but I'm too jet-lagged to do anything but curl up and take a nap."

"Let's celebrate after we break the second episode's arc."

Would she ever feel like celebrating again? She hated that what should have been a triumphant moment in her fledgling career as a producer was overshadowed by losing Jay. She couldn't even call her dad to tell him the good news about the show because he'd sense something was wrong, and she'd get some version of an "I told you so" speech.

Cami slept for an hour on Selena's office couch, then ate the salad Becca brought for her. She felt marginally better after that and another cup of coffee. Selena had been working nonstop on rounding up a mini writers' room.

"We'll work out of my house. You can stay there, too."

Cami stretched and yawned. "I have my own place," she reminded Selena.

Her friend cocked her head. "Oh, right. Sometimes I forget you do live in L.A."

Cami's grand plan to make a permanent move to Misty Harbor had been thrown into doubt, but she was still pretty sure she no longer wanted to keep her Los Angeles base. "I'm putting my house on the market, but I'll stay there for now. I need to check on things. And I need clothes."

"Whatever, you don't have to use my guest room, but you need to be at this week's writing sessions, most of them, anyway. We're going to need your input on the Parker/Amy arc."

Cami pressed a hand to her stomach, suddenly remembering she'd have to act with Jay in a couple of short months. "Right."

"Hey, you okay?"

"I will be."

"Yeah, you will." Selena smiled softly. "This is all going to be worth it."

"I want to believe you," Cami said.

"No fair quoting the show at me."

"Sorry, unintentional." *I want to believe you* had been one of the unofficial themes of the show—Amy's naiveté and hopefulness constantly battered by reality, until

Parker Wild's unwavering loyalty restores her faith in humanity. "And you're right. I can't not do things because I'm afraid of making a mistake. I have to believe that things will work out. And then I have to make them work out."

"Now you're talking like a producer."

"Are you sure I'm not talking like an over-optimistic control freak?"

"Same thing." Selena winked. "Now let's go write a new season of *Sawyer's Cove*."

Chapter Twenty-Six

From *The Sawyer's Cove Rewatch Project Podcast: The False Alarm*

After Jay ended the call with Cami, he immediately dialed the entertainment lawyer he'd been referred to, to discuss the *Sawyer's Cove* reboot deal. Nothing like going down a rabbit hole of contract law with an attorney to take your mind off someone telling you they love you.

Because he hadn't misheard. He'd told her there was no future for them, and Cami had said she loved him.

It only proved how right he'd been to break things off, because she should not be with someone so foolish as to reject the love of Camille Corsair.

The attorney said she'd review the contract by the end of the day.

That business completed, Jay dropped his head to the surface of his desk, a headache building at the base of his skull. He'd skipped his morning workout and come right to The Cove. He'd downed an energy drink in lieu of coffee and hadn't bothered to shave. Everything seemed pointless in the wake of Cami's departure and his realization that to do right by her, to make amends, he'd do the show *and* he'd cut her loose to focus on producing the thing.

Why did doing right by her make him feel like an oyster that had been dropped by a seagull onto the rocks from a great height? Not only did he feel shitty for making her feel shitty, which he clearly had, no matter what his intentions were, but even if he'd tried to play it cool on the phone, she'd hit him in the solar plexus with double-barreled jabs, accusing him of making decisions for her and then telling him she loved him.

And his mature, grown-up response had been to hang up on her.

His phone buzzed. He raised his head from the desk and stared at it uncomprehendingly. It buzzed again. Texts. He peered at the screen.

Where are you? We're supposed to be having lunch.

Am I being stood up?

Shit. He'd told Mimi last night he'd buy her lunch. He scooped his phone up and typed a quick reply.

I'm at work. Where should I meet you?

Bakeshop. Make it quick, little brother.

To make up for missing his workout, he left the Land Rover behind and jogged up Main Street. He caught sight of himself in the Bakeshop's window. He looked tired. Well, he was tired, dammit. And grumpy and...he wasn't going to use the term "heartbroken," because his heart hadn't technically been broken. He'd just taken his feelings and shoved them into a box, slapped a padlock on there to keep them out of the way. Only they seemed to be rattling around noisily, no matter how much he tried to ignore them.

The doorbell chimed as he pushed his way in. A couple of people waited in line, and he spotted Mimi standing off to the side reading a paperback. Trevor and another employee were running around taking care of the late lunchtime rush.

"There you are," Mimi said, joining him in line. "I haven't ordered yet."

"Sorry, sis. I got sidetracked today."

"You look like shit."

"Thanks for that," he said, nodding at Trevor when they got to the front of the line.

"Hello, Orlandos. What can I get you?"

Mimi ordered her usual salad and tea. "And he's paying." She pointed at Jay emphatically.

"I'll take a turkey avocado sandwich for here and six blueberry fritters to go, please." Fritters were Danica's favorite, and he owed her for covering for him while Cami was in town.

"You got it, babe." Trevor punched the order in. "Where's Miss Cami today?" He glanced between Jay and Mimi and wrinkled his forehead. "Should I make her latte?"

Jay didn't know how to feel that Cami had already insinuated herself into the community enough to have a regular order at the Bakeshop.

"No latte," Jay finally said, not looking at Mimi.

They took their number to an empty table by the window.

"What's going on?" Mimi hissed. "You were down last night, but today it's worse. Talk to me, I'm worried about you."

Jay looked at his sister. He didn't know what he could say that would stop her from fretting over him, so he decided to tell her the truth.

"It's really okay. In fact, I have good news," he said, forcing some cheer into his voice. "It hasn't been officially announced, but *Sawyer's Cove* is having another season. They're rebooting it with the entire original cast and adding a bunch of new young characters. I'm going to be playing Parker Wild again for ten episodes. Maybe more if it gets another order."

Mimi's eyes went round with surprise. "That's why Cami came to Misty Harbor?"

"She's producing it."

"And the whole cast, even—" Mimi stopped short, smiled. "Wow, this is incredibly exciting! I always wished you hadn't stopped acting."

"You what?"

"I wish you'd kept acting. I know you had offers. You were so good at it."

Jay looked at her in shock. "You thought I was good?"

"Of course. What—you thought all those times I complimented you on the show I was lying?"

Jay frowned, tried to remember. His mom and sister had been really supportive, but that's because they had to be. "I guess it didn't sink in."

"Well, you were. When you're on screen, no one can take their eyes off you. And this is so cool for Cami. Producer-slash-actress-slash-sister-in-law."

His heart seized. "Mimi, don't even joke about that."

She flashed him a grin. "Come on, you can't tell me there isn't something between you two. And if she's producing and acting in it, you'll be spending a lot of time together."

"That's why there isn't going to be anything between us. She needs to focus on the show. I have my life here. We'll be working together, nothing else." Sure, working with her would be slightly painful, but it wasn't anything he didn't deserve for messing around with her in the first place.

"But—"

"Seriously, Mimi, drop it. She's better off without me."

Mimi grabbed the wooden order number and slammed it down, making the metal table quiver and Jay jump. "Stop, for the love of all that is holy, and listen to me for a second."

Jay glanced around. Despite the scene Mimi was making, no one seemed to be paying them any attention. "I'm listening, Jesus."

"I don't care about Cami. I mean, I do, but not as much as I care about you. Who cares if she's better off without you, which I don't believe for a second, by the way. Are *you* better off without *her*?"

Jay gaped. He hadn't seen his sister this upset since a patron had returned a library book bookmarked by a greasy slice of pizza.

"Your entire life, you've always been there for me, for Mom, for the town. You go above and beyond every day for everyone else in your life, even if you lose out. But what about you—what do you want? Why shouldn't you get the girl?"

He swallowed. If he couldn't tell his sister, who could he tell? "I want her. I want her so much, Mimi. But she doesn't belong here, and I don't want to leave."

"Why would she be talking about moving if she didn't belong here? Hell, she's already got a regular order here. She likes Misty Harbor, and maybe that has something to do with you and your face, but that's not all there is to it. Did she tell you she doesn't belong?"

"She told me she loved me," Jay said miserably. He could guess what Mimi's reaction to that would be, but instead of screeching at him, her shoulders slumped forward, and she touched his hand across the table gently.

"Oh, sweetie. Then what the hell are you still doing here?" she asked quietly.

"What do you mean?"

"I've read enough romance novels to know this is the part where the guy makes the grand gesture to win back the girl. She loves you. You love her, right?"

He did love her. He knew very well he'd never truly stopped. He nodded warily.

"Grand gesture time, little brother. Be selfish for once in your life. Ask for what you want. It's what she wants, too."

"I can't just fly to California," Jay said, even as part of him was already mentally gassing up the Land Rover. "I have work and stuff to do on Harbor Fest and—"

"I'll call Danica, and she'll be fine. She is the manager, right? Let her be in charge for a few days. There's an entire Harbor Fest committee that can take up your slack. You don't have to carry Misty Harbor all on your own."

"What if it's too late?"

"When did she tell you she loves you?"

"A few hours ago."

"I don't think that's enough time for her to fall out of love with you, Jay. Get out of here, seriously. Don't come back unless you're bringing her back with you."

Jay surged up from the table just as Trevor appeared, a plate of food in each hand. "I'm going to have to take mine to go."

Chapter Twenty-Seven

Erika: I forgot how romantic this episode is.

Jules: I usually hate when shows do Valentine's Day stunt episodes, but they pull this off.

Erika: It's all worth it for Parker and Amy to get past what happened in the last episode. They give us hope that love can conquer all.

From *The Sawyer's Cove Rewatch Project Podcast: The Snow Day*

Selena's house was a hive of activity. She lived in a gorgeous thirties-era stucco home with a red tile roof, Mexican tile floors, and wrought-iron embellishments. It was basically the kind of place a noir movie femme fatale would live. There was never parking on her twisty street in the hills, so Cami was happy to hop out of the rideshare she'd taken and simply walk up the front path.

Becca answered the door and led her to the dining room, which had been turned into an impromptu writers' room. The big wooden table had four people around it, each with a laptop in front of them. A huge whiteboard was propped on one dining room chair, ten rectangles for each of the ten shows marked on it. Some of the rectangles had words scribbled inside, but most were empty. Cami sighed. It seemed there hadn't been any breakthroughs on the script front since she left late the night before.

She wasn't a writer, but she knew Amy Green better than anyone. She'd also watched a lot of the old episodes for research when she and Selena were preparing their original pitch to the studio. She'd watched the series finale five times alone. When they'd been unexpectedly canceled, they were about to film the last two episodes of the season. Ryan Saylor, the show's creator and showrunner, had done his best to wrap up as many storylines as he could with those final two episodes, but there was an open-endedness to the core relationships that Cami knew had frustrated viewers.

It made sense at the time that characters who were just leaving high school for the next phase of their lives wouldn't have everything resolved and figured out. Still, she hoped by revisiting these characters later in life, they could provide some closure for the audience. And maybe for her and the rest of the cast. They'd all thrown their hearts and souls into their characters. They'd grown up along with them. And saying goodbye so suddenly had been difficult.

She rolled up her proverbial sleeves, took a seat at the table, and went to work.

Becca was constantly bringing in takeout and coffee, but Cami was still on East Coast time, and by five she was dragging.

"I gotta take a break," she told the group before escaping to the living room. She lay down on Selena's shockingly uncomfortable Art Deco-replica sofa. She was happy with the way they'd finally cracked the nut of the story for the second and third episodes. The writers Selena had assembled were sharp and funny, and they all seemed to know the characters well—she'd been stunned when she learned that actually being a viewer of the show wasn't a prerequisite for a job writing said show.

She was drained. At first, she'd been relieved to have the deadline of Friday to focus her on what had to be done. It had given her a reason to push her conversation with Jay to the back burner. But whenever she thought of something funny she wanted to tell him, or idly wondered what the weather was like in Misty Harbor, her stomach and mood would plummet. She couldn't text him. She couldn't call. He'd taken all of that off the table. She'd lost him as suddenly as she'd found him again.

That was why she assumed she was more exhausted than she thought when her phone rang and Jay's name appeared on the screen. That couldn't be right. Why would he be calling? Had he changed his mind about doing the show?

"Hello?"

"Hey, Cami."

She flew up to sitting on the sofa. "Jay. Is everything okay?"

"Yeah, everything's fine. Hey, where are you?"

"Selena's. Where are you?" she asked reflexively.

"Your place. What's her address?"

Cami's brain, tired and full of bits of dialogue and worry and love and missing him, was moving turtle-slow. "My place? I don't have a place in Misty Harbor yet."

He chuckled—nervously? "Ah. Yeah. Where does Selena live?"

"Echo Park. Four-four-five Cuyama Street."

"Great. Stay there."

And then he hung up.

Cami looked at her phone. "The bastard hung up!" she said to the empty room.

It was a fifteen-minute drive from Cami's bungalow to Selena's abode, ten of which Cami spent splashing water on her face and finger-combing her hair into something that less resembled a rat's nest.

"Jay's coming here?" Selena said when Cami tracked her down in the kitchen, serving up take-out enchiladas to the hungry writers.

"I think so."

"Huh."

"What?"

Selena just smiled. "You can invite me to the wedding, but you are not allowed to ask me to be a bridesmaid. I don't do bridesmaid, okay?"

Cami could do nothing but stick her tongue out at her friend. That was the level of comeback she was capable of. Her heart felt like it was trying to jump out of her chest and race down the hill to reach Jay first.

Then the heavy iron knocker on the front door sounded.

"I'll get it," she said quickly. But she didn't move.

"Where's your spine, Cami? Get your man."

Cami had always been good at taking direction. She went to the front door.

She'd half-convinced herself this was all an elaborate prank. There was no way Jay was anywhere but Misty Harbor. But when she opened the door, it was him. Jay Orlando. Looking even more handsome than the last time she'd seen him, wearing jeans and his should-have-been-silly-but-was-somehow smoking-hot leather jacket.

"Cami."

"Jay."

"Can I come in?"

"Sure," she said brightly, as if she knew her lines by heart, though she had no idea what kind of scene they were in. "We're having some food. The writers are working on some story ideas. The studio wants to see two finished scripts by Friday."

"Oh, great. I hope you're writing some good stuff for Parker." He smiled, slightly bashfully.

They were, actually. "I think you'll be happy."

"Yeah?" He reached into his backpack and fished something out. She stared as he handed her a small sheaf of paper. "I signed the contract. And don't worry, I went over it with my lawyer. You'll see a few changes. Hopefully they'll be acceptable."

She took the stack, flipped to the end, where yes, his name was scrawled in black ink. "You actually printed this out and signed it."

His brow furrowed. "Yes?"

She laughed. "You are adorably old-school."

"Well, it seemed important."

"Thanks, Jay."

They stared at each other. Cami broke first. "Is that why you came here? You could have just emailed it."

"I came here because—"

"Cami, do you know where—oh. Sorry, I didn't realize you—" Becca walked into the foyer and looked up from her tablet. The girl's eyes widened behind her glasses.

Cami was screaming inside wanting Jay to finish his sentence, but she made introductions politely. "Becca, this is Jay. Jay, Selena's assistant, Becca."

Jay smiled and waved. "Hi."

Becca mumbled something that resembled a hello, then scurried out of the room. Since she wasn't the scurrying type, Cami could only imagine the blush on her face had something to do with Jay Orlando showing up out of nowhere.

Cami could relate. She wanted him to wrap her up in

his leather jacket, tuck her against the warm wall of his chest, and spirit her away. But he stayed stubbornly to himself.

"We've got enchiladas in the kitchen if you want," she offered when he didn't immediately launch into the explanation she was desperate for.

"Enchiladas sound good. Did you know they don't feed you in coach?"

"Been a while since you flew, huh?"

"Twelve years."

She decided not to touch that, just backed up through the house until they got to the kitchen. Selena looked up from shoving a forkful of enchiladas rancheros into her mouth.

"Selena, look who's here. And with a contract and everything!" Cami was aware her voice was fakely upbeat.

"Oh, wow!" Selena said with her mouth full. "Jay!"

"Hi, Selena," Jay said warmly.

She swallowed and glanced at Cami, who shook her head slightly. She didn't know what was going on either. "So, this is awesome timing," Selena said finally. "Can we pitch you on the arc of the show?"

"Uh. Sure." Jay sat at the big island in the kitchen, scrubbed a hand over his face. "Sorry, I'm just a little out of it. Big day. Plus, East Coast time."

"Tell me about it. I'm exhausted," Cami said with feeling. Jay's arrival had perked her up, but she was still sleep-deprived.

"Oh!" Selena looked between them, her mouth an

oval. "Well, this can wait. Are you going to be in town for a while, Jay? Maybe we could meet up tomorrow."

Jay glanced at Cami briefly. "I'll be here tomorrow."

Cami wanted to pull her weight, but she was also bone-tired and dying to get Jay alone and find out why he was really here. "Tomorrow would be better for me," she put in.

"Then how about we meet back here at ten?"

"That works for me." Cami yawned her appreciation.

"I'll be here," Jay said. "Can you recommend a hotel? I don't know the area at all."

Hotel? Cami felt her hopes that Jay was there for more than business dampen. "Oh. Well. I have a guest room," she offered.

This time, Jay looked at Selena, who looked like she was hiding a smile.

"Okay, thanks," Jay said cautiously.

"Do you have a car?"

"Yeah, I rented one."

It took a few minutes to gather her things and say goodbye to the writing crew, while Jay scarfed down a quick plate of food.

She said a short, grateful farewell to Selena. "Are you sure you're okay if I take off?"

"Please. We'll start fresh tomorrow, so don't stay up all night, if you know what I mean."

"Selena!" Cami would have been more scandalized, except part of her was hoping she'd have a reason to do exactly that. But Jay had been completely businesslike since his arrival. She didn't know what to think.

Jay had parked down the hill, so they walked through the pink evening light. The typical June marine layer had burned off by midday, and the evening was clear. Selena's neighbors' houses were all landscaped with drought-tolerant plants, beautiful succulents and cacti and desert tropicals. At the bend in the road, they had a view of Echo Park Lake below them, the greenish water glittering as the sun set.

"It's actually kind of pretty here," Jay said as he unlocked the generic black rental sedan.

"It can be," Cami agreed. She didn't know how to tell him she hadn't been able to appreciate the beauty until he'd arrived.

Jay drove them to Cami's mostly in silence. He didn't seem anxious to start talking, and Cami could keep up the illusion he was there for more than just work a little longer.

"I'll unlock the gate, and you can park in the driveway." Her house was smaller than Selena's, but more private, set back from the street and fenced in on all sides. She hopped out to key in the code for the gate, then walked up the driveway as Jay eased the car through and parked it.

He took his backpack out. It seemed to be the only luggage he had with him. "Cute place."

Cami unlocked the front door of the single-story mid-century modern house she'd only spent a handful of nights in since the beginning of the year. "Thanks. It's convenient." She flipped on some lights. "But I'm still thinking about putting it on the market." He might not want a relationship with her, but there was no law saying she couldn't move to Misty Harbor anyway.

He hummed, looked around her living room. His gaze snagged on a framed photo perched on a bookshelf. He dropped his backpack and crossed the room. She followed, looking over his shoulder as he picked it up.

It was a group shot, five teenagers on a beach at sunset. But not just any beach. The rocky beach at Misty Harbor. Crosby anchored one end, with Ariel tucked into his side, then Nash, then Jay. She was on the end, looking at the camera and smiling, as they all were. All but Jay. He had his head tilted slightly down, toward her, his gaze unmistakably on her face. His smile was supposed to be for the photographer taking the promotional shot, but it was all for her.

"I always liked that picture," she said.

"It's a good one," Jay agreed. He set the photo down and turned around to face her. "Even the first season, I knew how special you were. Classy and talented and beautiful. Way out of my league."

"I didn't think so," Cami said. "I thought you were too hot to look at, and when I found out how nice you were, it was like you couldn't be real."

"I guess we're lucky you tripped that day and we kissed, or we might never have gotten over ourselves and actually gotten together."

"Even though we screwed it up?"

"I wish I had been secure enough not to screw it up, but I could never regret being with you. I was lucky enough to strike gold once, and then you came back to

Misty Harbor, and I didn't think it was possible to be that lucky twice."

Cami's chest swelled with tenderness and hope, but she had to make something clear. "You're the only person I've ever been with who didn't care I was Camille Corsair. Except when you're making assumptions about how my career is more important than you."

"I'm sorry for that, then and now. I never thought I was worth it. In the cosmic accounting, I always valued your success and happiness above mine, and I made some pretty shitty decisions because of it." Jay reached out and took her hands in his. She shifted so they were less than a foot apart, echoing the pose of a couple making vows. Perhaps they were.

"I'm reformed, Cams. No more assumptions. No more trying to do the right thing and making both of us miserable in the process." His grip on her hands tightened. "You told me yesterday you loved me. That you wanted me. I'm here in front of you because apparently I am a lucky enough bastard to be getting a second chance—or maybe it's my third—to give you what you want."

She felt love radiating from the man who'd come all this way to give her what she wanted. She thought it was the same thing he wanted, too, but she had to be sure.

"What do *you* want, Jay?"

"I want you, Cams. I want you to let me love you. Because I do. I love you so much. I just never thought my love counted. And then this reboot business muddied everything. I didn't sign that contract to stay near you."

"And I didn't offer it to you to keep you near me. There are no contractual strings attached to the way I feel about you, you know that, right?"

"No assumptions, no strings, no expectations."

"It sounds like we're not getting much," Cami said. "Which is weird, because I feel like I'm getting the world."

Jay leaned down and kissed her sweetly. "We both are." He kissed her again, but when she tried to deepen the kiss, he pulled back. "Can I get a tour of the rest of the house now? I'm particularly interested in the bedroom portion of the tour."

"I thought you'd never ask."

Chapter Twenty-Eight

ERIKA: Not to mention, there is nothing like make-up sex.
JULES: Amen, sister.

FROM *THE SAWYER'S COVE REWATCH PROJECT PODCAST:
THE SNOW DAY*

Jay only got the barest glimpse of the rest of the house as Cami made a beeline for a door that opened to her bedroom. The entire back wall was made of windows covered by fancy shades that had already been drawn. Cami's bed was unmade, sky blue sheets tossed all over the place. Two more doors inside the room showed the way to a walk-in closet and bathroom.

Cami threw herself at him, literally, jumping into arms he'd instinctively held open for her. He laughed and squeezed her tight. She felt spectacular, like his past and future all rolled up into one. He took them to the bed, laid her down. She started pulling off her thin cotton sweater.

"Take off your clothes," she ordered.

He smiled. "Is there a rush?"

She dropped the sweater over the side of the bed, leaving her in a thin camisole. "I missed you. And we're both tired. I want to make sure I get to come before I fall asleep."

He laughed. "Doesn't coming make you fall asleep?"

"Best sleep aid I know. So come on. Let's get some sleep." She tugged at his hand and put it on her breast. He cupped the soft flesh through her top. She didn't seem to be wearing a bra. He felt her nipple harden up through the fabric, and he flicked it lightly with his finger. She gasped, and the sound went straight to his cock.

If she wanted it fast, he could oblige her.

He stopped touching her long enough to peel off his jacket and throw it over a nearby chair, then got to work on his shirt and belt. She shimmied out of her jeans, laid back against the messy sheets in just panties and that teasing scrap of material she was calling a shirt.

He'd lost everything by the time he crawled on top of her, underwear and all. He didn't want to have to stop for anything once he got going, which meant— "Wait. I have condoms in my pack."

She stopped him from going to get them with a hand on his arm. "Do we need them? I'm on birth control, and I'm clean. You were the first in almost a year."

He thought back to his last physical. "Yeah, I'm clean. You want to go without?"

She bit her blush pink lip and then licked the spot. "It's not a dealbreaker, but yeah. I want to feel you, Jay."

He caught her mouth and plunged his tongue inside. There was no time for finesse, and she didn't seem to want any. She groaned and wrapped her arms and legs around him, pulling him against her like an octopus reeling in its prey. He couldn't have been happier about being caught by her.

He pushed down the top of her camisole to expose her breasts and feasted on one after the other, until she was squirming underneath him. He gave her reprieve long enough to tear her panties down and off, then repeated the process on her clit and pussy until she was bucking into his mouth and crying out deliciously.

"Jay, fuck, wait. I want to come with you inside me." Her voice was so close to begging, his cock pulsed as it got impossibly harder.

"You sure you're ready?" He'd only been inside her once before, and it had seemed something of a tight fit. "You want to get on top again?"

Her eyes were heavy-lidded and her cheeks flushed as she propped herself up on her elbows to look at him. "Let's try it this way. I'll tell you if you need to stop, okay?"

She opened her legs, and he could see every gorgeous inch of her. He smoothed a finger over the mound of soft blonde curls, touched her clit, which was so engorged he could see the flesh standing up proudly, and continued through her slick folds, wet from his tongue and mouth and her juices.

Satisfied she was wet enough, he moved closer, kissed her once, hard and fast, then slid inside. He'd only meant to go in partway, but she tilted her hips, and her channel was so smoothly welcoming, he found himself buried to the hilt. She moaned and spread her legs wider.

"Okay, sweetheart?" he asked.

"Feels so good, Jay. You feel so good. Don't stop."

He started moving again, remembering how good it always felt with her, cataloging the various shades of pink that graced her body from the tips of her pert ears to her lush mouth to the part of her where they joined, his erection disappearing into her over and over, faster and faster, until she gripped his shoulders hard and told him she was coming. He'd have been able to tell by the way her entire body shuddered and opened even wider for him to take her ever deeper.

He let himself go, the incomparable feeling of coming bare inside her sweeping away every thought in his brain until only the knowledge of his love for this woman remained.

"Love you," she whispered as he slipped out of her, grabbed his T-shirt, and used it to catch the mess they'd made between them. She burrowed into a pillow with her sweaty face. He tossed the shirt into what looked like a laundry basket, climbed back into her bed, drawing the sheets up around them both.

"I love you, Cami," he said into her eucalyptus hair.

He wasn't sure she heard him, but it didn't matter. He'd be telling her every day, every night, for as long as she'd have him.

They woke before dawn, California time. They made love again, more slowly. Cami let herself savor Jay's weight and strength, and he kissed her so thoroughly, she'd half-forgotten her name. By the time they were both panting and sated, the sun was just seeping around the edges of the windows.

She was about to suggest one of them get up and make coffee when Jay said something unexpected.

"I was thinking maybe you should keep this place so we have somewhere to stay when you need to be in L.A. for work."

Had she heard him correctly? "So *we* have somewhere to stay?"

"I have the bar, but I don't have to be there all the time. Believe it or not, I trust my employees to do their jobs. Which means I can travel with you some of the time. If you'd want that." He sounded like he was trying for casual, but there was vulnerability in the question.

Instead of answering, she asked, "And what about when we're in Misty Harbor? I need to reschedule my appointment with the realtor."

"Yeah." He cleared his throat nervously. Could he be more adorable? "About that. I don't think you'll need to."

Her heart leapt. "Why not?"

"I thought, you know, I've got plenty of room. You

could have your own office. There's an empty bay in the garage for your car."

She smiled. Some people might think deciding to move in together at this point in a relationship was too fast, but as far as Cami was concerned, it was happening twelve years later than it should have. "I don't drive."

"Yeah, you're going to have to learn, Cams. I can't chauffeur you all over Misty Harbor."

"Will you teach me in the Land Rover?" she asked hopefully.

He laughed, then stopped. "Oh wait, you're serious. I'll teach you in something that doesn't weigh three tons."

"Then yes."

"Yes, what?"

"Yes, I'll move in with you. That's what you were asking me, isn't it?"

"You will?" His voice was hopefully disbelieving.

"Of course. I want to be where you are. I want to come home to you, Jay."

"I like the sound of that. Let's come home to each other."

"Deal."

Chapter Twenty-Nine

ERIKA: So get this, apparently the rumor of a *Sawyer's Cove* reboot is a rumor no more. It's happening!

JULES: I'm just like—what? I'm in shock.

ERIKA: I know. It's amazing, but maybe it's too good to be true.

JULES: Here's what we know so far. All five original cast members are coming back. Plus, several new cast members have already been announced. We don't know what their roles will be, but since they're all in the eighteen- to twenty-year-old range, one can only assume they're the next-generation *Cove* crew.

ERIKA: This is seriously so exciting. I just hope they don't ruin it. Oh, God. Wouldn't it suck if it was just anticlimactic and awful?

JULES: It's not going to suck. Apparently, Camille Corsair and Selena Echeveria are producing. You've got to assume they have the show's legacy in mind, since they were there the first time around.

ERIKA: I wonder if Ryan Saylor is going to be involved. The original creator. They at least had to get his blessing, right?

JULES: You're asking me like I have inside intel, E. I know exactly as much as you do about this thing.

ERIKA: I know, I know. Sorry. I'm just really excited!

FROM *THE SAWYER'S COVE REWATCH PROJECT PODCAST: SPECIAL DROP…IT'S HAPPENING*

"Harbor Fest is officially a success," Mimi declared as she flopped onto a folding chair at the table Deb and Cami were holding down within sight of the main stage. "My feet are killing me from working the library's booth all day, but on the plus side, I have funnel cake."

"Don't say funnel cake!" Cami groaned, putting her hand on her stomach. "I ate mine and most of Jay's. He's been too busy to eat."

Hundreds of people had cycled through the festival on its first day, patronizing the food trucks, shopping at dozens of booths, checking out local artisans at the craft fair. Kids were playing games put on by the rec center and standing in line for their turn on the Ferris wheel that rose high above downtown and the beach. It was closing in on dusk, but it seemed most folks were sticking around for the night's entertainment, a popular classic rock cover band Mimi had booked, and then for fireworks after.

Jay had been running around all day, the de facto

head of the event, making sure everyone was having a good time. He'd reported the event had so far already broken even, which meant the next two days were going to be profit—or at least, funds to help put on next year's festival.

"I was thinking maybe we should have a *Sawyer's Cove* fan event here next year," Mimi said. The town had been talking nonstop about the reboot once the news finally broke in *Variety* a few days after Jay signed his contract to join the cast.

"That is a genius idea." Cami had been working nonstop on pre-production for weeks, but she'd managed to do a lot of the work from Misty Harbor. From her cute office in what was now their house, in fact. She'd also had precisely two driving lessons with Kevin, a driving instructor who barely looked old enough to drive himself but who had the patience of a saint. Unfortunately, she wasn't anywhere close to passing the test she'd be required to to drive the sky blue Fiat her dad had bought her as a congratulations present for getting the show officially greenlit.

Barry was coming to Misty Harbor for the Fourth of July, and she looked forward to seeing him again, updating him on the progress on the show, and also doing family things like sharing meals and talking, maybe having a beach day or playing Scrabble. They'd slowly started communicating more, and he'd claimed he was pleased for her and Jay when she told him they were officially together.

"Get your own, Mom," Mimi said, smacking Deb's hand away from her funnel cake.

"Wow. I thought I taught you how to share," Deb grumbled. "I'd rather have ice cream, anyway. Cami, you need anything?"

"I'll come with you," she said, jumping to her feet. She and Deb hadn't gotten to spend much one-on-one time together since she'd made the move to Misty Harbor, and she was still partially convinced Jay's mom didn't like her. "Did I tell you Selena and the writers got rave reviews from the studio for the first two scripts?"

"That's terrific," Deb said, getting in line at the ice cream truck. "I was wondering how many rooms at the inn we should block off for the shoot."

"Great question. I'll have business affairs call you Monday."

"Sounds good. I have to thank you, Cami. This production is going to be great for business."

"You don't have to thank me. I—"

"And you don't have to treat me like the Queen of England. I'm Jay's mom, but I care about you, too. Anyone within a hundred-mile radius can look at the two of you and see the devotion there. Including me. So, maybe you could stop thinking of me as the big bad wolf, and just as Deb."

Cami winced. "I haven't been very subtle, have I?"

"It's okay. I just want you to know I'm glad you're back, Cami. You make my son really happy."

"Thanks." She threw her arms around Deb and gave her an enormous hug.

Deb let go, then patted her arm affectionately. "Now. What flavor do you want? I'm getting triple chocolate."

"As delicious as that sounds, I'm going to see if I can find Jay."

"All right. Try the stage or the beer garden."

The Cove was sponsoring the beer garden near the main stage, so Cami went there first. She waved to Danica, who was serving Warner. But no Jay. She spotted Pauline talking to Trevor and waved to them, too. "Have you seen Jay?"

"I think he was talking to the band," Trevor said.

She edged her way backstage, and there he was, the unofficial mayor of Misty Harbor, mind-meltingly hot in a simple black short-sleeved button down and jeans, two days of stubble speaking to how busy he'd been in the run-up to the festival, but also suiting him in a rakish way. His sunglasses were hooked to the front of his shirt. He looked every inch the heartthrob. She allowed her inner fangirl to sigh in appreciation before she went over and smiled at him brightly. "Hey, found you."

His answering smile was equally dazzling. "Cams! Come meet the band. I'm going to introduce them in a minute. Can you hang out here?"

"Okay."

She shook hands with the band members, posed for a picture with the drummer when he told her his daughter was a huge fan of hers. Then she crept to the edge of the backstage. Smaller groups of people began massing together on the grass in front of the stage when Jay bounded out and grabbed the microphone.

"Welcome to Harbor Fest!" he yelled. The audience whistled and clapped. "I'm here to introduce the rocking band we have, but first I have some very exciting news. Many of you know the television show *Sawyer's Cove* was filmed here a while back. We did three seasons, and they were the best three years of my life."

He looked over at her and winked. She felt a flush involuntarily spreading over her face.

"What you might not know," Jay went on, "is we're filming a ten-episode season for streaming this fall right here in Misty Harbor. And Misty Harbor's newest resident, the beautiful and talented Camille Corsair, is not only reprising her role as Amy Green, she's producing it as well. And I want to take a minute to thank her for bringing this opportunity to our town, and to me—she's levering me out of acting retirement with a crowbar, and I couldn't be happier about it. Join me in thanking Camille."

The roar of the crowd was deafening. Cami laughed as Jay gestured for her to join him on stage.

She waved and bowed. It was overwhelming being on the receiving end of in-person adulation. She'd never done live theater, and award shows weren't the same. "Thank you, Misty Harbor. I fell in love with this town fifteen years ago, and then I fell in love with this incredible man right here. Thanks for the warm welcome—it feels like I never left."

"Kiss her!" someone who sounded suspiciously like Trevor yelled.

Jay looked at Cami with a question on his face. "You wanna?"

"It'll be all over social media in about ten minutes," she warned.

"A little publicity never hurt," he said. And he swept her into a good old-fashioned Hollywood kiss.

Epilogue

Mimi snagged a bottle of water from the Harbor Fest beer garden and downed half of it in one gulp. She was sweaty after dancing all-out during the band's last set. The fireworks were about to start, and she wondered if she had enough time to grab a beer before the display.

Her phone buzzed several times in succession, and she took it out, startled by the name on the screen. Well, it wasn't really a name. It was just the way she'd entered him all those years ago, the first time they'd run into each other at The Cove when he was visiting her brother. Jay wasn't around, and *he* had started talking to her. Then, for some inexplicable reason that became explicable two drinks and one tipsy makeout session later, he'd given her his digits.

Labeling him as Mr. Actor Guy in her phone had been a joke at the time, but later she was glad she hadn't typed his real name. That would have been too formal for what were the most casual of encounters.

> Hey, so I guess you know about the reboot?

> I'm really looking forward to spending more time in Misty Harbor.

> I'm getting there in August. I rented a beach house for a couple of months.

> Hope you'll save some time for me.

She looked at the messages for a long while before replying.

> I heard. It's great news. I'm sure I'll see you around!

Her response was polite but noncommittal, noncommittal being the entire basis of their non-relationship. When he was in town, they hooked up. When he wasn't in town, she caught pictures of him on her social feeds and tried not to listen to his album more often than the average person. She always failed on that count.

Mimi was grateful for the thousandth time that Jay had never found out about their arrangement. That was a complication neither of them needed. Her phone buzzed again.

Cool.

Cool. She smiled, shook her head. Totally. Everything was totally cool. Nash Speedwell, aka Will O'Connell on *Sawyer's Cove*, more recently the frontman for The Nash Speedwell Experience, was going to be living in Misty Harbor for a couple of months. That was fine and normal and not at all a disaster waiting to happen.

She stuffed her phone back into her pocket as the first fireworks popped into fiery spangles over her head. The bass player of tonight's band—and heaven knew she had a weakness for bass players—had been eye fucking her all night. Might as well see if he was interested in taking things further. She wasn't hanging around, waiting for a huge Hollywood star to sweep her off her feet. She had more sense than that. This was how she liked her life. Independent. Free to hook up with whoever, whenever.

Mr. Actor Guy would just have to get in line.

Thank you for reading! Scan the code to sign up for my newsletter and download a free Sawyer's Cove: The Reboot story right now!

xoxo,

Libby

Acknowledgments

Thank you to all writers who so generously give their time and expertise to help other writers. Writing can be solitary, but it doesn't feel that way for me. I have such a lovely community of fellow writers that I feel supported and seen every single day. I'm so lucky that my community continues to expand and grow and that I'm able to contribute back as much as I can.

Thank you to the SALT Plotters, to the sprinting crew, my #twoweekgoals ladies, the Westport Writers' Workshop community, the Writers Rendezvous group, CTRWA, and the HEA Club.

Thanks to my family and friends for being more than politely interested in my work.

Thanks to Jessica Snyder for excellent plot advice, the Word Slayers team for stellar editing, and Sara Kettler for her rockstar proofreading.

Finally, thank you to Erin and Julia of *Dawson's Critique*, the best *Dawson's Creek* rewatch podcast out there. I've enjoyed being part of the DC community. Listening to their hilarious, fearless podcast helped me take my idle desire to write about nineties nostalgia and turn it into this series.

About the Author

Libby Waterford is the author of the Sawyer's Cove: The Reboot and the Never a Bride series. She's obsessed with her pollinator garden, DIY fermentation, and writing swoony first kisses and hopeful happily ever afters. Her steamy contemporary romances mix witty banter and all the feels with a solid dollop of good old-fashioned sexual tension. Libby wrangles her two ever-growing sons and a husband in Fairfield County, Connecticut.

Get a free story at libbywaterford.com and email Libby at libby@libbywaterford.com.

facebook.com/LibbyWaterford

instagram.com/libbywritesromance

bookbub.com/authors/libby-waterford

goodreads.com/libbywaterford

amazon.com/author/libbywaterford